THE SPIDER'S STRATEGY

When Carol Noeleen, 75, takes to her bed, seemingly for good, her patient husband, Mark, is at a loss to explain such a withdrawal from their comfortable life. Carol isn't ill, at least not physically, but she is afflicted, and the culprit is a loquacious spider that only she can perceive.

At first, Carol tries to reject the spectral presence in the upper corner of her bedroom. But the spider's insistent whispering, coaxing Carol into confronting memories that she'd just as soon consign to her "forgettery," proves too therapeutic to ignore.

The memories come then, some mundane, others harrowing, like that of the abortion she had as a young woman, or the abuse she suffered at the hands of her father. A sense of mystery builds from her unburdening, a feeling that there is a particular trauma, significant enough to be buried in the preconscious mind, toward which the spider is leading her.

Admirably, Darling doesn't indulge in pulp fiction, maintaining a cool, mature tone, appropriate for an older character looking back on a life fully lived... Carol needs to tell her stories, if only inwardly, and she won't return to life until they are sorted and ordered... A dinner party offers a chance connection that may allow Carol and Mark to rectify a tragedy suffered by their housekeeper, and the prospect draws the protagonist fully from her bed...

A graceful meditation on the value of confronting one's past...

Kirkus Review

"I found The Spider's Strategy a compelling and very thought-provoking read, for which the author must have undertaken extensive research on many subjects. I wish to convey both my thanks and respect for her amazing ability to write such an incredible book."

Pippa Lee, NSW who found
The Spider's Strategy at the **Wyee markets**.

THE SPIDER'S STRATEGY

JAN DARLING

Library of Congress Control Number: 2016918710

ISBN: Softcover 978-1-953048-06-6

Printed in the United States of America.
To order additional copies of this book, contact:

Writers Branding
1800-608-6550
www.writersbranding.com
orders@writersbranding.com

CONTENTS

I dedicate this story to my husband Arturo, who managed the house and garden, the kitchen, the kookaburras, magpies, butcher birds and Paco during my three months of writing. I am grateful for the sweet memories of past feline friendships with New Zealanders: Louis Quatorze, Napoleon Bonaparte and Seamus Fingall O'Flahertie; Londoners: Amy, Linus and Schroeder; Sydneysiders: Zapatos and Babuchas; Tesorita; Paco 1; Carlos Felipe and Consuelo and Central Coaster: Paco 2, el Magnifico, our current master.

CHAPTER ONE

Carol is drowsy, and a smile softens her lips as she drifts in and out of consciousness.

She is 75 and, in every way, appears healthy, but she took to her bed three months ago with no apparent reason. She just didn't get up one day, and she hasn't been out of bed since except for visits to the bathroom. She seems to treat each day as though it's an imposition. She tolerates it, and waits for it to pass, as though there is little left in her life worth living for.

This is not entirely new. She has habitually exhibited a vague sense of disaffection. It now seems to be developing itself into an affliction and is more omnipresent than ever before. Occasionally, she talks to herself animatedly. Occasionally, she will include her husband, Mark, causing him to hope for a change in her generally mute condition. His hopes are brief.

From Carol's perspective, she feels as though she is lost in some forgotten jungle where she lives parallel lives—a confusing state where the events of today and yesterday are intertwined.

Carol does not demand exactness from her memory; it is enough to be able to recall whole events. Placing them on a timeline is tricky, but now, she has decided to pursue the past and tie it down to make sense—at least to her.

Part of her problem is that she has always thought of life as being a temporary condition. Today, you're here; tomorrow, you're not. She imagines her life as a sine wave arriving from a distant past and continuing into an indistinct future.

She lives somewhere in between—the total of her past, and the anticipation of her future being experienced in the present.

Mark is increasingly worried by her lassitude. They've talked a little about it, but she's not inclined to discuss it. It's her life after all. She says she has examined how she feels about death in general and about her death in particular, and she can find no reason to fear it. At the end, there is either nothing or something. And by then, it will be too late to do anything about it, whichever it is.

It worries him that her current focus seems to be posited in the idea of death. It worries him more that she might be planning to experience it. She had been enjoying good health and spirits until the day she took to her bed. It was totally unaccountable. Or, at least, it had appeared that way.

She often says she doesn't care whether she lives or dies. Mark has been hurt by her attitude, and has tried to get her to think about the good times they have shared, the things they have done together. But Carol seems fixated on excluding him from her memories.

From Carol's point of view, he adds to her confusion. It's hard enough for her to fit her own memories together, let alone see where he fits in. It's not as though she's that difficult to get on with, she reassures herself. She has no secrets, no skeletons in the cupboard.

She has always, from as early as she can remember, felt a sort of transparency. As though people can see right through her. Not that she's ever had much to hide; it's just irritating that she feels she doesn't excite the intrigue in other people that they excite in her.

Right now, she's adrift in a fog of confusion. She is grasping at morsels of memory, and trying to hold them together to put them in their proper context. But every time she thinks she's got the time and place, she forgets what she was looking for. If she were fully awake, she would be anxious about this, but she's just drifting and dreaming. She doesn't know what she is losing, her mind or her memory. So she smiles. It's not important. Nothing is important. Today will be yesterday tomorrow.

Suddenly, a whole thought pops out of the fog. She's invisible, that's why she has the sensation of transparency. She either doesn't exist, or she's not who she thinks she is. There, very satisfying. Explains a lot.

CHAPTER TWO

She has often tried to imagine how it would be to be dead. Is dead just being dead, or is it being not alive? She realises that the idea of not being has nuanced her entire life. And now, it seems that what little sense of self she had, what little sense of her individual being is being swallowed up by shadows and uncertainties. It is becoming more and more difficult to locate the details of events in her mental filing system. Things that were perfectly clear to her yesterday seem vague and unsure today.

Yet sometimes, she is shocked by the sudden appearance and the unnerving power of very explicit memories. When she happens upon the fragrance of spring jonquils, she is immediately back in 1963, walking past Auckland suburban gardens on her way to catch the bus to work.

It never fails to impact her, and it works both ways. She thinks back to that year, and she can smell their fragrance. Or she catches the scent of jonquils and she is transported back to 1963 on her way to work.

She's in 1963 right now. It was both a good and bad year. Good because she was leaving an episode of her life behind, escaping from a three-year marriage she should never have made. Bad because she had left that marriage with nothing but her clothes, a pressure cooker, which she knew her husband would never use, and Louis, the cat. She remembers distinctly that even as she was walking down the aisle on her wedding day, she was thinking quite literally. *Oh, well, if this doesn't work out, I can always leave.* And eventually, she did.

A couple of years into the marriage, she found herself pregnant. She was delighted. She immediately set to work with the needles and knitted two lovely layettes. She smocked little genderless tops and sewed rompers. She knitted bonnets and booties until the expected baby had enough clothes to dress half a dozen babies.

Then one Saturday morning, she woke with pains in her stomach. She poked and prodded around herself until she was sure what degree of pressure applied where produced that shooting pain. She asked her husband, John, to ring the doctor. She became wobbly on her legs, sweaty across the forehead, and was vomiting.

The doctor came, felt around her belly, and decided she was having a miscarriage. She was well over sixteen weeks, and he opined that they should call for an ambulance and get her to hospital immediately. He would be there when she arrived. She wasn't thinking miscarriage herself. She was thinking appendicitis, the shooting pain matched what she had read about symptoms of the appendix. She was in surgery by 8 a.m., and the scalpel arrived just in time to remove her bursting appendix.

The Snucklebunny, John's name for the baby that was growing inside her, was lost at the same time. She would have lost it eventually, the doctor told her. The wall of her womb was damaged and probably not capable of sustaining a full-term pregnancy.

Carol, remembering, is swallowed up by the void that this created in her life. Her every waking moment is now spent in guilt. She had killed her first child by abortion, and that abortion had later killed her second child. She suddenly concluded that she was not proper mother material. That somehow, her mind had sensed this and had caused her body to expel the baby.

She lived as though in a trance. Nothing touched her, no tear was shed, she could not shake the pall of guilt that was consuming her day by day. So she parceled up the baby clothes and sent them off to her fecund sister-in-law.

She announced that she wanted a separation. They talked about it, but not a lot. John made one last attempt to convince her to stay with him, but she couldn't. She had found him sitting in the car at the side of the house, crying one day; and he couldn't, or wouldn't, tell her why. It was her fault, she knew that, but she didn't know why. So she moved on, shocked that she had made him cry alone in the car. She felt unable to continue in the marriage. She had to leave.

She didn't just leave to live in another part of the city, she went to another city altogether. The husband she was leaving was kind enough to drive her there with her suitcase, the pressure cooker, and Louis. It was a shame their marriage had ended so casually. They had been good friends. For her, marriage had meant escape with friendly support, escape from a town that held too many memories of a childhood, which she had survived rather than lived.

For him, it had been the security of a friendship made permanent. He was awkward and shy with women and they got on well together. They had a lot in common: local theatre, films, books, and they both had writing jobs. He was her boss, at least until they married, after which she continued to work at the same radio station but in a different department.

Entering the marriage had meant moving away, leaving unhappy reminders behind. It was convenient. Leaving the marriage had meant moving away again. It was, again, convenient.

She wondered what love was, what it felt like, if she would ever feel it. She saw other people 'in love' and envied them. They had something that she didn't understand, and she couldn't explain it to herself. She supposed that it was the trust their love implied. She had never understood trust, and she didn't trust anybody except her cats.

Ever since she was a child, her cats had been her companions and had shared her secrets.

Carol, in contemplative mood, has only recently come to realise that certain aspects of her behaviour are repetitive. She really needs this time resting in bed now to sort a few things out. For instance, whenever a problem occurs, she simply moves on, both mentally and physically; and in that way, she leaves the problem behind. It's her way of solving it. Behind the problem, nags the idea that she's taking the easy way out. Then she comes to her senses. No point in examining the why and how of it, it's already in the past. Get on with the next step. But somehow, the older she's become, the more conflicted are her feelings about events long gone and forgotten—at least she thought they were forgotten.

Now, at seventy-five, this way of dealing with her life by 'moving on' is causing her to question what she has missed. What she has missed out on, what she has left undone that she ought to have done.

CHAPTER THREE

She is still thinking about the 23-year-old Carol who has left a marriage behind and moved to Auckland where she is staying temporarily with a friend, a French woman, the widow of a British admiral.

She is excellent company, entertaining Carol with stories about her life as an early feminist. Madame Jeanne was a feminist at a time when feminism was not the narrow-minded male-demeaning bra-burning speciousness it later became. And she explained to Carol many times, we never pitched men against women, we never demeaned the role of raising our own children, we never expected women who had chosen to remain childless to pay for the raising of our children.

Madame Jeanne believed that once you abnegate the responsibility of creating a personal, ethical, and moral environment for your own family, you may as well throw your children to the wolves. She did not believe that it takes a village to raise a child. She believed it takes the family to raise a child. At the same time, she clearly understood the social and political implications of equality. In France, she had been part of the same political and social circles as Jean-Paul Sartre and Simone de Beauvoir, so she was well-versed in pre and post-war feminism.

Her personal experience was living testament to the truth of her convictions. After an education in France, she was pursuing further studies in Germany at the time that Hitler was embedding his doctrine of Aryan superiority. At first, she was able to accept the march toward Nazism as a rejection of the humiliation Germany had suffered as a result of the signing of the armistice that ended WWI. But by 1938, it was obvious that Hitler had monstrous plans to enslave Europe and whisperings that had begun in her university as mere gossip were daily becoming a vile reality.

Vile, anagram of evil; evil, anagram of live. How appropriate. Where exactly does live fit in? Carol indulges in a little wonder-wander, happy that today she's able to follow the thread of memory so rewardingly.

In Jeanne's world, lecturers disappeared, students denounced students, and Germany's teaching institutions officially and formally encouraged the denunciation of those not seen as loyal Nazis. One day, she was informed that a 'friend' had discovered that her fiancé was an admiral in the British Navy. She confided this to her mother and asked her advice. In France, news was increasingly focused on the likelihood of relations between Germany and Britain subsiding into war, so her mother acted swiftly.

Jeanne was told to pack a small bag, taking only what she needed immediately, and to go to a railway station where a farmer in a blue truck would confirm a password and take her to a safe place over the border in France. A few months later, she married her admiral and went to live in England just as war broke out. She worked with the free French in the underground movement, and supported the British Government war effort by visiting British factories at that time largely staffed by the women whose men were defending their country, and she made speeches that raised the workers' morale. She spoke about conditions in factories all over Britain, the importance of their contribution, and the hardships the whole country shared. And she shared as much as she was permitted about the underground efforts of her countrymen, the free French.

The intricacies and dangers of Madame Jeanne's life completely dwarfed Carol's current problems, so she put the problems behind her and moved on.

CHAPTER FOUR

In her reverie, Carol has left her husband, and is now in Auckland looking for employment and a place for her and Louis to live.

Happily, she finds both a job and a flat in one week, and she and Louis settle into a new life.

It's not long before she realises that by the time she's put aside the rent and money for power, she has very little left for bus fares and food. For several months, she buys a snapper every payday, pressure cooks it, divides the cold fish and jelly into seven slices, and that makes food for the week. Jelly and skin for Louis, flesh for her.

She doesn't have much of a social life. She goes to the theatre or a film with friends occasionally, and is having an affair with an in-the-process-of-divorce man who once or twice a week brings her presents of cold meats and cheese and bread. She sees him as a friend more than a lover, but has come to enjoy and depend on his company. She feels safe with him. He is more than twenty years older, but that doesn't bother either of them.

She's doing well at her new job as an ad agency writer, so when she sees a chance to be advertising manager for an upmarket British cosmetic company, she applies for it. Only after she has received a call from the managing director (a man who she discovered later was sharing a mistress with his own son), and has made an appointment for an interview, does she realise that the job she is apparently on the verge of getting is in another city.

She attends the interview and is duly appointed. Fortunately, the company is happy to relocate her and her pressure cooker and Louis, the cat, at their expense. So she moves on again from Auckland to Wellington, solving the cash problem by leaving it behind. The lover eventually moves to be with her, and they settle in a flat owned by her mother who lives downstairs. This suits both parties. Her mother, who is becoming a bit less independent, has company and they have security of tenure.

They decide to marry. It is more of a decision than a plan. Then one day in autumn, a month before the wedding, something happens that completely changes her idea of the future. Carol is in the kitchen; Pieter is finishing the planting of 150 saplings on the hillside, which is part of the property, when she hears him treading heavily and slowly up the outside stairs. It doesn't sound like his usual step. She senses that something bad is about to happen. She dries her hands and goes to the bedroom. He is sitting on the edge of the bed, blue-black in the face. Before she can say anything, he tumbles to the floor. He is dead. Heart attack or stroke.

Within days, she makes another decision. She will buy a round-the-world air ticket and have a look at Europe. She is twenty-nine, plenty of time to see the world. May as well start now.

She leaves the pressure cooker with her mother, and finds good new homes with friends for her (by now) three cats. A month later, she is moving on. Again, leaving it all behind.

CHAPTER FIVE

In her bed, in the sleepy late afternoon sun, Carol is becoming restless, making small throaty waking-up noises. Slowly, she opens her eyes, brushing the air as though to push away a veil from her face. She blinks once, twice, and then she lets out a terrifying shriek, high and loud. A door slams and there is the sound of hurrying footsteps. Her husband, Mark, disturbed from his reading, appears at her bedside. She's half-sitting, half-crouching in the bed, distraught, screaming.

'There, there, up there in the corner,' she's choking to get it out. 'Up', she shrieks, 'up there, it's hideous. Kill it!' She's waving her arms hysterically and trying to hide in the bedclothes at the same time. And she continues screaming.

Her husband follows her incoherent gestures with his eyes and sees nothing. He sits beside her on the bed and takes her shaking hands in his. 'Tell me what you see, Carol. What's up there?'

'It's a spider,' she whispers, hoarse now from screaming. 'It's going to jump on me and stick its hideous hooks into me and poison me. Kill it, please, kill it.'

Mark is staring at the ceiling trying to see something. There's nothing to see. 'It's only the way the garden shadows are reflected,' he says quietly, and he puts his arm around her trembling shoulders, trying to comfort her with a gentle squeeze.

'It's not just a shadow. It's a spider! You know I hate them! Get something and kill it! Please, please, before it kills me.' Her voice fades into a whimper again and she collapses into the covers.

Mark calms her, and eventually, she settles to rest waiting for him to leave her alone. She has had an idea. Mark sees her eyes close and he leaves.

CHAPTER SIX

She lies quietly for a few minutes then she reaches for a plastic bag from her bedside table. It contains a half wig made of her mother's hair. Her mother had saved it from the time she had cut her schoolgirl plaits at fifteen when she had been forced to leave school to stay at home on the farm to look after her newly born brother. Perhaps it had signified a rite of passage for her.

The hair had been sewn onto a mesh band, which could be fastened with elastic around the head, and worn under a hat or bonnet. She'd made it for Carol when she was part of the local theatre group.

She smoothes it out and strokes it. It doesn't feel as brittle as she expected. Not considering it has been dead for ninety-five years. It still has its auburn colour, but it lacks the texture of living hair. And she thinks how sad that her mother's one great regret was not being able to finish school and train to be a teacher. Was that why she had cut her hair and kept it? A symbol of a dream cut short?

There are three other keepsakes in the plastic bag—a school photo, and her baby book, which contains a few curls from her own first haircut. The old school photo was probably taken when she was seven. She could still remember some of the girls' names and wondered if any of them had kept the same photo. Three rows of 7 and 8-year-olds sitting, kneeling, or standing according to their height; primly gym-slipped with white blouses and school ties; front row cross-legged, hands neatly folded on laps; brushed hair off the face, tied with snug little bows. Everyone clean and healthy, and no-one pulling faces at the camera. The nuns had warned them not to be 'bold'.

The photo was creased; and in places, the blacks and greys were dissolving into sepia. She felt quite pleased that she could still recall names from sixty-seven years ago.

She had found the photo, the hair, the baby book, and her own first hair clippings all together when she was clearing out her mother's place before she was put into the home, a place where old people went to die. She must have connected the four things somehow.

CHAPTER SEVEN

Inside the baby book Story of Our Baby, subtitled Baby's First Five Years, she reads her details. She hadn't bothered to read it when she found it. There hadn't seemed much to read. Most of the spaces were blank just like, it occurs to her, the blank spaces of her life. She'd kept everything together and taken it back to Sydney with her. Now, quite suddenly, she feels the need to read it. Here she is as a baby, labeled and described in the fading pages of the little blue book.

Baby Arrives: Christmas Day, 1940
At: 10.20 a.m.
Place: Timaru Hospital
Escorted By: Doctor and Nurse names (both blank)
Is Named: Carol Noeleen
For: BLANK
By: Rev Fr Mannix
At: Timaru RC
Date: 26/1/41
In the section titled signatures:
Mother: BLANK

Father: full name, in her mother's handwriting!
Sponsors: BLANK
A Page for Marks of Identification

Fingerprints Right Hand: noted in pencil at 12 years old. Why had they not been taken at the time of her birth?

Colour of Hair: Gold
Eyes: Blue. They're green not blue, perhaps no one had ever really looked into them.
Complexion: Fair
Weight: 8lbs 12 ozs
Length: BLANK
Chest Measurement: BLANK
Pages for Congratulations and Gifts: BOTH BLANK
First Pictures: BLANK
First Discoveries
Grasping Objects: 4 mths
Recognition of Mother: 3 mths
Recognition of Father: 5 mths
Notice of Strangers: 3 mths
Recognition of Objects: 6 mths
Mother's handwriting on page called 'First Merry Christmas' reads:
In Timaru
Father in hospital
Baby visited and was badly frightened by the sister's veil
1 year old, 1941

Pages titled First Birthday, First Hair Cut, 2 Years Old, Playmates, Bright Sayings, 3 Years Old—How Celebrated, Those Present, Gifts, Growing Up—New Photographs, 4 Years Old—How Celebrated, Those Present, Gifts, 5 Years Old—How Celebrated, Those Present, Gifts—All blank.

Record of Growth
Age: One Week 8–12 lbs
Age: Two Weeks 8–15 lbs
Pages for One Month to Five Years: All blank

'Seems I had a lot of blanks,' she says aloud to herself. 'And no bright sayings.'

Her fingers are stroking and curling the golden blonde baby hair. She is thinking about the stories her mother had told her about how she was due on November the twenty-second, and how she had dug the garden, weeded the flowerbeds, and worked every day trying to encourage the labour pains to start. It had felt like an accusation at the time.

I knew better than that, Carol says, why leave a nice warm place where I was safe to be squeezed out into the cold? Strange, her mother had said once, years later, 'It's usually the first who's late, but you definitely were not in a hurry to be born. You were due November twenty-second.' She hears her mother's voice, mildly scolding. 'You disappointed your father, he would have seen you if you'd been on time. But by Christmas, the air force had sent him back to the islands, and he had already been invalided back out to Christchurch. He didn't see you for months.'

The voice continues, 'Where I noted in your baby book that you were badly frightened by the veil, that was a nun's veil. Not the hospital sisters. It was the nun who baptised you, a cousin of your father's. You were baptised three times in all. The hospital thought you weren't going to survive. You were blue, the cord was wrapped around your neck. So one of the nurses baptised you. Then Sister Vida (wearing the veil that frightened you) baptised you because a nun's baptism was better than a nurse's. Then when you were well enough, your grandmother insisted on a proper baptism in church because a priest's baptism is more effective than a nun's.'

Mark appears at the door and says, 'Hey there, you talking to yourself or can anyone join in? Who's the blonde?'

Carol smiles and offers her cheek to be kissed. 'It's me. I'm the blonde. And you know Mark, I actually remember that first haircut.'

'You do?' he replies, sitting dutifully at her side, but not quite masking his disinterest. She continues.

'Yes, very clearly, it was at Dressie's. She was a dressmaker we knew when we lived in Christchurch, so I must have been about eighteen months. I remember she was using a Singer sewing machine when mum and I arrived, and she stopped working, tipped the machine upside down and underneath to make a table, spread a newspaper on top, and then picked me up under my armpits and stood me on the paper. Then she got a pair of big silver shears, and I realised she was going to use them on me. I remember bursting into tears and being terrified by the shiny sharp-looking blades.

'Dressie gave me a hug and wiped my tears. She said "it won't hurt. I'm only going to cut your hair. You won't even feel it." I could barely hear her through the noise of my snuffling. "You'll look even lovelier with nicely shaped curls." So I stood still and squeezed my eyes shut, waiting to feel the shears until I realised that Mum was already collecting the cuttings and tucking them into a paper bag. It didn't hurt after all. Silly the things you think when you're a child. People don't explain stuff to you.' She yawns and closes her eyes, fingers still stroking her baby hair.

Mark pulls the curtains closed and sits with her until she's once again dozing. He's wondering whether she will ever get out of bed again. He goes back to his reading, closing the doors quietly. So he wouldn't hear her if she woke again?

CHAPTER EIGHT

Her sleep is deep and uneasy. She's dreaming that a big black spider is spinning webs in her head, so that her memories are all tangled up. In her dreams, she feels parts of the web sticking to her, and she frantically waves her arms in the air to free herself. She feels the sticky thread on her arms and face.

How can she feel it outside on her skin when the spider is spinning inside her head?

Then she remembers that you should move backwards when you walk into a spider web, not fight it. If she steps back from it, it will detach itself from her, and she will be free. '*Yes,*' says the spider, '*You will be free but only if you solve the puzzle.*'

'What puzzle?' Her dream self asks. 'Where is the puzzle?' She feels trapped like a fly in a spider web, struggling with legs and wings against an impossibly sticky substance that spreads itself all over her body, suffocating her, strangling her. 'I'm not a fly.'

'How do you know? You're trapped. You may as well be a fly.'

Did the spider think that into her head or did she think it herself? *'Think of it like this,'* the spider spins into her ear. '*Your life has been a series of episodes with nothing in between. It's like a cheap necklace, beads of different sizes and colours connected by uneven lengths of chain. Even when you're doing something, you're doing or thinking something else as well. You're not committed to your life. You don't know how to live in the moment.'*

In her troubled sleep, she flinches. Or is she awake? Truth hurts. She knows she often lives in two worlds at once. In one, she is doing; and in the other, she is watching herself doing. She seems to simply observe herself as though she were playing no part in what she is doing. It's more than simple detachment. If she were able to detach herself and live only in one world, which would she choose?

'Exactly,' breathes the spider, and a sticky silk thread wraps itself around her head and insinuates itself into her mind. *'That's the puzzle. Think why do you do that? Is it because you never stay in one place long enough to know where you truly are? How you fit in? You live like you're a spectator on your own life. You don't live the event. You live either side of it. You let others do all the work. You think you "go with the flow" that you're somehow more tuned in. But really, you simply can't be bothered to examine possibilities. You believe that somehow, magically, things happen when they should so there's no point fighting it. That "fullness of time" mentality is your way of protecting yourself against bad things that happen. You didn't cause them, it was all predestined. Or perhaps you just can't face up to the responsibility of making decisions?*

Her head jerks to the side, and she opens her eyes. What was that shadow that just exited stage left? She's turning her life into a script, she thinks. Why am I doing that? She's wide awake and certain she saw something at the edge of the proscenium arch of her dreaming life.

'Aha, there you are,' insinuates the spider, this time without a thread but straight into her now-alert ear. *'You're learning something. You just asked why.'*

Now wide awake, she finds the lock of baby hair still in her hand.

CHAPTER NINE

She is in the grip of an irresistible ennui. She can't remember the day she decided she wasn't getting out of bed. Did she decide?

Or did it just happen? It just happened.

Mark had come home after seven, and she was still in bed. He hadn't been angry, although he would probably have been justified. He was surprised. And as the days had passed, he had gone from surprise to being worried and then angry. She couldn't tell him what was wrong, she didn't know herself. Whenever he asked her, she just told him that she needed time and the peace to think. There was nothing wrong.

He eventually engaged a housekeeper to come in from ten to three each day, since the housework had to be done and meals had to be prepared. He didn't have time to do all that stuff and it wouldn't do itself. Carol had not been happy about the idea of someone else being in their house and messing with 'her things', but she had to admit that it was an obvious solution.

'Just until you feel better,' he had cajoled. So she acquiesced. It was easier.

She refuses to see a doctor. 'There's nothing wrong with me,' she says each time he tries to persuade her.

'Then why won't you get out of that bed?' he demands. 'Because I need time to remember.'

In the end, he had given up. She had been in bed nearly four weeks. Friends were asking after her, inviting them out, and in the end, he was going out alone inventing explanations for her absence.

One day, she asked him to move the picture board into the bedroom. It was just a piece of hardboard in a frame, so it was easy enough to unscrew and move. Then she asked him to rearrange the pictures so they were in some kind of time sequence. She had seemed nervous and uncertain about where some of them fitted.

'I wonder what started that spider nonsense,' he mused. And he was careful to close the curtains before the late afternoon cast its shadows onto her wall. 'Well, probably', he thought to himself, 'she won't be thinking spiders now that the picture board is in that corner.'

CHAPTER TEN

Carol is reading a magazine, while listening at the same time to a radio programme about bagpipes. The narrator is saying, 'History goes back far beyond two thousand years when it was common in Greek and Roman societies. Some form of the bagpipe is one of the oldest known traditional folk musical instruments popular in the middle ages in Italy, France, Spain, as well as Scotland and Ireland.' She's only catching part of it. He goes on, 'Over the years, it has spread through military contact to places as far from European life as Oman, Uganda, and Sri Lanka, used on ceremonial occasions to lead the troops into battle as a challenge to the enemy and announcement of attack. And after the battle, to mourn the passing of brave young men.'

The man on the radio continues the commentary, while Carol both listens to snatches and continues reading. She is quite pleased that she can still read and listen at the same time. It's useful occasionally. She's reminded of a TV programme she'd once watched about Pakistan and bagpipes.

She leans back on the pillow, brushes her hair off her face, and recalls one New Year's Eve in Wellington when a lone piper was playing on a hilltop exactly opposite to where she lived. It was midnight. She couldn't see him. But the mournful wail of the pipes travelled over the hilltops and into the valleys, and everyone in the area had commented on it afterwards. Nobody knew who the piper was. Just a sentimental Scot longing for home, they supposed.

The man on the radio is talking about the unique Scots festival of Hogmanay, and how it originated from the Yule rituals of the Vikings and Norsemen of the eighth century.

On New Year's Eve, one hoped that a tall, dark stranger would knock on the door at midnight; and by welcoming him into your house, he would bring you good luck for the year. Traditionally, he brought with him gifts of coal and salt and black bun and shortbread and a 'wee dram o' whisky'.

The man on the radio comments that in the eighth century, it may have been a tall, blonde stranger appearing at your door, bringing you very bad luck, and carrying a very big axe with which to deliver it.

'First footing' is still celebrated everywhere there are Scots. Carol remembers that she used to go 'first footing' too. It was a common custom in her childhood in the South Island. Some Southern Hemisphere Scots still clean the house and clear the ashes from the hearth to welcome the New Year in even though Yule occurs in midsummer in southern latitudes, and nobody has fires.

The sun's bright reflection on the glossy pages of the magazine is making her eyes feel tired. She puts it on the bedside table and listens as the pipes on the radio play a melancholic pibroch. Just before she feels her eyelids drooping to close completely, she catches sight of the edge of the picture board and a photo of herself age 8. She is wearing her kilt, squinting slightly into the camera, heels together, splayed feet looking too long for her little girl figure, a cockaded hat a little too big for her, and sleeves trimmed with lace that was much longer than her fingers. A monstrous cairngorm is perched on her shoulder.

Then suddenly, the breathy whoosh of the cat-o'-nine-tails whips through the air and lashes her memory into action. The girl in the kilt is feeling sick, stomach knotted, head aching, limbs shaking. She's not squinting, she's seeing what will soon be happening to her. If she squeezes up her eyes and shuts it out, maybe it won't happen.

Carol closes her eyes to remove the picture, but they won't close. They are glued wide open staring at the girl in the kilt. She tries to clear her head to think of something else, but her head is already busy juggling a mindful of fears she doesn't want to remember. Her eyes will not close. She can recall that same little girl fear right here, and now sixty-seven years away. She tears her gaze from the photo, but her eyes slide off the board, up the wall, and into the corner of the ceiling. She shrieks. It's back, and there's no one home to save her.

CHAPTER ELEVEN

She tries to get her thoughts in order. 'It was a long time ago. I have to forget it. I have to forgive. I can't forgive him. I will never forgive him. No matter what harm that does me. I hated him then, and I hate him now. At least I won't forget that. I'm not confused about that.'

'Oh, yes you are, Carol.' She struggles as the web descends onto her head, threading itself through her ears and nose and swimming upstream through her helpless tears into her head. *'You must think about it. We're only talking about beatings at the moment, mere physical assault. You know there's much worse than that can happen to a person. Tell me your story. Help us, both of us, to understand why this still hurts you so much.'*

Carol shudders and squeezes her head with both hands, but she still can't get the girl in the kilt out of it.

'Go on, there's no one else here. Talk to me. Just tell me like it was. No frills. No exaggeration.'

Carol considers this then thinks to herself. I'm not talking to a bloody spider. I'm not that mad. I'll just think it through quietly, and we'll see how smart that ugly little arachnid is. 'You can retire to your web and await a fly,' she says aloud.

CHAPTER TWELVE

So Carol starts to tell her story, straight, the unvarnished truth, to herself inside her own head where she feels safe. She forgets the threads of web that have sewn themselves into her, and she prepares herself to start. But it proves to be too difficult doing a silent monologue with no one to address. So she decides to address herself in her mind, and silently of course, to the spirit of her cat, Zapatos.

Zapatos had died in her arms during a late night dash to the vet's house in 1990. She had been under the balcony in the spa when Zapatos had come down the steps beside her, ears flat, eyes wild, body convulsing, and letting out a high-pitched pain-driven yowl. She had leapt out of the spa, wrapped a towel around herself, wrapped Zappie into a blanket, and driven like a fury up the hill and around the corner to the vet's house. She was too late. He gave one enormous wail and shuddered violently just as the vet came to his door. Zapatos had just announced his death.

Poison or maybe snakebite, the vet had said. 'Would you like me to look after him for you?' Unable to face the thought of burying Zapatos herself, let alone having to take him home to Babuchas, his sister, she had said yes. 'Thank you' and regretted it ever since.

Babuchas had died when Carol was away in Spain in 1993, and her neighbours had taken her to the same vet. Her next two cats, Paco and Tesorita, were unlucky. They had mysteriously disappeared, snakebite too, the Vet had supposed. There was a lot of bush in the area. She had no cat bodies to bury in her garden.

Horribly, there was a rumour circulating that cats had been disappearing all around the place, captured for meat (to be served up as rabbit in which restaurants?) and pelts, which were exported to China for the fur trade.

Carlos Felipe and Consuelo, her last two cats, had been respectfully honoured, and their funereal urns are sitting right now under their pictures in her living room. She could not at first believe how consoling it was to know their ashes were there in the room with her. Having processed these thoughts, she feels calmer now and prepares to commit herself to the spirit of Zapatos.

'Here's how it was, Zappy. I can only tell you from my point of view, so everything I say is only how I saw it. My mother wanted me to have all the opportunities that she never had. So I was sent to ballet, tap and highland dance lessons, then music lessons, and then elocution lessons. At ballet, I was too clumsy and I looked silly in a tutu. At tap dancing, I was agile but lacked a sense of rhythm. I had the strength and stamina for highland dancing, but I was never really good at it. The dance community held competitions every month, and all the highland dance teachers used to enter their dancers to improve them, and to make sure their standards were uniform.

'So every second Saturday, my mother would take me off to 'the comps'. I lived in acid stomach-churning fear of those days because if I did not win a prize, I knew what lay in store for me. My father thrashed me every time I did not come first, second or third. Highly commended was not enough. Now here's something I hadn't thought about before. How did he know that I hadn't won a prize? I certainly didn't tell him.

'I was sent to my room as soon as I got home. I would be told to undress and lie across the bed, and he would come into the bedroom stroking his cat-o'-nine-tails—a leather razor strop that he had sliced into nine strips, leaving just enough solid leather at the top to allow a good strong delivery. He would stand back and raise the leather right above his head and bring it down on my backside as hard as he could. It stung. It really hurt me, and I felt utterly helpless and utterly hopeless. He would strop me again and again, often more than ten times, until he felt that he had made his point. I used to beg for mercy and say I would try harder, so he wouldn't be ashamed of me, and he wouldn't be spending all that money for nothing. This went on for four or five years, Zappie.

'Where was my mother? I don't know. She was never a witness to these whippings. Yet, I used to think, she takes me off and brings me back each time. She must know what's going to happen to me. She was never there to see it. She must have heard me. She would certainly have heard the sound of the strap. The cat-o'-nine-tails was kept handy ready for use any time any of us needed it.

'She had a riding whip. It had been her father's during the Boer War. He was in the cavalry. Being handy with horses, Australians and New Zealanders often ended up in cavalry. From time to time, the riding whip was pressed into service on me—maybe on the three of us. I don't know, we didn't discuss it. Mine were ritual hidings. I don't think my brothers were involved in anything that provided the same opportunity for punishment. They were definitely strapped from time to time. I didn't know much about that; we didn't live in a very together way. We were just kids in not much of a family. How am I going, Zappie? I'm trying to be objective about it. It's hard though.

'That photo was taken when we lived in Invercargill. We lived in a house that had concrete steps at the back, leading up to the landing at the back door, which had a glass window in the upper half. The neighbourhood kids used to come and watch me through the window doing my highland fling and sword dance practise in the living room. My father would be half kneeling beside me with the billiard cue in his hand. Every time I lost my balance or wobbled or obviously got a step wrong, he whacked me around the legs with the billiard cue. It made bruises, and it hurt. The kids would watch this and laugh as though I was some sort of sideshow. In the end, I think my mother put a stop to them watching.

'I did try very hard to dance well, but I had no talent for it. I felt that I was living my life for my mother, not for me. I was reminded often how lucky I was to have all these opportunities.

'One day, while I was getting a thrashing, I realised that he was enjoying hitting me. I was probably about eight. While he was hitting me, he used to repeat over and over again, "This hurts me more than it hurts you."

'Something in my 8-year-old mind asked silently, "Why do it then?" And the grownup inside the 8-year-old said, "Because he enjoys it." And the 8-year-old thought, "What is it about hitting me like this does he enjoy? He knows he's hurting me because I'm crying and I'm asking him to stop and I'm saying that I'll do better next time. Does he like to hear me cry and beg for mercy? What will happen if I don't?" So I stopped crying. It didn't stop hurting, but I decided on that day never to cry again. He obviously didn't understand it. He strapped harder and harder. The more he strapped, the more I promised myself I would never even whimper.

'And I didn't, and eventually, he went back to same old thrashings as before. But they weren't the same for me. For me, each lash of that cat-o'-nine-tails was a tiny victory. Pain had lost its power.'

Carol lets out a huge sigh. The little girl in the kilt has been put to rest with Zapatos.

CHAPTER THIRTEEN

She wakes as she hears the front door slam. She does wish that Mark would make less noise when he comes home. She waits for his footsteps in the passageway, but there's no sound. She looks at the clock and realises that what she had just heard was the housekeeper leaving. She looks up to the window and remembers that she had been talking to herself and must have slipped into a doze. Now what was I thinking about? She wonders this aloud, and before she can stop herself remembering, it hits her.

'Stop it! Stop it! Get away…ugly, ugly, ugly!' she screams as loudly as she can. But the web is already quivering in her nostrils and tickling her around her neck.

'That was not so bad, was it? And you thought I couldn't hear it. Silly! You can't hide your thoughts from me. I'm part of you. I heard it all. And you told it just like you said you would. Did you realise you were crying all the time? See how your pillow is wet? You didn't do that with your glass of water, it's wet with your tears. So you did cry. You thought that you only cried on the inside, that's all. You must be careful about

that, Carol. Tears have to be shed. No use holding them back, or you'll both dry up. You and your tears. You must learn to feel pain and shed tears, or you'll forget how to use them.'

She can feel the web vibrating along with the voice in her ears. 'Forget, what do you mean forget how to use them?' she asks, and then she thinks, what's wrong with me? I'm talking to a bloody spider!

'I can hear you. I told you we're in this together now. You do really want to get out of this bed, don't you? Then you must continue the journey you started. It was just getting interesting. Have you asked yourself how you managed to keep your promise not to cry? It's part of the puzzle, but I'll give you a clue. Think about what you felt and how you managed those feelings. Think about it now, Carol.'

'I don't remember what I felt,' she thought. 'I only remember that I was busy trying not to feel.'

'That's good, that's good. You're getting closer. You were converting that pain into sensation. Sensations can be good or bad. You used yours to construct a wall between what you really felt and what you allowed yourself to feel. You decided to feel nothing. Not feeling the pain allowed you to keep your promise not to cry. I'm right, aren't I? That's an important part of the puzzle, Carol. Now, think about this. You taught yourself not to feel pain, you did it well too.

'You know how I know that, Carol? Remember what happens in the kitchen? Every time you go near the oven, you burn yourself. Every time you pick up a sharp blade, you cut yourself. You know why? You don't know when you're burning yourself until you see the burn, and you don't know when you've cut yourself until you see the blood, am I right? Because you don't feel the pain, and pain is the trigger that sends the message to the brain that tells you to stop doing what you're doing. And now think about this, did you stop yourself feeling everything? I mean not just the pain of the strap, but other kinds of pain as well? Pains of the heart and feelings I'm talking about. You know what they are, Carol? My apologies. I talk too much.'

'Yes, you do!' Carol shrieks up at the ceiling. 'You don't know anything. You don't know what I feel. You have no right to say these things to me. Go away, you're just an ugly little arachnid. I've never liked spiders, too many legs. You just have to look at them to feel the nasty little things crawling all over you. Go! Before I call Mark to spray you dead!'

'He'd have to see me first.'

CHAPTER FOURTEEN

Carol is feeling exhausted. Just as she has gathered her thoughts and started to feel better after the conversation with Zappie, she hears Mark at the door. She pretends to be asleep. 'How're you feeling, Carol? I have a surprise for you.' He hands her a bunch of beautiful spring flowers. 'The guy at the station kiosk can get flowers from any place in the world any season.'

She looks at them, and she's on her way to work in Auckland again. Jonquils, that most potent of spring memories, she is floating on the fragrance of jonquil, heady and high with it. 'They're lovely, Mark, thank you so much. I love jonquils. They remind me of a street I used to walk along where all the gardens had jonquils and daffodils and freesias. They're beautiful. Thank you.'

For a few minutes, she relaxes into the luxury of their perfume. Everything seems different to her now, somehow better and safer. 'How was your day?' It's a rhetorical question, really, but he answers enthusiastically.

'Good, good, fine, I saw the Thorndons this afternoon, and they invited us to dinner at the weekend. I knew you wouldn't want to go out, but I thought maybe it's time you gave yourself a treat, a break from your bed. So I invited them here instead.' Before she has a chance to respond, he goes on, cutting her off just as she was opening her mouth. 'Don't worry, you won't have to do anything. I've arranged for one of those "Chef in Your Own Kitchen" fellows to come and prepare whatever your little heart desires. They do all kinds of cuisine, and all you have to do is plan the menu. Which', he smiles genially trying to sound much more confident than he really feels, 'I have right here.' He brings his other arm from behind his back and hands her a heavily embossed folder.

'I don't know if I'll feel well enough.' She's struggling to find the right tone of voice. She has known this moment will come eventually. Now, how to handle it? She doesn't want to hurt him. She just needs to buy herself a few more days of peace in bed. 'Can we make it tentative?' 'I don't think so,' Mark replies. 'I don't think that would be fair on them. Besides, I really think it will be an effort worth making. You can rest all day, have a nice long soak in the spa, shower yourself with powders and perfume, and wear that lovely green dress that Paco gave you last Mother's Day.'

Paco is the second cat she has given that name. The first was as sleek as a seal, smooth short silken fur shining on his six month old body. That first Paco had disappeared, presumed dead. He had been with her only two months when he just didn't come home one day, and she had promised herself that she would never again have a cat who was so beautifully sleek that he might attract pelt catchers.

This Paco is the opposite, flamboyant, lion-ruffed face, crazy grey tabby fluff waving in all directions. Huge whiskers, clean white socks on grown-up paws, and a tail to shame a flag on a windy day. This Paco lives for cuddles, tickles, affection, and bikkies—in that order.

Carol's cats have never forgotten a birthday, Easter, Christmas, or Mothers' Day. She has no children and no regrets. She has tried not to dwell too long on her reason for childlessness. Seeing her friends' children and their children has been sufficient to make her appreciate the feline species in general and her cats, past and present, in particular, all the more.

Clever devil, she thinks, clever to put it that way. I'll feel as though I'm letting Paco down. 'All right then if you think it will be good for me. But I won't stay up late. I get so tired, and I'm doing nothing to make me tired these days.'

'Thank you, darling.' Mark is relieved. That was easier than he thought it would be. Of course, she gets tired these days, precisely because she is doing nothing. Not a thought he'd care to give voice to. Quit while you're ahead. 'No spiders today?' He wishes he hadn't said that. Why don't I take my own advice? That was too close for comfort.

Carol ignores the spider comment. She's too tired to respond. Besides, she's remembering something that has been escaping her for a while. That picture of the girl her father had called Eileen.

CHAPTER FIFTEEN

Why have I been thinking about that? The girl looks to be about three. She's in postcard size wooden photo frame. She's wearing a burgundy coloured dress (now why did I think that? that picture is black and white), smocked across the chest, tatted around the collar. She's sitting and looking at the camera, head slightly tipped forward, and a shy nearly smile at her lips.

Then the memories come tumbling in, tripping over each other, and jumbling themselves up until there are so many things going on in her head. She just wants to close her eyes and go to sleep.

'Oh, no, you're not getting away with that,' the voice is thick and sounds like dust caught in a cobweb except it's sticky as well. *'You said the magic word again. You asked why? You know you have to find the answer now, don't you! Let's start with who is she, the little blonde girl in the black and white photo wearing a burgundy coloured dress? Who is she? You know her name, don't you? Let's go back to the beginning. I'll stay up here in the corner, and I'll just spin some thread down to you from time to time to keep you on track. Where did you first see that photo?'*

'On their dressing table. It was sitting on the left hand side.' *'What else is there on the dressing table?'*

'Nothing, I can't see anything. That's weird, isn't it? No one has a dressing table with just one thing on it.'

'No, not weird, it just means that the only thing of importance to you was what you remember. The photo in the frame. Who is the girl in the photo?'

'He said it's Eileen.'

'Who said that? Who said it's Eileen?'

'He did. My father. There's another picture there. I can see it now. It's a man wearing an air force cap. It's him with my mother.'

'Then who is Eileen? Do you have a sister called Eileen? Do you have brothers?'

'Yes, two brothers, no sister, I don't have a sister.'

'When did you first meet Eileen?'

'I didn't. I never met her. I've only ever seen this picture of her. Who do you think she is?'

'It's not for me to think, Carol, that's your job. You have to answer the questions. Remember, all the questions are clues to the puzzle. You have to solve the puzzle. Then you can get out of bed!'

'What? What do you mean *then* I can get out of bed?'

'Exactly what I said, Carol. And you know it too. Why do you think you want to stay in bed? You want to think about each of the beads in the necklace, and how to put them together so that they're equally spaced. You want to rearrange the colours and the sizes and make a beautiful piece of jewellery with what you already have. So let's get back to the subject. Who do you think Eileen is? Think back to when you first noticed the photo.'

Carol is thinking. She's sure it was around the butter wouldn't melt time. That was when she first realised that adults not only don't explain stuff to you, like the scissors with Dressy, they tell lies as well. Yes, that's when it was. She'd had her pants pulled down and been smacked hard on the bottom by her father.

'What do you mean by the butter wouldn't melt time, Carol?' 'Bloody spider. I forgot he listens to thoughts.'

'I heard that. Now, tell me about the butter.' 'It's not that important.' *'Important enough for you to remember. Important enough to tell you that adults tell lies.'*

'It was during rationing time at the end of the war or just after. We all had separate little dishes for our week's butter. It wasn't much, about an inch square. One day, I heard a friend of my mother say, "Oh, her? Butter wouldn't melt in her mouth." I don't know who they were talking about, but I thought that was silly because butter would melt in your mouth. So I cut the rest of my ration in half, put it on my tongue, and ran into my parent's bedroom to look in the mirror to see if it melted.

'I hadn't noticed my father was in the bed. I was watching the butter melt, and suddenly, he was there and grabbing me by the shoulders shouting, "You little thief, don't you know that's rationed? You're not getting any more this week!" I said it was my butter, and I wouldn't expect any more. So he tore down my pants, threw me onto the bed, and whacked me for being cheeky.

'That's when I first noticed the photo. That's right, he was staying in bed all day, so he must have just come back from the hospital in Christchurch. He must have brought the photo with him. That's who Eileen was. One day I asked who's that in the photo and he said that's Eileen, she's my girl, she visited me in hospital. You weren't there. Eileen was. I looked very closely at that picture and said, "Do you think she looks like me?" He didn't answer.

'I went back to that picture time after time when he wasn't around, and held it up next to my face in the mirror. One day, I told him I thought it was me in the picture, and he said it wasn't, it was Eileen, his special little girl. I asked my mother, and she didn't contradict him. She just brushed me off. I was almost certain it was me. I had found the dress hanging up high in my parent's wardrobe, and I'd stood on a chair with the photo in one hand to look at it. It was the same dress, I was sure. It was a burgundy colour and smocked exactly the same as the dark dress in the picture.

'I told him I had found the dress in the wardrobe, and that it was my dress, so the girl in the picture had to be me. He sneered at me, and I suddenly hated him for it. "That's not you. You were never there. That is Eileen, she loved me, she was with me in hospital, *you* weren't." I was very confused and worried about me and my dress. The little girl looked like me, and she was wearing my dress, but he said it wasn't me and my mother wouldn't say it was me. If it was some kind of game, surely she would have let me in on the secret.

'The next time I looked in the wardrobe, the dress was gone. It was years before I could accept that it was some kind of mean madness in him, and my mother had been complicit. Who would lie to a child about something as important as their identity? My mother never admitted the deception, and she never referred to those questions that confused and worried me. But I had learned one big lesson. Trust no one. You will be betrayed.'

Carol is now feeling very tired, but also, she feels strangely relieved.

'Well done, Carol. You can put that photo into the filing cabinet now. That's another piece of the puzzle. Your father was vindictive and unfeeling. And your mother failed to protect you. Why? Perhaps she was frightened of him too. Perhaps putting it out of her mind was her way to survive.

'Think of this, perhaps she also trusted you to work it out one day because you're strong and clever. Perhaps she hoped you would understand her. You didn't deserve to be treated like that. The girl in the frame is you. They lied to you.

'Perhaps he was angry that he wasn't there to see you when you were born. Perhaps he felt guilty about being in hospital. After all, he was injured through his own carelessness. Imagine a PT instructor taking a class of pilots on bailing out techniques, and having of one of your students land on you from a great height, knocking you unconscious. Looking the wrong way is no excuse. He's the teacher, he's responsible. He

betrayed his students. He betrayed you. Perhaps the only way he could live with not seeing you was by inventing another girl completely. And think about this, he could control the little girl in the frame. He couldn't control you. Tell me something about your father, Carol. What did he do?'

'He was a professional boxer until my mother married him. She said she wouldn't marry him until he gave it up. In the end, I wonder whether he regretted giving up. He always said he had the killer instinct. And I wonder whether she regretted the marriage.'

Carol notices the slightest hint of a tickle around her neck and ears like having a silk thread lightly tracing a pattern on her skin.

CHAPTER SIXTEEN

Paco has crept up to Carol's pillow and settled himself over her head like one of those clutch hats we used to wear in the fifties. Doris Day had lots of them. In those years, Carol used to buy the stiffened and shaped net frames to make her own. The bases were shaped like today's huge earphones, band over the top, and bulging each side above the ears. She had covered them with materials that matched her outfits.

Paco is arched over her head, paws in pairs resting on each of her shoulders, making a splendid display of fluff, and is purring softly into her ear.

She is thinking feline thoughts. She imagines that she is stroking Louis Quatorze who is sitting on her knees. Lovely white Louis who had left her marriage with her and the pressure cooker, and gone with her to live in Auckland, and later, Wellington. She's remembering Louis as a kitten, being delivered to her in a baby's bassinette, tiny white furball tucked close to a new baby's head. The father of the family who had given her Louis delivered him on the way back from

Napier Hospital when he had collected his wife and their new baby. Louis was a placid home loving cat.

One day, Carol arrived home with a companion for Louis, Seamus. Seamus was one of the latter breeding stages of the pure white Siamese, a breed being developed by the neighbour of her astrology tutor—a philosophy lecturer at the University in Wellington. The face and ears were perfect, his bright china blue eyes amazing, but the breeder had yet to get the muscle structure corrected.

Seamus was not only named after literary royalty, but he had the gift of being able to check everything, instantaneously, on entering a room and matching it to its mental imprint. He identified changes immediately and inspected them. Move just one chair a few centimetres from its place, and he would notice it. Carol liked the idea of Seamus being a shamus.

Seamus settled into the house on the hill upstairs with Pieter and Carol and Louis and the pressure cooker, with Carol's mother downstairs. Louis was happy to have company, and he and Seamus amused each other.

Then, one afternoon, when Carol was at work, she received a call from a neighbour reporting that there was a white cat lying on the side of the road down by the golf course. She jumped into the car and went off in search. She found a white cat, but it was not one of hers. She took a rug from the car and gently slid it under the cat. It looked at her with cool green suffering eyes and made a stifled mewing sound. It barely moved. It didn't even blink. She wrapped it up, laid it carefully into a cardboard carton, and drove off to the vet. His report was shocking. The white cat had been hit on the head, probably to kill him, and dumped. He could barely drag his back legs behind him. The vet suggested that the kindest act would be to put him down.

Carol asked if there was an alternative. Vet said he couldn't guarantee recovery, but if she was prepared to look after him, together, they would see what they could do.

So the throwaway cat was named Napoleon Bonaparte and taken to live with Louis and Seamus. He was put on a diet of DYC yeast tablets to strengthen his nervous system, and regular gentle exercise to try to restore strength to his back legs. In six weeks, Napoleon was walking normally and able to jump from the floor to the bed. He wasn't a demanding cat. When the fridge door was opened, the other two raced to the kitchen. Napoleon waited until he saw them eating before he joined them at the plates.

Arriving home from work one day, Carol went straight to the bedroom to drop her bags and coat. Napoleon was asleep at the foot of the bed. She leaned over to pat him, he jerked his head toward her and leapt into the air, ears flattened, eyes flashing, wildly startled. Then she got it. The knock on the head had affected his hearing. That's why she had surprised him. He doesn't respond to the sound of the fridge door because he doesn't hear it.

So it was back to the vet who, serendipitously, had a friend at the university whose specific study was feline neurology. After laboratory tests, he was declared irrevocably deaf. Nerves all dead, nothing to work with.

Carol is rolling all these thoughts around her head in a deliciously sleepy haze of fur and purr.

CHAPTER SEVENTEEN

Paco trills that little interrogative rrrrrr that cats do. He stretches his front legs, opens his fingers momentarily, revealing curved claws, and relaxes back onto Carol's head. Carol's now remembering Amy, Linus, and Schroeder, her London cats. They were a wonderful story of starvation and salvation.

She and her husband had returned from nine months in Spain where she had been working in an ad agency. She had remarried in 1972, a creative director she was working with in London. They were moving into the basement (euphemistically called garden) flat that a friend had lent them. Carol's mother, who'd met them in Spain, was with them.

Carol was going back to the same company she had been with before she had accepted the Spanish contract, so she didn't have to find a new job. And her husband planned to go back to freelance design and illustration and his old clients.

It was September 1973 and London was already anticipating the dreary drizzles of winter. The flat was accessed by a dozen stairs down from the footpath in front, and the obligatory second exterior access was at the back where French windows opened onto a three metre by four metre paved area, surrounded by a three metre high concrete retaining wall, which held the lawn and garden above at bay. In the event of an emergency at the front, there was no way you could escape via the rear windows unless you could handle a three-metre levitation from a standing start.

The day they moved in it was raining, and the patio was strewn with the litter of twigs and pretty gold and red autumn leaves. It was too chilly to have the windows open, so they unpacked their suitcases and lit the electric fire. They had bought sandwiches for their first night meal and planned to get in some supplies the next day—Sunday. That gave Carol one day to get things organised before she started work on Monday. They made up beds for themselves and Carol's mother and retired early. It had been a long five-day drive back from Torrenostra where they had an apartment on the Mediterranean coast just north or Valencia.

They had loaded Carol's mother, who had been with them for a month in Spain, along with everything they owned into the Seat 127, just managing to leave the minimum legal space for driver vision, and they had set off from the beach very early in the morning. It had been hard getting up early. They'd had a long farewell with friends the day before; and before daylight, they had stripped the beds, put everything in order, washed the floor, and left the linen for Carmen, a close friend, to launder and return to the cupboards.

They took the coast road to Valencia and the motorway via Madrid from there to the French border, stopping on the way at various places to buy provisions for the road. Luis, the chef who owned the bar-restaurant-pensions in their playa, had prepared an enormous tortilla for their journey. Luis had never been further away from his home village than Valencia, eighty kilometres to the south, and looked upon their journey across Spain and up through France to Calais as truly a voyage of exploration.

Carol's mother saw Spain, the Pyrenees, the Massif Central, and Channel Coast squashed into the back seat surrounded by packages and clothing, barely able to breathe without dislodging something. But she was looking forward to the journey because for the last three weeks, to save money for the trip back, they had virtually lived on snails, which were free for the taking from the rosemary bushes in the hills. Her poor mother had never eaten snails before this and hoped she never would again. Surprisingly, Carol had found many culinary disguises for them, some even looked edible, but it's hard to hide the texture of snails.

Little did her mother know that within days of arriving in London, she would be feeling the same way about duck, which in the past she had really quite enjoyed. Carol had a butcher friend from her previous years in London who sold her what he called 'wanky ducks' for fifty pence each. There was nothing wrong with the ducks except that they had been packed in the bottom of the delivery box, and what should have been nicely rounded duck carcasses were squashed absolutely flat.

Back to the London drizzle, the first morning was dreary. Cold and intermittent light rain. Light, but penetratingly wet. Very different from the Mediterranean sunshine they had just left behind.

Carol checked the patio for temperature—too cool and no room to sit outside at any rate. They did their shopping, took mum for a drive around Kensington to show her the flash part, as distinct from the nouveau-arty but shabby part, where they were staying.

The next morning, as Carol was getting ready to go to work, she glanced out at the patio and noticed that the leaves had been swept into one corner. That's odd, she thought, the wind surely can't get down that low. As she was contemplating how a pile of leaves had been made out of an untidy scatter without apparent intervention by broom, the leaves stirred then rustled and started to move apart. She stepped closer as a tiny little head poked out, all eyes and ears. A ginger tabby kitten, barely old enough to have a cover of fur, eyes huge and blue. 'You poor wee thing, you can't be more than a week old. You're too small for your eyes to be open, and you're so scrawny.'

Carol looked around, and there was no sign of a mother cat. She looked up at the top of the wall. How the hell did that kitten get down here? The kitten wriggled and mewed such a little mew.

She asked her husband and mother to go to the chemist she had seen in the strip of shops around the corner. And she set about finding a cushion and a soft blanket to put the wee kitten on in front of the fire. She found a cardboard carton, tore up some newspaper into tiny pieces, and made a makeshift litter tray. Not that the kitten looked as though it was bursting.

They came back with Farex, which was mixed onto a saucer with warm milk and marmite that they'd found in a cupboard. The kitten sniffed and tried to pick it up with his tongue, but he was too little or too weak. So when she left for work, her mother was feeding it by finger.

The next morning, she got up early and flung open the curtains, not having any idea why or what she expected to find. It was raining heavily, and the patio was soaked. She felt strangely disappointed. She left for work just as her mother was feeding the kitten who was, by that time, enthusiastically licking Farex off her finger.

Carol had also bought an eyedropper to make sure the kitten was getting plenty of liquid. It had looked as though it was close to dehydration, and it obviously had not learned to lap. It knew how to suck though and wrapped its tiny mouth around the plastic eyedropper, which was about the same size as a nipple, and worked at it furiously.

The following day, the sky was clearing, and the rain had all but stopped. Carol thought to herself, 'Silly, what do you expect to see?' But she opened the curtains straight away at any rate. She scanned the patio and froze. 'I'll look away, and then I'll look outside again. I'm imagining it.' She was not imagining it. There, in the corner, was a neat little pile of leaves. She knew what she was going to find. Without hesitation, she bent down and wrapped her hands around a little ginger and white kitten, tiny, wriggling, and mewing. Blue eyes wide with what? Hope?

She called to the others. 'You won't believe this! We have *two* kittens!' She turned to go inside, and out of the corner of her eye, caught a flash of ginger. The flash landed beside her, looked up at the kitten in her hands, and walked straight into the room and lay down in front of the heater. Carol was elated. She put the new kitten in front of the fire with the other one.

The skinny ginger flash presented her belly, and both kittens mewed and tottered toward it. She smelt and licked each one and nudged them closer to her. Carol could see that she had no milk to give them. She could barely be six months old and was nothing but skin and bone with dangly chewed nipples, red and sore looking. She stroked the cat's side and felt the sharp ridges of her hungry ribs. She opened a can of sardines and put them onto a saucer, and the mother cat devoured them. Probably the first decent meal she's had in months.

'I wonder how many others there were?' Carol mused. She knew that only these two had survived. If there were more, the mother would have waited and brought them one by one until she was sure they were welcome. She would not have shown herself, she wouldn't abandon a baby.

Amy and Linus and Schroeder had arrived into their new lives. Carol and her husband were thrilled with their ready-made family. The feline nature is a strange one. It has its secrets, and special ways of communicating with nature. The night in 1968 when the inter-island ferry, Wahine, had foundered in a violent storm in Wellington, Louis, Seamus, and Napoleon had squeezed themselves into the space between the floor and the bookshelves (planks on bricks) and had hidden there for fully six hours before the severe storm alert was broadcast. They must have sensed the change in atmospheric pressure. Nature told them to find a safe place and stay there. Just like nature had urged Amy to test a kitten.

Carol and the family were in the London basement flat for two months in all, and their final week was made amazing by the scene that greeted them one afternoon of rare winter sunshine. Amy and her kittens were soaking up the warmth among the leaves on the patio, and sitting above them at the edge of the lawn, looking down at them, were two full-grown cats; one ginger tabby identical to Amy and Schroeder, the other ginger and white identical to Linus.

Visiting time at the nursery.

CHAPTER EIGHTEEN

Carol is still luxuriating in the memory of her London cats as Paco stirs and stretches and thinks it's time he had another bikkie.

He jumps off the pillow onto the side table, knocking the bedside clock onto the polished wood floor. Carol wakes with the sudden noise. What time is it? She reaches out to retrieve the fallen clock and it shows 4.30. The housekeeper has been and gone, and Mark will be home before seven. What does she have time to do?

'Bathroom first then I'll have a snoop around and see if I can find a book to read. Or I might just have a rest.' At the bookshelves, she finds an old photo album. Another walk down memory lane? Sounds good to me.

She turns the pages absent-mindedly, tucking photos back into their frilly little black photo corners, much more practical than the predesigned spaces photo albums offer today. Not all photos are the same size, and what do you do with the too big or too small ones? She pauses at a picture of her favourite aunt, Aunty Margaret.

Something flutters at the side of her face, and she brushes it away impatiently. It sticks to her hand, and she tries to shake it off. She scrutinizes it closely, and it dawns on her that it is grey web. Cobweb, old and dusty. Her eyes flicker upwards to the corner of the room and it's there! 'I hate you!' she screams at it. 'Go away! I can kill you!'

'Then why don't you try?' comes the hideous leggy voice of the spider. *'See, I've got all these legs to trample on your dreams. Time to do some more work if you ask me.'*

'Which I didn't!' Oh, God, I'm talking to a spider again. What's wrong with me?

'Aaah, now you're getting the idea. What is wrong with you? That's what we're here to discover. You keep secrets, things you think are shameful. Things you have done that you have never really faced. They're not really shameful. The real shame is that you've never processed them, integrated them, tucked them away some place where they can't harm you because you've already neutralised them. Don't know what I mean? Let's think about that. Nice photo, the one of Aunty Margaret. She looks very regal. I know, I know, you made the dress. Very regal too.'

'Don't patronise me, you ugly hairy little arachnid. You know nothing. Nothing!'

'Possibly not, but probably yes. You didn't say that just then, you only thought it. I heard it because I spin your thoughts for you. You just follow the threads. Tricky, isn't it? People are pretty tricky little numbers. You're trickier than most, but you don't know it. You think you're transparent, that people can see right through you, so you try to complicate things by keeping secrets. That doesn't work with me. I've been asleep in your head a long, long time, and you woke me up with that silly priest nonsense. So now, it serves you right.'

'What silly priest nonsense? What are you talking about?'

'I don't think you're ready for the priest stuff yet. Let's just stick (you understand sticky don't you?) with family stuff.'

Carol feels the sticky web trailing across her forehead and tries to brush it away, but it just sticks to her hand, and she feels like crying. She wipes her hand on the bedcover, but she's not even sure there's anything there at all.

'You loved your aunty, didn't you?'

Despite her misgivings about talking to a spider, Carol wants to talk about Margaret. 'Yes, yes, she meant more to me than anyone. I really used to look forward to her visits. She only came once or twice a year, but I loved it when she was with us. I spent school holidays with her sometimes. It was difficult for her because she had the lending library to run and me to look after as well.

'Her mother sent her off to a nunnery as soon as she turned fifteen. She was old school Irish, had to give one child to the church. She'd sent one of Margaret's brothers off to the seminary to become a priest, but he only lasted two years. Another brother was sent to become a brother, and he didn't even last eighteen months.

'Margaret was the youngest and the only one of the five left, so she was bundled off at fifteen. She told me that Nan made the decision one Saturday evening when she arrived home from church, and found some of the neighbours' kids and Margaret in the living room with the lights off. Margaret was hiding behind the couch with a boy when Nan went into the room, saw what she thought was going on, and went ballistic. So she was sent off to a convent where she stayed for fourteen years until my father and one of my uncles took her out for the day and never took her back. She hated the convent.

'She went to live with my great-aunt and uncle who doted on her. They gave her a good life, but she never felt free enough to make a life of her own. She didn't know how to. Imagine she'd spent the best years of her life locked away in a convent with a lot of other girls who'd been "given to god" by Irish parents.

'Great-Aunty Kitty died when I was very young, and I don't remember her. But Great-Uncle Jack lived till I was in my twenties. He'd started life as a hairdresser, managed a string of country hotels around Otago, and went on to own and train trotters. By the time I met him, he was pretty well off. He and Aunty Kitty made a good home for Margaret, and she was very fond of them. She was fun, and she loved me. If you've been living in my head all the time, how come you're asking me about her?'

'There are limits to my interests, Carol. I can't be everywhere at once, and to be honest, I only come when you call me.'

'Call you? I never call you. You told me you know everything about me. Why are you asking me about Margaret?'

'Here, let me clear that web off your hand. I can tell it's annoying you. I'm asking you about Margaret because your answers will lead you somewhere. She was good at telling jokes, wasn't she? And she told you some pretty funny real things as well. That little carved camphorwood box over there, she gave it to you and told you its story. Tell me the story.'

Carol is surprised. She really is enjoying the memory of Margaret. And if I forget the mad spider bit and just talk to myself, it could be fun. 'Well', she addresses herself in the mirror of the dresser, 'it goes like this. Margaret's next-door neighbour, Alva, was a spinster like Margaret. Funny word, isn't it? Spinster, sort of spidery.'

'Not to me, my lovely, I spin and spin and spin enough to make you dizzy.'

'She lived with her parents who had never encouraged Alva to go out and enjoy herself. In fact, they kept a pretty tight rein on her. They were elderly, and Alva must have been late thirties, early forties herself when this happened. She'd managed to have a few affairs, like with the bank manager who looked after her parents' business. Margaret had also had her fling with him. But he wasn't the only one according to Margaret. And she'd had a few close shaves. Abortions, I mean. It wouldn't do to become pregnant. What would that do to her narrow-minded parents? So when she was "up the duff", she would visit Mrs Haggerty for the knitting needle treatment, and then go to Dr Scott for the aftercare in case anything went wrong. She was pretty reliable, Mrs Haggerty, and by all reports, she serviced a fair number of Dunedin's residents. She was considered to be the most experienced abortionist around.

'Well, Alva was pregnant for the fifth time over about fifteen years. She remembered that Dr Scott had warned her the last time that if she got herself up the duff again, she would be facing real danger. Because she'd been using some kind of ring contraceptive, Dr Scott had told her that it had worn away some of the surrounding tissue, and another abortion would weaken it so much that she might hemorrhage and die.

'So Alva gives Margaret that little camphorwood box and makes her promise that if anything happens to her, she will take it to the cliffs above St Clare Beach and throw it into the sea. Margaret promises. Alva makes her swear on it. Margaret asks what's in the box? Alva tells her, "All my best jewellery, rings that boyfriends have given me over the years. I can't let my parents find them." Well, Margaret has seen some of those rings, and has already made up her mind and crosses her fingers behind her back as she swears to throw the box over the cliff.

'Margaret takes the box home and shakes it to see if it rattles. Alva has already told her that everything is wrapped in tissue paper. The box doesn't seem heavy enough to contain many rings and brooches.'

CHAPTER NINETEEN

Alva has her termination, is checked over by Dr Scott, and given the all-clear with a stern warning to be extra careful in future. Which is a bit of a laugh because both Alva and Margaret have had affairs with Dr Scott. Margaret's current affair is the owner of the grocery shop next door to the library. Alva fancies him as well.

'Back at Margaret's house where she'd lived with her uncle and aunt since she escaped from the convent, Alva asks her if she wants to see what's in the camphorwood box. She fits the fancy key and opens it, and it's full of used French letters! Alva was too frightened to flush them in the toilet because they float, and there was a certain sentimentality about them. She couldn't bring herself to drown her dreams, I suppose. So she locked them away in the little camphorwood box.

'When she gave the box to Margaret, she hadn't given her the key, which was such an unusual shape that the front of the box would have been damaged if the lock had to be forced. Margaret, who had been rehearsing the explanation she would make to the locksmith when she took the box to be opened after Alva died, all but collapsed laughing!

She confessed her plan for her betrayal to Alva. I was going to get done up in my fur coat and jewels and take it to the locksmith and explain that I had accidentally dropped the key down the sink as I was cleaning some rings. "You bitch, Alva." She giggled. Can you picture the scene? "Bitch yourself," said Alva. "Do you think I'd trust you with my jewels? I knew damn well you'd be at the locksmith before I turned cold."

'That's the story behind the box.' Carol looked pleased with herself and fancied she could hear the sound of eight hands clapping.

'Very good, but very good, very amusing. Now tell me about your trip to the same lady.'

Carol cringes. She cannot believe she has walked straight into that one. However, since she's in the storytelling mood and she hasn't had to introduce the subject herself, she's thinking get it done and over with. It's not as though the bloody spider's a priest.

'Aah, there you go again, Carol. Don't tell me you'd tell a spider something you wouldn't trust to a priest.'

'I'll do it quickly and that will be it, right?' What am I thinking, it's a bloody spider.

'Bloody's not a bad word for this bit, is it? Just think of Zappy or Babuchas or Paco or Tesorita or Amy and Linus and Schroeder and tell it like it happened. No exaggerating, no omissions. You know you will feel better afterwards.'

CHAPTER TWENTY

Carol knows she will feel better once she has connected all the details of that time in her life. Forget the bloody spider, she thinks. I have to do this eventually, so why not now? Perhaps it will be therapeutic. Where to start this little episode? She's looking for a thread she can trace back to the event's genesis.

She is thinking 20 December 1957, five days before her seventeenth birthday. It's 7 a.m., and she's getting ready for her first day at work. She was one of only two in her sixth form class who had chosen to make their own ways in the world instead of going to training college or uni. This was her first job. She was starting at the local radio station to train as a copywriter.

Suddenly, she hears raised voices coming from the kitchen. Her father is yelling, 'You're a liar! I did tell you, you're a bloody liar!'

Her mother's voice reaches her, shrunken, defeated, 'Well, I must have forgotten or not heard you.'

'You did bloody hear!' he was shouting at her.

Something snapped inside her, and she charged through the kitchen door and stood defiantly between her mother and father, looked him full in the face, and said coldly and slowly, enunciating clearly, 'That's the last time you speak to my mother like that.'

He raised his arm, as though to punch, and clenched his fist at her and snarled, 'Get out of my way, you slut! Mind your own business, get out of my house, and don't come back.'

She looked at her mother who looked away. 'Right. I will. I will go.' 'And I went.' Carol's right back in the moment. 'I felt all kinds of sick and frightened, but I was glad that I had finally stood up to him for her. Even if it meant I had to find somewhere to live, I could do it.

I was so relieved that I hadn't been the cause of the scene.'

Carol knows she's talking to herself. Aloud. It doesn't worry her any more. In fact, she quite likes the idea of giving it all to the universe. Once things have been given voice, they belong to the universe. Anyone can listen in. The important thing is that they have been said aloud and can no longer be taken back. That's why you need to say the truth. You don't want your lies pursuing you all your life.

'I went off to my first day at work and later called Miriam, a school friend, to ask if I could stay with her family for a while just until I got myself sorted out. They both knew that my father had been a professional boxer before his marriage, and that some people believed he was a punch-drunk. They'd probably heard a few reports of his behaviour from Miriam.

'The family situation was sad for my mother because relations between her family and my father had never been very friendly, with the result that we grew up barely knowing our cousins. So later that day, before my father was home from work, I rode my bike back to the house, packed a bag, strapped it onto the back of the bike, and pedalled off to Miriam's house. Over the next week, I made surreptitious trips back until I had taken all that was mine. Each time my mother begged me to stay. Each time she begged, I quietly said no. I wasn't angry, I wasn't sad. I just knew I couldn't go back. Not on my word. Not back to the house when he was there. I felt nothing.

'She rang me at work day after day. She had my oldest brother plead with me. He worked as a sound engineer (technician in those days) at the radio station. It was through him I had obtained the cadetship. It was hard to take the calls, but easy to refuse to go back. I'd had my fill of my father's bullying and punching and sneering and humiliation. Once I passed him when he was walking with another man on the main street and heard the man say, 'There's your daughter.' And he replied, turning, and looking straight through me, "I have no daughter".'

CHAPTER TWENTY-ONE

Carol is still locked in that moment. She consoles herself by continuing her soliloquy. 'I stayed with Miriam's family until she went off to teacher training college at the end of January, and then moved into a small flat in a very big house close to the centre of town. Am I really still talking to that spider? Oh, well.

'The house was owned by a couple of maiden ladies, the Misses Vincent. My mother had given me some sheets and blankets, and the people I worked with at the radio station contributed odd pieces of cutlery and china, so I had enough things to be able to cook and eat. The place had furniture, fortunately. However, it took nearly every penny I earned to pay the rent. I had less than five shillings left for food every fortnight. A couple of techs and an announcer had a place just up the road, and we made a deal. If I did their washing, their flat had a washing machine, and did some cooking for them, they would buy food for me. And I could use their washer.

'Things were looking up. Mum had found some old dark pink curtains that just fitted my front windows, and I finally felt almost respectable. Then one day, when I arrived home from work, one of the maiden ladies knocked at the door and asked me to come upstairs to their place. I was mildly surprised, but followed, wondering what had happened. She opened the door of her living room and indicated a seat for me and said she would be back in a minute. The door on the other side of the room opened, and my mother was shepherded into the room by the other sister and sat down opposite me!

'It transpired that the elderly sisters had been scandalised by the appearance of red curtains at the front window. "You're too innocent to know what that means in a port town, dear." So they had imported my mother to explain to both of us why I would have to remove them!'

CHAPTER TWENTY-TWO

'A week later, I moved out of the Misses Vincent's bordello to share a flat with Beryl, a new girl at work who had been transferred from another station. Our boss, John, was the man I married three years later. Am I repeating myself, arachnid?'

'A little, it doesn't matter. You don't have to remember things in the order they happened. Things have a way of grouping themselves to make a point to you. Just go on telling your story.'

'Our friendship was based on shared interests. Neither of us had close friends in the town, everyone I knew was either away at college or uni. And he was pretty much a loner. We started a relationship. I never went to his place, but he would stay over in my shared flat at weekends. I had a sun porch bedroom to myself, and the living room between Beryl and me. The only idea I had about contraception in those days was the douche. When necessary, I kept a basin of hot water, heavy with the odour of disinfectant, under the bed with the black plastic and rubber douche. It was a crude device and a crude and unsafe way to run a romance. Eventually, of course, I became pregnant.

'I called Aunty Margaret. I was terrified. If my father found out, he had already called me a slut entirely without reason, I would be calling all kinds of shame down on my mother, and my father would be jubilant. Bullyingly, sneeringly, nastily jubilant, I would have proved his words correct.

'Aunty Margaret told me to see Harry Yung, a local businessman who was a friend of the family. He had had an affair with Margaret at some stage. He was Chinese, and I had worked after school in his shop. I liked him and trusted him, and I knew from Margaret that he was not overfond of my father. Harry had been studying medicine until his father died when, as the oldest son, it fell to him to become head of the family. He had five younger brothers and sisters to help to educate into adulthood, so he left his degree unfulfilled and returned to work in our town.

'Margaret rang Harry from Dunedin and asked if he could help me. Harry asked me how far along I was, and when I told him, he asked why hadn't I come to him sooner. Of course, I had no idea about his "other" business activities. He didn't think he could help me now, but he would try. It took him a couple of days to get the ingredients together then he called me and gave me a thick sludgy green mixture to drink, while sitting in a bath as hot as I could possibly take it. "Stay in the bath as long as you can bear to. Don't take any risks. I don't want to get into trouble. Call me first if anything happens. Don't call a doctor."

'I rang him the next day to report nothing had happened. He rang Margaret to advise her, and she called me to get to Dunedin the next day. This was soon after Easter, 1960. John knew I was pregnant. We had agreed there would be no marriage in these conditions, but he would pay whatever fees were charged.

'So I made the excuse at work that my aunty was ill and had asked for help, and I was allowed that Friday and two days off the following week. Five days in all. I took the Thursday late train to

Dunedin where Margaret met me and took me first thing Friday morning to Mrs Haggerty. She left me there and went to open the library, a private lending library and news agency in St Kilda that her uncle had bought for her, so that she had a secure job. She assured me that Dr Scott would care for me if anything dangerous happened.

'Mrs Haggerty showed me into the kitchen. She took the tablecloth off and placed a roll of plastic over the wooden tabletop. I had no idea what was going to happen to me, and I was too terrified to ask. I hadn't asked Margaret either. She put a kettle of water to boil on the stove, and got some towels and cheap thick sanitary pads ready beside the bench. She told me to remove my lower underwear and squat on the table, holding onto the back of a high wooden chair.

'I don't know whether it was a knitting needle or a length of wire that she inserted, but she was careful enough and was obviously experienced at guiding it by feel. I could feel it, but it didn't really hurt. She moved it around for what seemed like several minutes, and then withdrew it and removed her hand from holding my haunches. "There you are," she said. "Take these pads with you, and use them every day until you don't need them. Now, straight home to bed. You will have cramps and they may be strong. There's no way to tell. Everyone's different, and this is your first. If you feel movement down there, go straight to the toilet and try to put a plastic bag into it first so you can see what is expelled." 'I had put my mind into neutral, but I was still struggling to keep myself calm. I thanked her, gave her the envelope with fifty pounds in it, and made my way to the tram stop. I only had to wait ten minutes, but I was already feeling dizzy and having cramps. I was panic-stricken by the time I got off the tram. My belly felt like it had rubber balls rolling around in it, banging against each other. Every so often, they stopped and just tore away at something. I imagined slices being stripped away from my sides, and then a row of sharp needles digging into me. I thought of the way a butcher pulls and trims lamb flaps, and it felt just like that looks. I made it to the house and my bed and lay down with sweat pouring off my forehead.

'A few hours later, I felt my belly violently suck itself in and then the pressure of something about to be released. I flew to the bathroom, plastic bag in hand. I sat and was too frightened to relax and let whatever had to happen, happen. What if I bleed to death? There's no one here to help me. Finally, I stopped holding my breath and relaxed. I felt a solid bubble expel itself from my vagina. I quickly shoved my hand through my legs, and felt the soft plop of something like a heavy lump of slimy jelly fall onto my hand.

'I sat for ages not knowing what to do. Wanting to see what it was that fell. Not wanting to look at it. Suddenly, I was seized by an overwhelming need to touch it, turn it over, feel it. It was a tiny foetus, features forming already, curled in typical foetal position. I knew it was a male. I looked at it a long time, but I don't know whether I saw anything or just believed it was male. I couldn't think the word boy. That was too close to being human. I willed the world to stop turning, I tried to make the clocks stand still, I was trying to squeeze my action into some kind of nano-space between seconds where it would not be recorded. Then none of this would ever have happened.

'I flushed the toilet. And there was nothing left.'

CHAPTER TWENTY-THREE

Carol is sweating and trembling. One tear slips from under an eyelid and quivers on her cheek. She brushes it away, but it clings to her fingers. It's not a tear, it's a piece of spider web and it's so sticky. She shakes her fingers wildly then lets her hand fall lifeless to the cover. Oh, God, the placenta, she remembers. The placenta came away with a big fat bloody splash two days later. It looked like a lump of liver. How could something so small leave something that big behind?

'And did you examine it?' Dr Arachnid enquires. *'You were told to examine it to make sure it was whole. But tell me, what happened next? There's more to this story, isn't there, Carol? Something was left behind. Not the placenta, not the baby. Yes, baby. You have to face it. That was not just a little foetus, it was a piece of human being. I'll give you a clue. It rhymes with quilt. That's what was left behind. And you know why? Because you wanted to forget it. That was a little potential person, Carol, and you treated it as though it was an inconvenience. You didn't mourn it.'*

'I didn't have time,' Carol whimpers. 'I couldn't face it. I had to get back to work. You forget I had to make a living for myself.'

'Oh, yes, a living. Is that what you call it? Sounds more like a slow dying to me. But there's still time, you said so yourself. You have taken to your bed to give yourself time to think. So think about that, and keep thinking until you accept it. When you can see it as just another run in the great pantyhose of life, you will be on your way to being perpendicular again. I'm saying understand it for what it was and forgive yourself, Carol. But you can only forgive what you have taken the time to understand.

'Now keep going, Carol. There's more, the most embarrassing bit. The bit you were not prepared for. The bit no one told you about. I'm surprised you didn't prepare yourself better, Carol. There were books you could have read.'

Carol feels herself shrinking, tugging at the bedclothes to cover her insecurity.

'Are you with me, Carol? I can see you. Tell me about the funeral. If it's easier, pretend I'm not here and just tell the air in the room.'

Carol needs to remember it now, partly because she has never shared this with anyone in her life. She wants to give it to the universe and be done with it. 'I don't need to pretend you're not there, spider. I know you hear my thoughts, so I may as well tell you.

'A week after the abortion, I was invited to my eldest brother's engagement party. It was held at our, my parents', house. I tried to get out of it, but he asked me to be there. So I went. I sat all night in the same room as my father, and he never looked in my direction once. I didn't want him to at any rate. But it must have looked odd to everyone else, not a word between us.

'The next morning, around 6 a.m., there was a knock at the door of my flat. I didn't even take time to think who can it be at this hour. I knew, I knew before I opened that door that it would be my brother telling me that my father had died. I opened the door, and before he could say anything, I put my arms around his neck and said I'm sorry for you. And, I thought, but pleased for me.

'He was astonished. Who told you? I didn't have a telephone. "No one," I said. "As soon as I heard your knock, I knew what had happened." So I spent time with my mother over the next few days and overheard someone in the kitchen saying very quietly that he had left a letter in which he had specifically disowned me. How sad that was for my mother. Of course she would never tell me. And of course, she never did even when I asked her what was in the letter that I knew he had left. I wondered what his instructions were about burying him. It was a long time since he had seen the inside of a church, and even longer since his last charitable thought.

'The funeral was to be in Christchurch. I never asked why, and I don't remember where. It was a dreary two-hour drive in perfect funeral weather, overcast, intermittent rain, chill wind. I had searched my minimal wardrobe for something suitable and had chosen a dull mid gray jacket and skirt suit.

'One of my mother's brothers was driving Mum and me. I was alone in the back seat. Suddenly, I felt a prickling around my nipples and scratched it. A few minutes later, I felt it again. I was going to put my hand inside my jacket when I saw two dark circles staining my grey jacket. I was panic-stricken. I guessed I must be leaking the milk that my baby would never need. No one had warned me. I was completely unnerved. I hadn't expected it. How could I cover my shame? I had a couple of hankies in my bag, and I surreptitiously tucked them into my blouse to prevent any further leakage. By the time we got to Christchurch, my jacket was drying into stiff crusty circles.

'What could I do? I made straight for the ladies room when we reached the crematorium, and was relieved to find that the taps spewed forth a decent splash. So I made sure I soaked enough of my jacket front to hide the telltale stains and then, pleading cold, I asked if anyone had a shawl I could cover my bathroom disaster with. Someone produced a knitted jacket.' Carol heaves a sigh and relaxes. 'My god,' she says. 'I'd tried to forget all that.'

'What did I say to you, Carol? You do feel better now, don't you?' 'Yes, I'm damn glad to be rid of it. And I don't care if I am talking to

a bloody spider. At least I can hang onto a thought for a while now. And my memory's getting a bit better.'

CHAPTER TWENTY-FOUR

The front door slams shut, and Mark comes hurrying up the stairs to the bedroom, plants a kiss on her forehead, and sits beside her on the bed. He is all smiles. 'I have news! I have news!'

Carol thinks whatever it is, he's pretty excited. I quite like it. A surprise would be good for both of us. 'What news, darling?'

'Good news, very good news. The conference, you know the one I told you was coming up soon? Well, guess what? It's in a place you like, but you'll have to get out of bed to go with me.'

Carol flinches. She wishes he hadn't said that. Doesn't he realise that she wouldn't be in bed if she felt well. She just can't think about all the things she has to think about and get sorted and be up and about at the same time. She forces a tight smile. 'Yes, I suppose I will.'

'Well,' he goes on, not noticing her reaction. 'It's been moved to the end of next month, and it's going to be in', he performs an exaggerated flourish, one leg kicked out behind him and removes an imaginary hat as he bows low toward her, 'New York, New York! That's a helluva town.'

Carol feels her heart give a tiny bounce. New York. She loves New York, and she hasn't been there for thirty years. Thirty years! It's hard to believe that she'll be there in just two months. She's already making a mental list of the shops she'll be hitting.

'So how do you feel about that, sweet Carol baby?'

'I love it,' Carol replies. 'And I can show you some more than decent restaurants too. And we can go down to the garment district and give the plastic a fright, and I know some silk shirt shops that have the biggest selection of the best merchandise you can find anywhere in the world. Shirts from Italy, Spain, France, the latest of everything gorgeous.' She shudders with pleasure.

'Yep, I knew you'd know where to go for everything. The hotel's in the centre of Manhattan, just off Fifth Avenue.'

'Good,' says Carol. 'I can nip into the Manny Hanny. It's right there on the corner of Fifth and 57th, and demand back the $240 they swallowed from my account for doing nothing! Not a single transaction, and they took darn near the whole $240 telling me four years later that it was used to cover fees. I left that money there when I moved back to Sydney specifically, so I would have something available on my next visit.'

Splendid, thinks Mark, that's got her going. Perhaps she'll get out of bed one day after all. 'You can do what you like, my dear Carol, but I don't think you'll get anything out of a bank. I'd like to be there to see you try though.'

'I already tried years ago. I couldn't believe it. They'd sucked it up in fees! And the thing that really pissed me off, Mark, was that the day I went there to withdraw the miserable few dollars that were left, they were doing a customer survey on using ATMs. Explaining how convenient it was going to be, you could handle (control was the word they used like it was some kind of customer advantage) all your transactions in the foyer yourself. You didn't have to go near the teller. They get to charge you for the work that you are doing on their behalf! Don't get me going on banks!'

That wound her up, thinks Mark, maybe there's a spring after all.

'Hell, that tells you how long ago it was. They were trialing ATMs on customers, they had a mobile one, and they were testing how clear the screen prompts were and how customers reacted to the idea. Late 70s. I suppose a lot will have changed, but it's New York, it could only get better. It's shopping heaven. You'll love it. I'm glad you've never been there. I can show you *my* NY. Mind you, it was always shopping heaven, but it started out as working hell.'

'How did you get to New York? How long did you work there?'
'I was working for a multi-national in London. They needed a creative manager in their Sydney offices, so I was relocated. I became director for Australasia and then they decided to create international zones administered from New York. So I moved to New York where I was responsible for Asia, the Pacific, and Canada. If you can see the cultural connections there, I'd be happy if you would explain them.'

'That's obvious,' Mark replies with a knowing smile, rubbing his thumb and forefinger together. 'There are people in each place. That means customers, customers mean sales, sales mean profits, internationally transferable expensing opportunities, accounting-created profits, and useful losses. Money doesn't recognise cultural differences, dear Carol, it all smells the same.'

'At any rate, I resigned and returned to Australia in just under a year. I was too old for New York. Or New York was too young and brash for me. One or the other. Hell started pouring crap on me the day I arrived in the Apple. Well, almost the first day. I was booked into a hotel on 58th St. close to where I was working on 57th. The room was so small, not to mention on the dark side of the building, dark side of the world probably. I had no space to put my two suitcases anywhere but on the floor. No stand, the smallest of bedside tables either side of a double bed that took up so much of the room that you had to shuffle along sideways to get to the bathroom. And the shower was made for midgets. I complained and was moved the next day, but the tone had been set.

'I answered an ad for an apartment on West 57th, good view, nice part of town, etc. Met the Argentinian guy who said it was his and moved in straight away. It was Saturday, so I did a big shop to stock up with kitchen stuff, some wine and vodka, which I used to keep in the freezer for a quick nip, a few utensils that I noticed were missing and a mop and broom. I bought all the basic foodstuff a kitchen needs. I spent the Sunday sorting stuff out and stashing the goodies I'd brought with me.

'These included a really heavy antique Burmese garnet necklace with dozens of large stones set in brass, very overstated, with matching earrings and two garnet bracelets. My mother had been gifted them by a friend and had just passed them on to me. There was a pair of exquisite pearl earrings I had bought in Tokyo on the way from London, assorted gold rings and bracelets, and matching blue and white sapphire earrings and ring. And of course, my clothes, which I hung in the wardrobe.

'Sunday night I started to feel very unwell, and during the night, I had high fevers, sweating right through the foam mattress (ugh!). And on Monday, I called work to say I was sick. They sent the company doctor to see me. He took a blood sample, my temperature, and asked me a few questions like which countries had I been to recently and how long I had been sweating like this. Later that day, he diagnosed malaria. Turned out that I'd actually had a mild form of it for a few years. Contracted it in the near east (far east to Londoners) after taking a full course of anti-malaria tablets for a trip with some stops in the east from London to New Zealand. I'd had what I thought was a huge dose of flu when we'd returned to London, and had been two weeks getting over it. I didn't see a doctor, so no tests were done. Dumb London doctor (I'm not sure whether he was Indian or Pakistani) had prescribed protection for a totally different strain of malaria. African rather than Asian. Well, that's what the New York doctor presumed.

'So I had three days bed rest in my new apartment and then back to work well-medicated. I did a half-day my first day, so was back at the apartment by one o'clock. Imagine my panic when I found my door taped with what looked like police tape! I went straight to the concierge who announced that he had himself called the mayor's department to report the illegal let! I'm occupying an illegal let? I couldn't believe my ears. "Yes," he told me. "The apartment is let to a Chilean girl." But I did the paperwork with an Argentinian man! "Yes," he said again. "And he doesn't have the right to sublet. Nobody does in this building. We know who he is and what he does. It's happened before. He runs a sublet scheme for lots of South Americans. Contracts in this building don't allow sublets, but that doesn't stop it happening."

'So what do I do? I asked. He said, "You use my phone and call the Argentinian and tell him to get down here straight away. I'll call the mayor's department and get the bailiff down here to open the door. It's taped now. I don't have authority to break the tape." The bailiff arrived and I got in. Not a thing was left in the apartment! No clothes, no mop, no broom, no booze, no provisions, no jewels. Can you imagine how very pissed off I was? I demanded to know what had happened and why. "Illegal let, contents are confiscated into a storage unit up on 126th. Nobody, but nobody goes near 126th without protection."

'"Why?"' I asked. "Bad part of town, black, very black. Poor people who want clothes and brooms and booze and jewels." Is there a list of what they took? Bailiff said there would be, but he didn't have it. Meanwhile, the Argentinian piece of shit had turned up, wringing his hands, wearing just the suit you'd expect a sleazy pimp to be in. At this stage, I was interested in only two things. One, get my belongings back.

And two, get me a legal place to stay. Meanwhile, I said, I am contacting the company legal department to sort this out. They told me to confirm my position before end of the day when they would help if I needed it.

'The Argentinian pimp conferred with the bailiff and was given permission to go to the 126th St. address. I said I was going with him. He made a call, and a huge stretch limo turned up and he hustled me into the back seat and got in beside me. During the ride, up the west side of Central Park and deep into the badlands, he opened his briefcase and was sorting through some of its contents when I saw that the case was stuffed half-full of banded bank notes. Shit! I thought. What kind of crap am I in!

'I ostentatiously looked out the window at the rundown ramshackle buildings we were passing, and just out of the corner of my eye, I saw the revolver in the briefcase. Right, that kind of crap. I will make a lot of noise and try to hurt a lot of people with very little provocation if anything looks like happening to me.

'We arrived at 126th, he knocked on the steel door, and it was opened by a fat slob in stained overalls. He conferred with the pimp, grubby dollar bills changed hands, and I was invited to enter and identify my stuff. The clothes were there, the broom was there, the food was not, the booze was not, the jewels were not. I asked where the missing items were. "That's all that arrived," fat slob said. "You ask the bailiff or the mayor. He's in charge of illegal lets." 'I later found out that this is how the system works. An illegal let is reported. The mayor or town hall sends the bailiff. The bailiff, together with a sidekick, make a list of everything (well, some things, a few might miss getting on the list), they confiscate it, and ship it straight up to the holding pens.

'When you check the list, I didn't get to check it until the company legal department had extricated it from the mayor's office, you find that it matches what you found. There, perfect. Every item on the list has been returned. How good is that?

'While I am getting more and more pissed off, as the only available alternative to feeling terrified of the shit I had found myself in, the pimp is making calls. He eventually announces that he has located accommodation on 7th Avenue, nice place, available for a week, which will give me time to find another place of course. Not even anything to pay! Again, how good is that?

'I move into the less than salubrious dwelling, farewell the pimp, and note that it has a door that looks as though it belongs to a strongroom. I dump my stuff and try to feel as safe as the door suggests. Looking out the window, I see a dance studio opposite at my level and feel a bit better. If there's a dance studio, they can't all be wild animals. You can tell I had just arrived in New York.

'I went out to get something to eat, took the industrial lift three floors to the street, and returned half an hour later with a hamburger and something for breakfast. The lift was straight out of a horror movie. It was no effort at all to imagine a group slaying inside it. I might have even looked for blood spatter.

'Later that night, I understood why the place had a strongroom door fitted, and why the door had three locks inside. It was not to make me feel safe. It was to keep the werewolves out. About eleven o'clock, the banging started at my door. It was so loud and constant that I really thought the door would be smashed in. I didn't get much sleep. It had obviously been used as a knocking shop at some time, some very recent time.

'Next day at lunchtime, I went back to the Chilean girl's apartment building and asked to see the manager who recognised me. I asked whether he had any apartments free and signed up for one on the 27th floor and moved right back into the building. I did, of course, discuss the whole affair with the legal department. There was nothing they could do after the fact—the company had offered me the services of their preferred letting agency, and I had declined them.

'The head of personnel, a tall handsome black guy in a very smart suit, offered to show me some nightlife. He was being very, very persuasive. I declined the offer. They don't miss a step in New York. Yeah, it'll be good to see that helluva town again.'

CHAPTER TWENTY-FIVE

Mark hadn't heard the whole apartment story before and was quite impressed. His wife was tough. 'Why go back to the same building?' he asked. 'No way would I be inviting trouble like that'.

'Well, it was the newest one nearest to where I was working, and you know what my sense of direction's like. It was three blocks along from work on the opposite side of the street. Didn't stop me from exiting the building on the wrong side one day and panicking because I didn't recognise anything about the street. Fortunately, the concierge was checking the rear parking entrance, so I just followed him back in and straight through the hallway to the side I recognised.' Carol is realising that for the first time in maybe years, she is relaxed and feeling like chatting. Things are looking up, she thinks to herself. And I'm finally free of that bloody spider.

'Don't speak too soon, Carol, I'm still the puppet master, pulling the threads so to speak.'

She adjusts herself against the sea of pillows she has spread on her bed, and steals a sneak peek at the ceiling. Nothing there. Well, there's some sort of shadow, but it could be just dusk falling.

'You know, Mark, the best piece of advice I got in all the time I was in New York was from one of the Puerto Rican girls who worked out of the bar on the ground floor of that building. There were half a dozen girls, all Central or South American, working as call girls. The bar was owned by a Yugoslav who ran some kind of numbers game or betting shop out the back, he was good to the girls who helped behind the counter as well, so there was always one there for me to drop in and have a chat with on my way home at night.

'First thing, Maria—they're all called Maria—told me was to always carry a Spanish language newspaper in clear view. "It's New York," she said. "And there's every kind of animal hanging around Manhattan. The place is falling apart, the city's broke, they say, and you can see for yourself it's not exactly bulging with the boys in blue. And the ones you see are fat and probably half drunk on the freebies they get from all the bars around here. See that apple crate in the middle of the road there? That's not fallen off anything, that's been placed there by one of the shop owners as a cover to warn traffic there's a hole in the road."

'She wasn't exaggerating the situation. The city was all but bankrupt. By ten o'clock on a weeknight, the doorways would be full of huddled bodies covered with vegetable sacking or newspapers. Even there in the centre of Manhattan adjacent to the city's swankiest stores, Saks one corner, Cartier just around the next. And in the upmarket doorways at night, the downmarket side of the human coin, derelicts, drunks, homeless, or just poor Latinos arrived yesterday looking for an opportunity to escape from their dreamless poverty.

'On my second night in that apartment, I'd gone out to buy my Spanish paper and had seen a pudgy policeman bending over a drunk, curled with his knees right up to his neck in the gutter, whimpering as the pig struck him alternately on the head and feet with his nightstick. I could almost feel the shooting pains the poor sod must have suffered. I watched for a few minutes, the bottom dropping out of my belly with horror and anger until I turned away, ashamed I didn't know how to stop it.

'The next day, I went to an art supply store on West 57th, just around the corner from where I had witnessed the previous night's beating, and bought a stuffed pig dressed in a police uniform, carrying a nightstick. New York was the first time I had ever connected police and pig in the same sentence.'

'So', asks Mark, 'what's with the Spanish paper?'

'That's because a woman alone and in that city was as attractive to roaming gangs as a sticky doorknob is to flies, the Spanish newspaper implied Hispanic connections. The black gangs wouldn't touch me. They didn't want to mess with Spics. The Hispanics wouldn't touch me either in case I was associated with another Hispanic gang. Good advice. I stalked the streets safely alone.

'And, yes, I did stalk. I felt so angry all the time I was there I positively glowed with anger. Millions of people on the sidewalks but no one looks at anyone. I walked up the west side of the park one weekend and was nearly knocked over by a black guy wearing nothing but a sack, yelling to himself while speeding along on a skateboard. Hundreds of people, not one word.

'My second day on Sixth Avenue down between 55th and 56th, I saw a knifing. Broad daylight. The assassin crossed from one side of the sidewalk to the other, less than two metres in front of me, grabbed a guy in a leather jacket who appeared to be window shopping, took him by the arm, swung him around, and plunged a knife into his gut. By the smooth way he carried it off, not the first time he'd done it. Not one pedestrian stopped. The world just hurried on past and averted its eyes. I turned back and stood in the nearest shop alcove and watched as two men appeared from nowhere and hustled both of them into a van, one leaking blood from his open jacket, the other too ordinary to be memorable for anything but the blankness of his face. Drug deal gone wrong was the word in the bar downstairs later.

'Another day at lunchtime, I was walking west along 57th, just off Fifth Avenue, I stopped at the traffic lights. And while they were still red, a woman, mid-thirties or so, stepped out into the traffic from the corner opposite and pulled her flowing dress right up over her head revealing her naked body.'

'Hell, Carol, didn't anything happy happen to you?'

Carol smiles as she sees in her mind's eye the black guy who danced for her on the street at eight o'clock one morning. 'You know how I told you I never carried more than $20 cash at any time?'

Mark nods.

'Well, one morning on my way to work, a black guy, decent looking, clean jeans, and a denim jacket approached me, hand held out asking for money. "What do you need it for?" I was surprised that a beggar was out so early. I expected him to just go on his way and ignore my question. "Lady, I need it to buy a train ticket to an audition."

'"An audition? What for? Are you an actor?"

'"They're auditioning for a musical play, and I need $24 for the train ticket. I've only got five."

"Well, how about this. You do a dance for me, and I'll pay you $20." "Wow! Are you for real? Right here on the sidewalk?"

'"Sure. You dance, I pay." So he danced and sang and he looked more than competent. I gave him the $20 note I was carrying and told him to go break a leg. He kissed my hand, and acknowledging the small crowd that had stopped to watch, hurried off toward the underground. That was happy. And not every policeman's a pig in New York.

'The one New Year's Eve I was there, I went to eat with friends in Bangkok 54, a good Thai place. About eleven, we went off to Eddie Condon's to see the New Year in with some jazz. Just as we arrived at the doorway, I put my hand up to my left ear and found that I'd lost an earring, new black sapphire and diamonds. "Damn," I said. "You guys get a table not too close to the double bass, and I'll go back to the restaurant." I probably knocked it off while I was getting into my coat. A big puffy purple and pink affair. You remember it, Mark? You said I looked like an ice cream sundae in it.'

Mark smiles and nods.

'So off I hurry just in time to find them vacuuming the floor. I explained what had happened, and they had a good look around the table, finding nothing. They opened the vac bag and emptied it onto a newspaper. Nothing! I thank them and leave. Now this is where I really show how smart I am. There was already a thin layer of snow on the sidewalk, so I walked head down, eyes scanning the path until I arrived down to 54th St. where there was not quite so much light. So I stopped purposefully under each street lamp and scanned all around the pool of light.

'Suddenly, I am aware of a big shadow beside me. This was New York, a place where you don't take chances. Out of the corner of my eye, the shadow looks very big indeed. I gauged its height where I thought its belly would be, sucked in a deep breath, and turned swinging my fist as hard as I could into the belly. It feels like I'm hitting a concrete post. I step back. I'd damn near knocked myself over. The post is a big black policeman, and he hasn't even been moved by my attack. I stand stunned, hand already aching, searching for an opening phrase. The big man steps back, his face beaming hugely. "Hello, little lady, and what's a little lady like you doing out alone looking around lamp posts on a night like this?" Then it hits me. How could I explain it? I'm looking for an earring I could have dropped anywhere within five blocks, and the only place I'm looking is where there is light.

'"I lost my earring," I said quietly, realising how unbelievably stupid I must sound. "So I'm looking for it."

'"You sure you lost it under a lamp post?" His question was kindly, he knew I wasn't trouble or drunk. "It's the only place there's any light," I replied. "Where are you going, little lady? A little lady like you shouldn't be out alone on a night like this. There are bad people around." So I explained how when we'd got to Eddie Condon's, I felt for my earring and it wasn't there, so I'd come back to look for it. It wasn't at the restaurant, so I must have dropped it on the way there. "Why don't I walk with you and see you safely to your friends, and we can look on the way. Where there is a light, that is." I felt pretty damn silly.

'Just as we arrive at the cellar door, I slip my hand into my pocket for the $20 note I always kept accessible to thank him for his escort services. And my fingers close around my earring! It had slipped off my ear, over the smooth puffery of my coat, and straight into the pocket. Good God! It's in my pocket! I was all kinds of embarrassed. "Please, come in and have a drink with us and celebrate the return of my earring, and the New Year. And please have this." I handed him the note. He looks at it and with a small bow, he declines graciously. "No, little lady, I'm on duty, and it has been a pleasure escorting you. You have yourself a good time and a Happy New Year. Tomorrow, it will be 1980." He turned and disappeared into the soft snowflakes of the night.'

'You tell a good story,' says Mark. 'You should tell them more often.'

CHAPTER TWENTY-SIX

Mark is in the kitchen organising the dinner the housekeeper has prepared for them. Carol, lightheaded and delighted with her newly discovered energy, is rearranging her pillows to accommodate her dinner tray. Mark brings it in with a tiny vase holding three jonquils, fragrant and full of spring memories. She is touched by this thoughtfulness.

'Let's discuss our Saturday dinner date,' Mark says, settling himself at the card table he has moved in so he can eat with her. 'You give me your selection from the menu, and I'll do the rest.'

Carol is beginning to quite like the idea of dressing up and enjoying a nice dinner without having to go out. So they make the selection together and Mark texts it through, so that they have a record of what they've requested.

That night, Carol sleeps like a baby. Things are looking up. She already has more energy, and the thinking time is doing her good.

Just before settling down for the night, she had glanced up to the ceiling and fancied she saw a light going out inside what looked like a spider web. 'Well, fancy that, we're going to bed together. I wonder what it's like to be a spider, hanging around in your web, waiting for a fly to happen by. Or', she thought, a smile suddenly painting her face with glee, 'racing to hide under a leaf as that hungry looking butcher-bird cruises around looking for a bedtime snack.'

'Carol, dear, you know I'm not that kind of spider. I live in your head. I don't need to eat and no bird can eat me. I feed off your thoughts. I'm only here because you need me. You don't know, but the part of you that wants to understand it all created me, and now I have to stay here until I've fulfilled my part of our little contract. You thought me into life, Carol, and as long as you need me, I'll be here.

Carol's already dead to the world.

CHAPTER TWENTY-SEVEN

It's the morning of the day of the dinner party, and Carol's mood is bright and optimistic. Mark is thrilled with her recovery and is even beginning to encourage her to make plans for the future.

'Why don't we take a cruise when I retire at the end of the year?' he suggests without pressing for a response. 'Or we could do a river tour of France and Spain.'

Carol doesn't answer. At the mention of Spain, she's back in Torrenostra. It's Easter and chilly. The spring equinox has brought gales and intermittent icy rain. Odd birds, separated from the rest, swoop past shrieking their defiance at the wild air currents that have blown them off course. She is standing at the floor to ceiling windows of her apartment, listening to the wind whistling and moaning around the fifth floor rooftop.

The view straight out over the Mediterranean is steely gray and stretches forever. Sea and sky meet on the distant horizon with barely a shade between them. The building seems to sway slightly, and the late afternoon light shudders across the glass, making it appear to move.

The outlook has not changed all day. Gray. She feels the temperature drop, announcing the arrival of dusk. She turns toward the kitchen to make tea, or maybe to pour a glass of red. She'll decide when she gets there. Just as she leans across the cooker to switch on the kitchen light, she hears a soft thud against the window and sees a bunch of feathers disappear below the sill. Poor birds, she thinks, they're being blown out of their own sky.

She selects a glass and pours a red from a huge two-litre bottle, part of Pascual's welcome gift when she and her husband had arrived last weekend. She thinks she hears a tiny sound like a bird chirping. As she settles onto the cane couch with her glass, she hears the noise again.

Surely it can't be a bird. Where could it be? The sky is birdless. We're five floors up, sound doesn't travel that far. And it can't be coming from the roof.

'Are you okay, Carol? You just shivered. Shall I put on the heater for you? Would you like a wrap for your shoulders?' Mark brings her back from Spain with a jolt.

'No, thanks, darling. I'm fine. You mentioned Spain, and I was thinking of the bird I rescued from a storm one Easter.'

'Tell me about it. I like rescue stories. What kind of bird, what happened to it?'

'It was a young swallow. It must have been caught in a down draught and was thrown against our kitchen window. I just saw a wing disappearing below the sill, and a few minutes later, found it huddled on the ledge below the window. Just a bunch of feathers with useless legs and crooked wings. It must have hit the building with a lot of force. Its little beak was opening and closing, and only managing an occasional barely audible chirrup. But my heart had heard it. I hooked it in through the bedroom window with the long-handled fishing net.'

'Please don't tell me you fed it sherry!'

Carol had once rescued a mouse from her cat and then killed it with kindness, sherry, and asphyxiation by hot water bottle.

'No, I cut the top off a sock, checked his wings for broken feathers, folded them against his body, and tucked him into the sock.

And put him in the bedside drawer to keep him warm overnight. The weather was wild, and I was hoping that the best approach would be to keep him warm and rested. And that being cosy in a drawer would inspire a feeling of safety. As it turned out, I later thought he might feel abandoned alone in a strange drawer, so I spent most of the night on my back with him in his sock on my chest. Occasionally, I popped his head into my mouth, so I could breathe warmth onto him.

'Next morning, the wind had died down to a breeze, the sun was trying to get out from behind the clouds, and the marble floor in front of the windows was nicely warmed up. So I slipped him out of the sock to see if he could stand up. He tried, but he was unsteady, so I sat him on the floor, propped up with more socks, and hoped that the sunshine would make him better. Yes, I did moisten a breadcrumb with water to hold against his beak, but he showed no interest. I didn't force him.'

Mark smiles.

'As soon as he started to chirp again we took him up to the roof, and I held him up to feel the breeze. He didn't seem too interested, so I tried gently throwing him up in the air, but he just sort of fell out of the air back onto my hands. Then I had a brilliant idea. One of my favourite pieces of music was Pablo Casals playing a traditional Catalan melody "El Cant dels Ocells," the Song of the Birds. In the fifties, it was widely adopted as a theme against oppression. It has an exquisitely expressive melancholic longing about it, and the vinyl we had included birdsong in the background. I'm sure it's on YouTube now. But I'm talking about 1974, a bit before YouTube.

'So I sat the bird down again on the socks and put on the Casals. Now, believe me or believe me not, this is absolutely true. When he heard the birdsong through the music, he actually stood up on his little shaky legs and looked around! I was amazed. He recognised the birdsong? At the end of the piece, we took him back up to the roof, and I just stood there with him on my hand, letting him feel the breeze in his feathers. There were a few swallows way up in the distance calling to each other.

'When they started flying toward our building, our little one chirped and flapped his wings a little. They kept on coming, and when they were about two metres away from us, I threw the little one straight up into the air and two of them swooped down, tucked their wings under his body, and carried him away with them. It was heartbreakingly beautiful. It took my breath away.

'About ten minutes later, while we were still standing there just looking at the sky and marveling at what we had just witnessed, dozens of birds appeared from all directions as if from nowhere. They formed themselves into a flock, and flew three huge circles around the building before disappearing out over the sea. There was no doubt in my mind that they were acknowledging the rescue.'

She didn't add that there was another aspect to the story. It was Easter Sunday, and she had just witnessed a resurrection—an observation that the priest had made later when she told him how it had happened.

CHAPTER TWENTY-EIGHT

'Wow, that's a great story,' Mark says. 'That's really beautiful. Now', he continues, 'let's talk about tonight. What about we set a theme for the evening? It won't be exactly the *Thousand and One Nights*, but what if we each tell a story, funny or horror, but a true story about something weird or wonderful that has happened to us. One rule only, it must be true.'

'We've never done anything like that before,' says Carol. 'Do you think Judy and Colin would enjoy that? I mean, some people would probably be embarrassed to have that sprung on them at the last moment.'

'Okay, Carol my lovely, how about this. I'll call them and ask if the idea appeals to them. And that'll give them a chance to decline, or a chance to ransack their memories for an entertaining tale.'

Carol hasn't felt this awake, for it seems like years. She's keeping her fingers crossed that Judy and Colin like the idea. She's definitely warming to it herself. 'Good idea, darling.'

Mark is very pleased with himself. She hasn't 'darlinged' me in ages. Once yesterday and twice today. Not bad. Perhaps I should have suggested she take to her bed a couple of years ago. Bed therapy seems to be doing its thing, whatever that is.

'Do you mind using the downstairs bathroom, darling?' Carol asks. 'I'd like to take a long hot bath this afternoon. I shall block out the sun and luxuriate in candlelight and fragrance and think about the tale I shall tell.'

Mark smiles and nods his agreement and notches up a third darling for the day.

'And what tale will you tell, mine hostess? Something you have to search for in those murky recesses of memory, or something you don't have to drag kicking and screaming out of the shadows?'

Carol brushes something from her forehead. She's wondering suddenly if the stories are a good idea. She feels a vague sense of danger. But she reassures herself it is a good idea, and it's high time I got back into the world. Judy and Colin are intelligent, broadminded, educated people. What is there to worry about? She will choose a story she can tell easily, one that won't send her into floods of tears, one that she would happily tell a priest, or a cat.

Damn, she thinks, I wish that priest hadn't opened the floodgates.

CHAPTER TWENTY-NINE

It's seven o'clock, and Judy and Colin are at the front door. Carol has just poured herself a G and T, the first one she's had in at least three months, and is settling herself in for an enjoyable evening. The Chef in Your Own Kitchen is in their kitchen, and Mark has arranged the signals between himself and the chef, so that their conversation will not be interrupted mid-story by food being offered or served at inconvenient times. He seems jubilant. Confident that the dinner party will be a big success.

He compliments Carol on her appearance. 'Stunning, you look absolutely stunning.' He plants a delicate kiss on her neck. 'Jonquil! You're wearing that fragrance I gave you last birthday. It's so spring, and you look so perfectly spring in that gorgeous dress.' Carol relaxes and sips her drink. 'I'll just get the door.' He ushers Judy and Colin in, and in next to no time, they're into conversation and toasts.

'It's so nice to see you looking so well, Carol. We were concerned for you. I know Mark said it's nothing to worry about, but well, you know.' She trails off, feeling she doesn't want to spoil the mood of the evening. Judy is sincere. She likes Carol and she has missed seeing her.

Carol smiles at her. 'I've missed you too, Judy. I don't know what's been wrong with me. Somehow or other, everything got on top of me and I suddenly felt overwhelmed. It's unfinished business. I read that it happens to a lot of people my age, not just women. It's something to do with coming to terms with yourself and everything and everyone else. It's some sense of one's mortality, tying up loose ends. Moments of introspection, I suppose. Mine just seem to be lasting longer.'

'You've probably had plenty to deal with. You've certainly tucked a few experiences under that trim little belt.' Colin compliments her. 'You are looking splendid. I wish I could take a few months off from the daily grind to get to grips with myself. Seriously, I think it's something we all should do at some stage. We simply don't give ourselves enough time to digest what's happening to us. At least I always seem to be not quite at the end of one thing before I need to attend to another.'

Carol is grateful for Colin's unexpected empathy. She's surprised at the warmth and sincerity of his statement, but empathy? That's a funny word for me to think. What's the difference between empathy and sympathy? Suddenly, it's important to her to understand this because she knows she often falls short of really feeling for other people in their distress. She can feel sympathy, but she can't identify with other people completely, not in the way she's noticed on other occasions that Colin does. He seems to feel their distress, regardless of its reason, where she looks for the reason first and sympathises later.

'Well,' says Mark. 'Sounds as though we're in the right mood for telling secrets. I'm in charge of the kitchen, everything has been timed to avoid unnecessary interruptions so we can eat, drink, and chat as much as we like. The chef and I have worked out a code. Food will appear, glasses will be filled, courses will be served, it'll all happen as if by magic.'

So the evening commences, each with a personal entertainment to offer. Only thing to do is decide who goes first.

'Do we have titles for our stories?' Mark asks. 'I'll call mine Foresight. No, don't stop to think about it, just sum it up in one word.' He looks at Carol. 'Yours?'

'Toesucker,' Carol answers instantly. He looks at Colin. 'Yours?'

'Window shopping.' 'And Judy?' 'Wigman.'

They all answer obediently.

'Now, who's going first?' Nobody accepts the offer. 'Well, let's make it easy and do it alphabetically. So that'll be Foresight, Toesucker, Wigman, and Window shopping. I go first then.'

CHAPTER THIRTY

Mark settles himself with a glass of scotch and starts by announcing the title, 'Foresight. Have you ever felt you might have dreamt something, but never been sure whether it happened or whether you only dreamt it? Or maybe you feel you did both. I've always been fascinated by the supernatural. So this is not so much a story about one specific thing, as a few odd things that I've experienced that I can't explain.

'Years ago, I was introduced to a hypnotist at a cocktail party, and we got talking about telepathy and things like that. And he suggested, since I was interested, I might like to try some exercises for myself. He explained that many people have natural, or supernatural, gifts that they may not even be aware of. He said, "Simple test. Sit in a café or any other place, and choose someone to stare at, willing them to look at you. Pick a subject who doesn't know you're there and concentrate on making them notice you. You'll be surprised how often it works. And the more you practise it, the more often and more quickly it will work. Or try this. Pick someone you know reasonably well (or they'll think you're bonkers), and agree to try to establish a mental contact with that person at a specific time when you are apart. Like at nine one night, the two of you agree to concentrate on contacting each other. You will be trying to communicate something very specific like an image or a word or a number to your friend. It won't work the first time, but you'll be surprised that eventually, it probably will work."

'I tried it with a guy I was working with, and the third time we tried, he got the image I was sending him. It was nothing associated with his work or mine. It was flames. And I think I was successful because I took it slowly. I first visualised him knitting himself a scarf! Yes, he really was knitting a scarf at work, and he was at it morning and afternoon tea times and lunch.

'Once that scarf-knitting image was firmly in my mind, I let my mind travel from the bottom of the scarf up through the knitting needles along his arms, and into his head. And created in my imagination a conflagration. I built an image of a huge fire with flames leaping upwards and outwards in all directions. And he got the message. He said he thought the word fire and then the image of flames came into his mind.

'Once I dreamt that I was in a car that stopped at the side of a country road that had a strip of tussock on the roadside and a barbed wire fence separating the road from a hill that ran down to a water inlet. At the water's edge, there was a small wharf and a shed. The dream was very detailed. The ground was covered with dry pine needles from the pine trees scattered over the hillside. I was making my way down the hill, and noticed broken brown beer bottles at the base of some trees. I then realised that I was being chased and was frightened I was going to slip on the dry needles and fall on the broken glass. Then the dream stopped.

'Some years later, my brother was driving me along a road I had never been on before, and I asked him to stop. I got out of the car and walked to the wire fence. It was the fence I had seen in my dream with a piece of sheep's wool caught on the barbed wire exactly as I had seen it. I climbed over the fence and saw the broken beer bottles, the pine needles, the tiny wharf, and the shed. How do you explain that? I have no idea what it meant, or whether there was any meaning at all, but it certainly happened.

'On another occasion, I was trying to astral travel. I was lying on my bed. I was above my body, but somehow looking at the scene as though I were an onlooker. I saw my body on my bed, and I saw myself hovering above it. My bedroom opened through a half glass door onto a small balcony. My astral body was on the balcony and watched as a car came down the driveway to the battle-ax section I lived on. The car stopped at the house opposite. A man and a woman got out of the car and walked to the door. The man knocked, the neighbour answered the door. The man stepped forward and handed over a brown paper bag that obviously contained a bottle, then he stepped back. And the woman who was with him, entered, he followed. The neighbour closed his door. I suddenly realised I could see myself lying on my bed and panicked. What if I can't get back into my body? I felt a sharp rough jerk and was back in my body on my bed again.

'While I was lying there thinking it over, I heard a car coming down the driveway. I went to the balcony and watched the scene in every detail that I had just witnessed in my out-of-body experience, exactly as though it were a rerun!

'I often visualise exactly what I will see when I turn a corner, known or unknown territory. I often know who is calling before I answer the phone. There's a lot of weird stuff going on out there that we simply don't understand. What I have told you is true.'

Everyone's flesh is creeping.

CHAPTER THIRTY-ONE

Mark turns to Carol who has removed her shoes and is wiggling her toes. 'Just getting myself in the mood,' she snickers. 'Here goes. Toesucker.

'My tale happens in London. I have been there for a few months, and realise that leaving a fresh veggie diet behind and living in the big city has led to my eating a lot of comfort food. Like breads, varieties that I had never seen before in calorie quantities my body had never handled before, and flavoured yogurts (fat and sugar in one hit) that I consumed by the half dozen. I was putting on weight, and fast!

'So I signed onto a nearby gym just off the Edgeware Road behind Marble Arch. The instructor, whom I assumed was also the owner, saw new clients on arrival and made a plan with them to meet their targets. Some were there for weight training and serious stuff, and some, like me, were there just to exercise as part of a plan to lose weight. One of the instructors was a Scottish girl named Heather who was a shot-put champion. That's just, by the way, to show you that it was a serious gym.

'The first visit there, I had a tour of the machines and was shown how to use everything, had a conflab with the owner, and a programme to gently ease me out of the bread and yogurt figure into something slightly less solid. Although I did feel quite slim alongside Heather who had a shot-putter's build.

'Before I was to start the course, I did a quick and vicious assessment of my figure and decided that the programme, as prescribed by the owner, was not going to get me to where I wanted to be fast enough. I needed something much more efficient. So that first evening, I cut loose and went for it. I did twice as long on each machine as my programme called for. After about two hours, the owner approached me to warn me that I was doing dangerously too much. What the hell would he know?

'I felt quite elated. I'd done everything twice and then some. As I was leaving, he approached me again and said, "If you can't walk tomorrow, come back for a massage." I must have looked at him as though I was offended. "I'm serious, you've done far too much. I'll be surprised if you can get out of bed tomorrow." Of course I dismissed him. Crap. Too much? What does he know? To begin with, he's ugly, he has bad breath, he has pictures of himself all around the gym, weightlifting and posing and looking absolutely repulsive. And he's hairy, all ugly muscle. Looks like some kind of ugly ape, Yukko. And he drives a red E-type Jag, probably into men not women. I had noted that there were several pictures of him muscle-posing with some sweet looking glistening boys.

'Next day, I could scarcely get out of my bed. I was aching so much and so stiff that I could barely straighten my legs, let alone move them in any meaningful way. I swear it took me five minutes to crawl out of my bed and get to the bathroom. I had a shower. I was hanging onto the walls because I was afraid my legs would give out. It took ages to get dressed, and I had to choose clothing that I could get into without too much twisting and bending.

'I finally got into the lift and onto the street. I had to walk two blocks to Marble Arch where I usually caught the bus that went down Regent Street where I worked. I walked the two blocks, aching all over. The bus arrived, and I tried to step up into the doorway. I couldn't bend my knee far enough for my foot to reach the first step! I was in a world of pain.

'Fortunately, I was the last in the queue to get on, so I was spared the embarrassment of pretending that I'd suddenly changed my mind about taking the bus. I walked as fast as I could manage, a euphemism for very slow and dignified, along Oxford Street and down Regent Street, wishing I had never got out of bed. I was a half hour late. My pains didn't improve during the day. In fact, after sitting for an hour at my typewriter, I had a hell of a job just trying to stand up straight. I had to hang onto the desk.

'Straight after work, I collected my shorts and singlet from the flat and went to the gym. I signed in, had a chat with Heather who said I definitely needed to see the owner. I can't remember his name. I've always thought of him as Toesucker. She advised me not to attempt any exercise until after I had spoken with him.

'He wasn't due back from wherever he was until 7.30, so I waited. When he arrived, he took one look at me, said, "Touch your toes." Of course I couldn't, I could barely bend. He said, "No exercise today. Wait back tonight, and I'll do a massage, but it won't be till we close. And if you still can't touch your toes tomorrow, don't come to the gym. You need a few days of rest." I waited and waited until finally, the gym closed at nine o'clock.

'Everyone had left by the time he called me over to the massage area and told me to take off my shirt and shorts (I was wearing knickers) and get up on the table. I was a little nervous at being alone half-naked with a stranger in such a huge basement. Nothing was partitioned off, machinery was allocated spaces defined by lines painted on the concrete, and vaulting horses and parallel bars were just separated by rubber mats and space. The only structures you could see were the square concrete pillars holding up the building. I convinced myself that open plan was good, closed would have been more intimidating. Even though the massage tables were on the far side from the door, right at the end of the gym, making a quick exit next to impossible if I need to make one.

'I was told to lie face up, hands at my sides. He poured massage oil down my legs, slapped his hands together, and started on my feet. God, it hurt. Even my feet ached. He gradually worked his way up my legs then took my arms, and starting at the wrists, he worked up to the shoulders. He didn't touch my chest, I felt hugely relieved. "Turn over," he said. "Now, this side is going to take longer. I've just warmed you up, now I have to get some circulation going to feed those muscles. The ones you should have, that is."

'He started at the shoulders, and worked down my arms, then across my back and then to my thighs. By this time, I was almost asleep. I was surprised that I felt so relaxed after the day of so much pain.

'Then I thought, that's funny. My right toe feels warm, and there's only one hand massaging my left leg. I lifted my arm and snuck a look. He was sucking my toe! He's a weirdo! I thought about this for a while until I realised that the movement of the massaging hand and the sucking rhythm had synchronised. Double weirdo! I snuck another peak. He was half-squatting behind me, massaging my leg with his mouth clamped around my big toe, which he was sucking vigorously. Definitely pathetic, but possibly also a dangerous weirdo! Then I got the full picture. His other hand was clamped around his dick. He was wanking!

'Holy Shit! What am I doing here with a crazy wanking toesucker? What can I do? He's twice my size and probably ten times as strong. So I'm going to have to find a way to talk myself out of this situation. I scanned the distance between me and the door, about twenty good paces. Shit! The door was bolted. Hope the bolt doesn't stick just in case I need to make a sudden exit. Shit again! Where are my clothes? Between me and the door. Good.

'Best thing is not to let on I know what he's doing until I have decided on an escape plan. I decided on the plan. The plan was to turn over onto my back suddenly, kick him in the head, and make a run for it, grabbing my clothes on the way. With a mouthful of toe, and his dick in his hand, I might just surprise him enough for it to work.

'So I swivelled my hips quickly (as quickly as I could, and yes, it was excruciating), extracted my toe, and tried to kick his head at the same time. He ducked away from me, and suddenly was standing beside the massage bed, dick dripping, looking very bloody angry indeed. I was half-sitting on the table, and sounding as matter of fact as possible, I said, "Why don't you put that away, and I'll go home and say nothing about this." He pushed his fist toward me, index finger extended, and poked me in the chest so hard that I fell backwards onto the bed. "Don't get smart with me, bitch. And don't think you can get away from me. I'm stronger than you." He hung onto the word and stretched out the stronger. "Where do you think you're going? What do you think you're going to do?" Spittle was running down his chin and I got a whiff of his stinking breath. That gave me just the adrenalin feed I needed.

'I pointed to his dick and said, "Put it away, it's dribbling. You don't really think a little thing like that would impress me?" This was me speaking, probably the least experienced 29-year-old in the world. I went on, "I'm going to get dressed now, and I'm going to walk out that door."

'Extended finger still sticking into my chest, he yelled at me, "You can make as much noise as you like down here, no one's going to hear you. Go on, try screaming, and by the way, the door's locked."

'So what's that? I was a whole lot more scared than my voice let on, thank God for drama lessons. "Kidnapping as well as assault? I don't intend yelling, I'm not completely stupid. I'm going to get my clothes and leave here. You have to be open tomorrow, what are you going to do with me? My flat is just around the corner, right opposite the police barracks, and my flatmates know exactly where I am. They're probably wondering where I am right now. Are those my things over there?" And I pointed behind him. He turned to look and I took off, leaving my shoes, shirt, and shorts behind. I raced to the door, pulled the bolt back, and I was outside. I flew up the stairs onto the pavement, not caring that I was nearly naked. I wrapped my arms around my boobs to cover me, and ran back to the flat as fast as I could.

'God only knows what I looked like. Edgware Road is one of the busiest streets in the city by day, but fortunately, it was after ten, after the shopping traffic. Late night traffic hadn't yet started, and there was only one restaurant to attract people in that area. There was no one at the lift. Thank you, guardian angel. I took it up the three floors to the flat and made it to the door without being seen. Shee-it. I was dead scared. I collapsed on my bed and tried to catch my breath.

'I knew he wouldn't be in the gym until late the next afternoon, so I went back straight after work to get my clothes and arranged to meet Heather later when I told her the story. She resigned from the gym at the end of that month. She wasn't frightened of him, I imagine she could handle him quite easily, but she was disgusted. She'd heard similar stories before.'

'You haven't told me that little tale before,' says Mark. 'Even I knew better than to mess with you the first time I met you. Frightening, you are. Did you really tell him to put that little thing away?'

CHAPTER THIRTY-TWO

'Yes, I did. And it was dribbling too. Now, allow me to introduce to you Colin. He's not our mystery shopper so much as our *window shopper*.' Carol sweeps the air with a dramatic gesture.

Colin stands up, bows, and starts his story. 'I had to make a last minute business trip in 1977 to KL, and the company booked me into their regular conference place, which happened to be where an important regional summit was being held. I arrived from the airport at 7 p.m. and was greeted by the concierge and placed in the hands of a bellboy to escort my luggage up to the seventh floor. He certainly didn't seem to be there to escort me. He took the key from the concierge, loaded my briefcase and suit bag onto his trolley, called the lift, and pressed the button for the seventh floor. He did this without once looking at me.

'It wasn't until he had pushed the trolley into my room that he acknowledged me by looking expectantly at my pocket and holding out his hand in a gesture that could be interpreted as either 'there you are, sir' or 'where's my tip?'

'I was staying for three days, so I unpacked and hung my clothes in the wardrobe straight away before I went off in search of refreshment. Unpacking took about fifteen minutes. I had a quick shower and left my room no more than forty-five minutes after arrival.

'My room opened off the main corridor, and I was surprised to see a lot more activity in the area than there had been when I arrived. It was usually a quiet part of the hotel. About to close my door behind me, I noticed a guard in army uniform lounging at the end of the corridor, leaning back, smoking, with his feet on a desk. Was that desk there before? I didn't think so, and I wondered what the army was doing on the same floor as my room.

'It has been my experience that in Asia, in particular, the less important a person is, if you dress him up in a uniform, he becomes an instant supremo. This one certainly fit the bill. A professional serviceman would never lounge about like this one. And his sudden appearance had alerted me to the fact that something was going on, and I needed to find out what it was.

'I took a minute to gather my senses then turned back into my room and switched on the news channel. That's when I realised the big summit was in my hotel. There was a high degree of nervousness all around Asia, it was the first time that Japan was participating, and those Asian nations were not yet used to the idea of peaceful cooperation.

'While I was watching a report covering the airport greetings as the participants arrived, my mind wandered back to the man at the end of the corridor. There was something odd about him. He was wearing a service holster, that's normal. So what was it that was odd about him? Then my memory suddenly placed what looked like a machine gun leaning against his desk!

'Night had already fallen, and the hotel delivery and pickup and parking spaces were brightly lit by flood lamps. I went to the window to get my bearings. Was I in the front or back or at the side of the building? By the amount of traffic I saw passing and heard parking around the corner, I assumed I was at the back. There was what looked like a park just beyond the flood-lit area. I pulled the flimsy curtain to one side, and leaning lightly against the floor to ceiling window, I strained to see some detail of the park, thinking to go for an early morning run. I noticed the lights on balconies below and to the right of my room. My room had no exit other than to the corridor via the door. As I leaned, I felt the glass give. Just a little, but enough to make me feel that something was wrong. I gingerly pushed it again. It seemed very flexible. Strange, I thought. What kind of glass is this?

'I don't know what made me do it, but I turned off the room lights, went back to the window, and felt all down the side of the pane. The glass was not fixed! It was held in by a narrow strip of moulded rubber flashing, the kind I have on the boat windscreen. I pressed the window at the side using more but controlled pressure, and it was immediately clear the whole pane could be popped by a couple of people intent on getting in or out.

'No way was I going to stay in that room. At that moment, there was a knock at my door. "Sir, Sir," I heard a voice call. I opened the door, and there was the same bellboy with his trolley and the hotel manager. Both were flushed and appeared anxious. The bellboy looked at his carriage, avoiding any eye contact, while the manager explained that an unfortunate mistake had been made. The room clerk was new, and he had mistakenly allocated this room to me. It had been pre-booked. In fact, the whole floor had been booked by the summit. He was most apologetic and quick to assure me that there was a suite being prepared for me at that very moment, one of our best, overlooking the cocktail terrace and pool. "You will be very happy there," he bowed and attempted to usher me out. "Wait a minute," I said. "I've just unpacked and all my clothes are in your wardrobe. I'll have to repack them."

'"No, no, that won't be necessary. We have inconvenienced you too far already, he", indicating the bellboy, "will load your things onto his trolley and deliver them to your new suite. And he will put everything away in your new big wardrobe. Very large, very exclusive. I'm sure you will be very, very pleased with it."

'"Can you give me ten minutes, then, to use the bathroom and collect my toiletries? I prefer to do that myself. You can take everything from the wardrobe right now. But I need a few minutes to myself. I'll call reception as soon as I'm ready, I won't be long."

'The manager started to apologise again and tell me how much better the new suite was. I thanked him, damn near pushed him through the door, and closed it. What would you have done? I'd love to have known who would be occupying that room, and I didn't like his chances of having an uninterrupted night, or even being there in the morning. So I decided to find out more.

'Leaving the toiletries un-repacked, I hurried off down the hall to the man with the machine gun. He stood up when he heard me and came toward me, hand held up flat in front of him as though to stop me. "There's something you ought to see," I said. His hand went to his pistol. "I think there is something I have to show you," I said, miming, returning along the corridor, and opening the door to my room. He turned and barked something over his shoulder. A more important-looking person arrived to look at me. Not yet important enough to speak English. I repeated what I had said before. He, more or less, shrugged his shoulders and said something to the machine gun man.

He turned and gestured to me to stay where I was.

'I was getting impatient. I wanted to get someone with authority into my room to see the window. I was realising it could only mean a kidnap or assassination attempt unless they had a guest who liked breaking out of buildings and jumping onto other guest's terraces. I amused myself with this thought, partly to calm myself down. I was becoming pretty anxious about my own safety by then.

'Finally, two more uniforms arrived, wrapped about with gold cord and jackets ablaze with stripes. They each sported holstered pistols and shouldered machine guns, nuzzles tenderly caressed by neatly manicured hands. Officer material, obviously, no English though.

'I finally convinced them to follow me back to my room where I strode over to the window, pulled back the curtain, and pushed the glass. They looked at each other, mystified. So I tried to get one by the hand. The other immediately grabbed my shoulder and grunted something. I said, "All right, both of you. Come here, look at this." I realised I was using the time honoured English way of getting yourself understood. Say it slowly and loudly then repeat it with gestures. I think they understood me.

'They both moved behind me to the window. They both observed me as I peeled back the rubber and mimed the window falling out, and me falling out with it. They looked at each other, suddenly getting my drift. One checked out the room, and realizing there was nothing under the bed or in the wardrobe, checked the bathroom and indicated to me to put the shaving stuff I had laid out back into the toilet bag.

'Meanwhile, another knock at the door. The manager. He entered the room and darn near dragged me out, toiletries in my hand, babbling what I supposed was an apology, and an explanation to the two goons. That was it. A narrow escape? I think so. I tried, but I couldn't find out who was booked into that room. But whoever it was, I probably saved his life.'

CHAPTER THIRTY-THREE

'Hey, what a great idea for a dinner party,' Colin said. 'This is fun. Now it's your turn, Judy.'

'Just a minute while I check my hair,' said Judy, looking around for a handy mirror. Then taking a compact from her handbag, she smiled at her image, checked her hair each side, tucked a stray whisk back behind her ear, and started. 'That's better,' she primped once more into the tiny mirror. 'I guess I'm about ready to tell you about *wigman*!

'I had just arrived at my Hong Kong hotel from Bangkok on a business trip. It was a last minute detour at the height of the tourist season, and all the suites at the Mandarin, where I usually stay, had been taken. I couldn't be bothered looking for another hotel, so I accepted a smallish room on the top floor. It had a good view, but no space. I don't usually spend much time in hotel lounges, I'm normally working when I'm on business and like to spend most of my time in a decent suite with a lounge or at least a TV room. There was a TV in my room, but it was hanging on the wall looking down at me as though it was threatening to fall on me.

'Little did I know that that was the best offer I would get that evening. At any rate, I decided to pass my time with a book in the main lounge. Apart from needing space and time to work, I usually avoid hotel lounges because they're all the same. Business people are all the same too. It's only their faces that are different. They just sit there with one hand wrapped around their drink, while they stare somberly into the middle distance. I like to imagine they're planning a company coup, or knifing their boss in order to get a promotion.

'Tourists are always the same too. Noisy, always on the way somewhere, nagging each other to hurry up or you'll miss the hotel bus, or the worst ones who are at the main desk complaining about lost luggage or a robbery or a lost handbag. Well, I seated myself in an alcove where there were only two other armchairs and a large heavy glass and cane coffee table. There was no ashtray. Never choose a chair close to an ashtray, and never sit too close to the bar. Unless you want one of the lizards hanging out at the counter quaffing cocktails to engage you in idle chatter to tell you how interesting and available he is.

'Soon after choosing my little island of isolation, a diminutive Chinese gent arrived and sat in the chair nearest me. I looked around for an empty space, but couldn't see an escape route to freedom before he had started to introduce himself. "Good afternoon, Mrs." They do that a lot in Asia, I hate it, it makes me feel like a schoolteacher. "May I introduce myself", myserif, "my name is Wen and I travel in wigs." Wow! What an introduction.

'Now, before I go any further, I should tell you that this was in the seventies, around the time the Vietnam War ended. I was fascinated and encouraged Wen to tell me more. What does someone who travels in wigs do? Wen was happy to enlarge upon his occupation and launched into the grisly details of what I had supposed was a glamorous business.

'This is what I gleaned from our tortuous conversation. Hair has many different textures and degrees of suitability for wig making. The best hair is living hair. Poor people in China and Asia sell their hair to buy food. The most expensive hair is naturally blond hair cut while living. That is cut from a living person. The grisly details continued.

'Some hair is cut from corpses, and if cut from a recently dead corpse, fetches a higher price than hair cut later from dead corpses. "How?" I asked. "Do you get hair cut from a corpse?"

'"In battlefields, Vietnam War big business for wig men. Many people rook for corpse with rong hair for serring. No say where it come from. Many people not rike idea. In India, rerigious people have head shaved before entering horry prace or horry temple. People correct hair flom froor and serr it. No good hair, furr of rice and dirt. But any plice good plice better than nothing."

'I'm not being mean. His accent was hilarious. It even got so tangled at times that I literally had to translate what he was saying. It's not that he couldn't pronounce *R* or *L*, he just got them mixed up. Thus, I understood that wig men were not quite in the beauty business. Most of his wigs were made from Indian, Chinese, or Mongolian hair. He also had some browns. But they're more difficult. Shades of brown usually start out as black. The hair has to be stripped of all colour first and then re-dyed. So it's rendered transparent and then coloured, which is why they're more expensive.

"Actually, I was reading the other day that in the UK, a good quality wig with a full head of long hair today can cost up to 900 sterling. And get this, it only lasts about six months.

'Well, back to my wig man. "Would you rike to see my samples?" he asked. "Yes, I'd love to." So he indicated to me to follow him. And I did, thinking that he had a sample book or photos and swatches or something nearby. But I found myself following him to the lifts and then to his room. To his room? I was considering my escape clause when he opened the door and bowed low and said, "Be my honoured guest." I took another look at him. Small enough to handle if I had to protect myself, very unlikely that it would come to that. He appeared, in every way, to be no more than pleased to find someone to talk to and who was interested in dead people's dead hair.

'So I entered the room. It was less than half the size of mine, and I thought that was small. There was no window. One light, which he had switched on as he entered. No bedside lamp, not that I was considering needing one. One huge wardrobe, the old-fashioned type with a drawer at the base and two doors and a space with a carved wood dragon themed edging above for luggage or whatever. Not even a dresser, but I think that the narrow door beside the wardrobe led to a miniature bathroom. There was no room left for any furniture other than a bed, not even for a small chair.

'I sat on the edge of the bed and watched as he indicated the top of the wardrobe, and said samples up there. He opened the right hand door, moved his right hand to support his weight on the dragon motif, and perched his right leg on the edge of the inside of the wardrobe. He turned his back momentarily whilst appearing to feel behind the upper edging with his left arm outstretched. Then suddenly, he swung around and launched himself at me. I was too stunned to move out of his way, but fortunately, his aim was inaccurate. While he was hurtling in my direction, I turned toward the hallway door just in time for him to land head first on the bed beside me!

'What was he thinking! What was his next move going to be? I didn't wait around, I was out that door and into the lift in no time, lurid headlines flashing before me, *Wigman Murders Blonde. Blonde Found Dead in Liftwell.* I've decided against ever wearing a wig. I don't care if I go bald, you'll never get me into a wig. You won't get me into a room with a TV threatening to leap off the wall at me either.

CHAPTER THIRTY-FOUR

The evening was hugely successful and the food delicious. They congratulated each other on their stories and vowed to repeat the evening's entertainment. It was agreed that a new theme would be set by Judy and Colin, and next time, the dinner would be at their place. Using the excellent culinary services of Chef in Your Own Kitchen.

Farewells said, Carol peeked into the kitchen—her kitchen—and was delighted to find it exactly the same as always. That was a good idea, she thought, and said to Mark, 'Thank you, darling. Thanks for pushing me. The chef idea was terrific. I really did enjoy it, and now I am absolutely done in. Couldn't pick up a glass of water if the place was on fire. I'm off to bed. It was successful, wasn't it?'

'Yes,' replied Mark. 'It was. And you were amazingly good, considering that it was your first night "out" in ages. I'll be along soon, I just want to watch the end of the game and set the recording for the match tomorrow.'

Carol undresses and slips into bed, too exhausted to even wash her make-up off. That can wait, she says to herself. Everything can wait.

She closes her eyes and brushes her hand across her brow, irritated by a vague tickling at the side of her face.

'I don't think so,' a spindly voice slips furtively into her disintegrating consciousness. *'I don't think everything can wait.'*

'Go away, spindle-shanks, I'm too tired to deal with you. I'm off to sleep.' And Carol slips off into a dreamworld where she is tracing her way through a maze. The possible paths are defined by tiny sparkling lights just like dew on a spider web, she thinks.

'Good, we're on the same page,' the spindly voice whispers as it slides across her brow and slips into her ear. *'Now, I want you to listen to me carefully, Carol. Do you know what dreaming about spiders means? It's another rhyme—spider, outsider. You don't want to get tangled up with me. You don't want to be part of my web. That would mean you would have to participate. And to participate, you have to understand and accept things and then become an insider.*

'You think I look like a spider and you don't like spiders, but you know that I'm not really a spider, don't you, Carol? When our day-to-day selves can't cope with things, there's a magic place inside of us that creates a totem to be an interpreter. You chose me even though you weren't aware that's what you were doing. I reflect some of your virtues, things I can use to help us. Like me, you are patient. That's why you know you have to think about your whole life, everything, now.

'Why did you take to your bed, Carol? To give yourself time to think. About what? You're still not sure. You just know you have to think. That's good. The dream you are having now, Carol, is not really a dream. You are communing with your spirit nature, our nature, yours and mine. You have just found yours. But I have always been there waiting for you to recognise me. Now, we can move on and solve some of the puzzles we have accumulated, Carol?

'You've been very patient, waiting, gathering, weaving even, weaving all your experiences into a puzzle called life. That's what most

people's lives are, puzzles, mostly to themselves. But now, Carol, you have decided to solve your puzzle. Why are you as you are?'

'I don't know,' Carol whispers to herself. 'I don't even know who I am, so how can I know how I am or why I am or even *if* I am? I'm still looking for me.'

'You're a lot closer to finding all those answers than you think. Think about this, Carol. Why did you choose me as your totem? Because like you, I am creative. I do weave beautiful webs. I am a weaver of your fate. But you're still in control, Carol. I just do the weaving. I just weave what you do. Did you know that I, a humble spider, am a symbol of feminine energy? I am. And energy is power, Carol. My power is also the power of integration. My beautiful web is the story of your many gifts and talents that I can help you bring together and use to make a beautiful pattern. But you're only seeing me as a shadow, a crumpled dried up dusty old web at the moment, Carol. I need you to help me shake off the dust and put my threads together into a divine pattern.

'Remember what the priest said about hate and acceptance, about accepting what has happened and using it to help you understand, about how when you understand and accept, hate dissipates? And you are free. When you understand, but still don't accept, the hate hides itself in the background of your life, watching, waiting to pounce. Do you think it is pouncing right now, Carol?'

Carol turns her head to one side, and a tear slips from the corner of her eyelid. She's dreaming that there is something she has to do. It's very important, but she can't remember what it is. She is retracing her journey from inside the maze back to where she started. Perhaps she'll remember then.

CHAPTER THIRTY-FIVE

Perhaps I'm looking at this from the wrong angle, thinks Carol. She is still in her dream, still looking for the pathway back to the beginning. She is asleep in the room with the picture board.

Or could she be awake?

'Why am I looking at myself in a pushchair? I remember the day that picture was taken. I was wearing my teddy bear coat, the warm brown one with the collar that tickled my chin. Mum told me it was taken by a friend who had a new camera when I was 10 months old, and she was taking Barry and me to meet Kevin at the school. It was his first week. On the way back, Kevin found a toy potty in the gutter. It was made of white china and Mum wouldn't let him take it home. She said it was dirty. Why do I remember that?'

Suddenly, she is 3 years old and running along the beach at Brighton with blood running from a gash on her chin. She had been standing in front of the swings watching some boys playing, hoping someone would ask her to play with them, when one of them pushed the swing very hard, and it shot up toward her and hit her on the chin.

She had run back along the beach, crying, and lost her new orange satin hair ribbon on the way.

She found her mother who wiped away the blood and put a plaster over the small gash on her chin. In her reverie, Carol wonders who carries a plaster when they go to the beach? Probably because plasters were a novelty then, and her mother was always practical. 'Then she told me to go back and look for the orange satin ribbon. I remember that ribbon as though it was yesterday,' she thinks. 'I found it, and it still had the bow in it. Why am I remembering these things now?'

She's still in Christchurch and sitting on the front steps of the house with the green and red fancy glass squares up the sides of the door. Her mother is making her a golliwog for Christmas. So she's still three. She has watched each stage of the golly's growth.

First, the cutting, and then the stuffing of the black stocking material with kapok, then the sewing of the legs and arms onto the rectangular body, then the flat round head with black rabbit fur for hair. He's now wearing black and white striped trousers, green jacket, and red bow tie. Her mother asks her to choose eyes from a tobacco tin full of odd trouser and shirt buttons. She chooses brown tortoise shell eyes.

It's a delicious dream.

Now, she can smell fish and chips, and she is in a cinema sitting with lots of mothers with young children. It's a community sing-song. There's a man on the stage, and he's talking about the newsreels they were showing of soldiers going off and coming home from the war. The homecoming scenes had been filmed at city docks, the wharves swamped by hundreds of anxious looking women and bewildered children, amidst shouting, brass bands playing, groups singing, and wives falling into outstretched arms weeping with relief.

There were similar scenes at smaller country stations where a handful of weary uniformed boys and men on crutches, heavily bandaged or with limbs in plaster, fell out of carriages into the arms of their relieved loved ones.

Occasionally, there was great grief. A loved father or mother was missing, dead, tired of waiting for the war to be over, or perhaps even worse, a child with shrivelled legs in irons, afflicted by polio—the epidemic rife at the time. The scenes are both touching and shocking in their rawness.

Most of the women in the audience are knitting balaclavas or gloves for the troops. She can barely hear the newsreel voice for the sound of knitting needles clicking. They were mostly metal needles then, she's thinking, plastic ones came later. At half time, they'll have fish and chips wrapped in newspaper.

Both her brothers are at school, so there's just Carol and her mother. The sing-song starts each day at 10.30 and goes till two o'clock, with people coming and going most of the time. It's to keep spirits up, while husbands and fathers are away overseas.

In her head, Carol's both the dreamer and the little girl, and she's thrilled that she's able to follow the same thread for so long. Perhaps she's not losing her mind after all. She's trying to remember more details from that time, but there's a wall in the way. It's the picture board, and she doesn't want to see the girl in the kilt.

Another picture pops into her dream, and it's Bunty, her pet lamb, wearing lensless horn-rim specs, a sun bonnet, a green cardigan, and a pair of Carol's shorts. Bunty is hitched up to an apple case on wheels. There's a doll in the apple case holding string reins. Bunty was second in the pets' parade at Caroline Bay that year. Bunty was a motherless lamb given to her father by someone whose farm he visited regularly as a fruit inspector. She had kept him for ten months until he grew horns and started galloping up behind people and bunting the back of their knees. She was told Bunty had to go. From the time Bunty disappeared from the garden, he was spoken about every time they ate lamb or any meat. 'This is probably Bunty' or 'I wonder if this is Bunty' or 'Gosh, Bunty tastes good'.

Her brothers joined in and she hated it. It was mean and it was cruel. She's hunting around in her dream head for something she did with her brothers. She's at the Opihi River, and there are seven kids on the back of a big horse. It's Bonny, the Clydesdale from Baron's farm. Bonny has a sweet nature, and when she's not pulling the plough, the river kids are sometimes allowed to ride her down to the river while they go for a swim.

She's on Bonny's back showing off with an arabesque, standing on a potato sack draped over Bonny's broad back. Bonny breaks into a slow trot along the grass space that serves as playground, cricket pitch, and picnic area for the summer houses and huts, either side of it, and takes the track that goes right under the willows at the side.

Thwack, a willow whacks Carol across her chest and in the face, and she falls off! Bonny stops, instantly aware that her rider is missing, and steps backwards right onto Carol's leg. No damage done, but a good fright for both of them.

Earwigs. The whole family is in the 'hut' they have built to live in, while a new house is built in Timaru. Everyone has an Edmonds baking powder tin or something similar, and they're chasing earwigs and squashing them on the raw wood of the walls and ceiling. The wood is full of earwigs, and they'll have to keep killing them till there are no more. Then it can be painted.

The hut is one rectangle with a small bedroom off it at the back, and a wide verandah in front, divided into two porches. The boys sleep one side in bunks and Carol sleeps in the other.

Abruptly, she's woken by the alarm. Damn, she'd forgotten to turn it off last night. She's awake at seven, needlessly. She'd been dreaming of the river and Bonny and Bunty. 'Poor Bunty, I wish I'd never had him to begin with,' she thinks. 'I still think of him often when I eat meat, and how mean my father was.' She wipes her hand across her forehead and feels the slight tugging of something close to her ear.

'You're doing okay, Carol. First, you have to dredge all that stuff back from where you've put it in the ante-chamber of your forgettery. Just keep going. Rest in bed and try to remember, bits and pieces. It's all good. Sooner or later, you'll hit the mother lode.'

CHAPTER THIRTY-SIX

It's Sunday, and Mark is off early for a golfing day. He may already be entertaining the club at breakfast with last night's tales. Carol did enjoy the evening. Dinner was delicious, and the storytelling such a good idea. She's looking forward to a relaxed day with Paco purring at her side, and looking through the photo albums on the bedside table.

But not just yet, 'I think I'll take a shower to wake me up a bit.' Freshly fragranced Carol has the croissant and coffee breakfast that Mark has left for her and returns to the pillows and Paco. 'Now, spindle-shanks, where are you in the bright light of morning?' She peers up into the corner of the ceiling and sees absolutely nothing. 'See, you're gone. Not there. Absent. Not present.' She brushes the hair off her forehead and feels the faintest vibration in her ear.

'Of course I'm not there, my dear Carol, I'm here with you. And we have work to do. I've been thinking about that dream we had about you when you were young. You don't seem to remember much about that

time. Would you believe me if I suggested that you have devoted a lot of energy to trying to forget it?'

'I don't remember much, truly.' Good grief, now I think it's normal to conduct a conversation with a spider.

'Let's talk about your mother. I know we've been there before, but I want to revisit this. Tell me your most intimate memory of her.'

'I suppose that was the day Pieter died. After people had been to the house for statements, and his body had been taken away, I went downstairs to see her. She put her arms around me and embraced me and said, "You poor thing, you don't deserve this." That was it. That is the only time I remember my mother embracing me.

'It was a weird day. First, I had rung the ambulance then his doctor then his solicitor. I told the solicitor I had called him to tell him that Pieter was dead. He said, "What happened, what did you do?" I said that he was working in the garden and came upstairs and died. I didn't do anything. It looked like a stroke. He was almost black in the face.

'Later, when I asked the solicitor why he thought I had done something to cause it, he said I had worded it strangely. I had said Pieter is dead, not Pieter has died, and I didn't sound upset. He said he immediately thought that I must have killed him! Kill him? How bloody stupid is that? I was upset, but I didn't cry because I hadn't cried in years. At least twenty years. Later, our neighbours, a young couple that we were friendly with, came over with a bottle of gin. Don, who knew I wasn't the crying kind, was worried that I was showing no emotion at all (he told me this later), so he tried pouring alcohol down my throat.

'I needed something, but it was just sympathy, not gin. Don sat beside me for at least an hour and held a basin, while I threw up. He felt that it was good for me, and he was probably right. That night, I dreamed that I was on a very narrow path around a mountainside, and I came to a blank wall where there was no path, just a bridge over a deep valley. I clearly heard Pieter say to me, "Go on, step onto it. You have to cross it, and I'll be with you until you safely get to the other side." When I woke, I knew that I had been given permission and encouragement and strength to go on. My goodness, I haven't thought about that for many years.'

'And now you feel a bit better, don't you? You have honoured the memory. That's what this is all about. Good and bad, it's about accepting things and honouring their memory. Now, back to your mother.'

'Don't ask me about that. I have tried and tried over the years to remember her hugging me, but I can't. I suppose she did, I just don't remember it. And it's not that I want to forget, I do want to remember.

'I remember plenty of sad things and things that made me angry like my first period. She hadn't had "that" conversation with me. I was in school one day, and stood up and felt that a waterfall had swamped me. There was blood running down my legs, and I was so embarrassed that someone would notice. I clenched my stomach muscles (shows you how much I knew of anatomy), and fortunately was wearing black stockings and black gymslip, so it didn't show. I stayed behind after class, it was the last of the day, and wiped the seat down with my sports rompers. We all wore rompers in those days for Phys Ed. We made them in the first sewing class of the year.

'I was working after school on Fridays at a gift shop, and at the weekends, at a fruit shop, so I had enough money to buy pads. I said nothing to her, I just felt angry with her. She found out a couple of months later when I must have spotted my bed, and she said, "You've had a little visitor." I nearly choked. I was angry with her inability to treat me like an adult, but I said nothing. She went on "You've become a woman now, and this will happen every month." And that was it. She gave me some cloth napkins to use, and I gave them back to her and told her I had bought pads. Not another word was said about it. That was how intimate our relationship was. Do I have to go on?'

'No, you need to rest now. But may I suggest you cast your mind back to the subject of tears. We need to talk about pain and tears and yes, the priest.' Carol closes her eyes and gives in to the warmth of the

sunshine on her pillow. 'I'm getting quite used to spindle-shanks,' she thought.

Almost fondly.

CHAPTER THIRTY-SEVEN

Carol drifts off again with pain on her mind. She's never been afraid of it, but she can't bear seeing it. She hates to see an animal in pain or a parent smacking a child. Even the sound of angry people arguing with loud voices causes pain and sometimes panic in her.

She knows how to deal with pain. It is just another sensation. She's thinking of the time in Napier she had her four wisdom teeth all out together. They'd been problematic, cutting through her gums, and making it difficult to chew. So she made an appointment with the dentist, having explained that it was for extractions.

The dentist asked her what she wanted, gas or general. She said neither. He suggested painless injection. She declined. She had determined that she was going to study the pain and concentrate on treating it simply as a sensation. So she lay back in the chair, mind focused on controlling the sensation. She was studying it to see how it worked. She concentrated on the sounds of the tools and the swishing of the rinse bowl that was running permanently beside her.

She felt the swab as he first painted the surface area where he had to cut the gum from around the emerging tooth, and then he inserted something to grip the exposed tooth. He wrapped the tooth in a little metal jacket, then tightened it, and got a good grip on the jacket and started manipulating the tooth to loosen it first and then extract it.

Poor sod, two came out with reasonable encouragement. But the two upper ones caused him all kinds of frustration. He kept apologising to her. He had his foot between her knees braced against the chair, as he maneuvered each one back and forth and tried rocking and twisting until exhausted, then he and the tooth fell away together. The second one made a spectacular exit. She thought the dentist was going to fly backwards out the door when it came away suddenly after a long struggle. Gleeful, she had controlled her pain perfectly, nothing but objective sensation. Pain is merely a sensation you don't enjoy, so don't feel it.

The dentist warned her to remain in the chair for ten minutes to recuperate. Recuperate? He might need to recuperate, but I need to get back to work. So she stood up, staggered a little as a film of silvery shimmery black descended on her, and she slumped to the floor unconscious. She was only out a couple of minutes, and she was grateful for the cup of warm tea handed to her with a straw and instructions to suck gently into the back of her mouth, which had been packed with tight cotton wool rolls.

As she left the surgery, gathering her bag and coat, the dentist shook her enthusiastically by the hand, and congratulated her on her control. Carol was very pleased. The experiment had gone off as planned.

'Do you think you may be a little masochistic?'

Carol wasn't sure whether she thought this herself or whether the arachnid had asked it. Does it matter? If he's in my head, he knows at any rate.

She rolled onto her side, tucking her legs up under her chin, and fell into a profound sleep.

CHAPTER THIRTY-EIGHT

Carol wakes just as Mark comes into her room. 'Home so soon?' she asks.

'Soon? It's nearly four.' 'Good lord,' says Carol. 'I must have slept all day. That's why I feel so good. Funny though, I had a dream about going to the dentist.'

'And you feel good?' Mark questions. 'I don't think dentist and good go together.'

'I was just turning over a few things in my head. Actually, I was thinking about mind over matter. I believe in it. I knew a guy once who showed me how to tear a London telephone directory in half.'

'Come on, Carol, even I can do that. The trick is to snap the spine with one twist.'

'Okay, strong man, how about this? I could thread a safety pin right through the skin on my arm and close it. Without shedding one drop of blood. Then I could remove it, and tell my arm when to bleed. How is that done?'

'I've no idea, Carol, but I hope you were careful about using a clean safety pin. But go on, you're itching to tell me. How is it done?'

'It's simple mind over matter. You talk to yourself, and tell yourself what you are going to do and what you want to happen when you do it. But you must believe in it.'

'What do you mean believe in it?'

'You have to believe that you have domination over your own body. It's like controlling pain by telling yourself it's only an unpleasant sensation. You concentrate on what you're doing, and you believe that your body will follow your instruction. I know it sounds crazy, but I really, really could stop my arm from bleeding until I gave it my permission. I used to do it in pubs in London, not as a performance of course. A group of us used to meet most nights in the pub across the road from where I worked. Just for a G and T or a glass of vino before we went off to catch our various buses or tubes. If we got onto the subject of mind over matter, which was a pretty popular concept in the seventies, I would do my safety pin trick. It never failed.

'A Japanese guy I used to know showed me another one too, based on the same principle, mind over matter. He would get a piece of timber, say a couple of centimetres thick, something that was solid at any rate, and set it up on a couple of bricks, and then take bets on whether he could chop the wood using only his bare hand.

'He would raise his hand flat on its side with fingers facing forward, about up to his shoulder, and use the leading side of his palm as the cutting edge. One thwack, and he would smash right through the wood. The trick is to not see the wood as a barrier. You focus on seeing your hand on the other side of the snapped wood. But you have to convince yourself you can do it. I failed the first time because I forgot to project my mind to the other side of the plank.'

'Holy hell,' Mark muttered as he moved toward the door. 'What's brought this on? Like a cup of tea? I'm going to make one for me. The stuff at the clubhouse gets stewed in the urn.'

'Come on, Carol, let's talk about pain. That subject interests both of us, doesn't it? You've just explained how you can control it. But we both knew you could do that, didn't we? What is more interesting is this. How do you prevent that control from damaging the rest of your life? For instance, when you burn yourself. If you're not looking, you don't notice until afterwards, do you? The burn's real, the skin is damaged, you just were not aware of what you were doing because you have trained yourself not to feel pain. You might have to retrain yourself to feel certain things, Carol. Have you thought about that?'

Carol is starting to understand what spindle-shanks is on about. 'How can I do that? I don't want to go around feeling hurt every time I bump into something or cut myself. It's enough to see the cuts and bruises. They hurt later on, it's just that they don't hurt at the time.' Can Mark hear her? She's not sure whether she's only thinking this, or saying it aloud.

'Don't worry, Carol, you won't be overheard. We can talk anytime and no one will hear us. One thing though, I really don't like being called spindle-shanks. It's very uncomplimentary. I prefer it when you call me doctor.

'Now back to pain. Do you remember telling me how you first stopped feeling pain? I'll give you a little clue. Feel and squeal, do you get it? When you were getting your hidings, you refused to let yourself squeal by training yourself not to feel. You thought that you were refusing to squeal because that's what your father wanted to enjoy. And that's true, as far as it goes. But what you were really doing was detaching yourself from the moment, from the experience. And you weren't old enough to know how to use the skill properly. So you switched off to all feeling.

'The really negative thing about that is that you sublimated your empathy. You can see how other people feel and imagine how other people feel, but you can't empathise. That is you can't feel how other people feel. Saved by the bell, Carol. Have a think about this, and we'll come back to it later. I think I hear Mark with the tea.'

'Here we are, Carol, I'm interested. What brought on all that mind over matter stuff?'

'I was thinking about our conditioning. You know how from the time we are infants, we are conditioned by absolutely everything that touches us. Environment, kindergarten, school, our parents' attitudes, the kinds of toys we have, and how we learn certain behaviours to make ourselves acceptable to, and protect ourselves from, others. Well,

I was wondering whether you can see in me any example of specific conditioning. Since most of that happens in childhood, I probably wouldn't recognise my reactions as being the results of conditioning. But you might have noticed something. So do I have any habits or attitudes that you find odd?'

'Now, there's an invitation. You don't salivate at the sound of a bell if that's what you mean. Sorry, I know you're being serious. I suppose what you were talking about before, mind over matter, is a form of conditioning, but I can't honestly say I see anything unusual or peculiar about you.'

Carol let out a small giggle. 'What's funny?' asked Mark.

'When you said peculiar then I had a sudden vision of a funny thing that happened in a teahouse in London. It was the early seventies and midsummer, I was walking along the Strand on my way to meet some friends for lunch. I was wearing a blue and white check mini shirt dress, you know, buttoned down the front. I found the place and was halfway down the centre aisle when someone called my name from behind. I turned around, saw it was one of the girls I was having lunch with, and she was gesturing over my shoulder at a table toward the back of the shop.

'I turned and started on my way again when I felt my dress suddenly tighten at thigh level. I looked down and saw that I had walked right into a dwarf who, by that time, had his face pushing at the back of my dress, trying to escape from the inside! Quickly, I lifted my leg up over his head, took a step backwards to release him, and hurried down the aisle to the sound of suppressed laughter. The place was full. I didn't dare look behind me to see how the dwarf had fared, but I got a round of quiet applause from nearby tables.'

'Nice,' says Mark. 'Glad I'm not a dwarf.'

They have their tea, and Mark goes back to watching the game he'd tuned into in the kitchen.

CHAPTER THIRTY-NINE

Carol picks up the photo album, and idly flips over the pages, barely looking at the pictures. She's thinking about what Dr Arachnid had said about detachment. 'That's exactly it. I can do two things at once without really investing myself in either of them. And I know how I learned to do that. When I was copywriting, I used to listen to our own radio station and monitor another at the same time as I was writing copy.

'In restaurants, I could engage in the conversation at our table, eavesdrop on another table, and mentally record the conversation at yet another. I didn't take the time to understand it, I just automatically recorded it. And if I picked up any juicy bits, I could play the tape back in my head later.'

'Knock knock, Dr Arachnid here, I believe we have an appointment to talk about pain. And I believe you have a question for me.'

'Yes, I have.' Carol hoped she sounded firm, but not aggressive. What am I doing? That eight-legged little web weaver knows exactly how I want to sound because he's listening to my thoughts. 'I want to know about empathy. What's the difference between empathy and sympathy? Answer me that.'

'That's easy, my dear Carol. Empathy requires feeling.'

'Well, I can feel. I feel sorry for people who have fallen on hard times or are sick or have lost a loved relative or who have been abandoned in some way. I can be comforting and supportive, and I can try to console them.'

'Yes, you can, I know. But that's sympathy, not empathy. Empathy is when you can really put yourself in their shoes and feel what they feel when you really feel at one with them.'

'Well isn't that the same as sympathy? I feel sorry for lots of people.'

'That's it, Carol. You've put your finger right on it. ***For****. Sympathy is feeling for. Empathy is feeling into. Remember when you looked it up, and you read that a psychologist called Edward Titchener identified the German word "einfuhlung" and had defined it as empathy, feeling into. There was actually no one word that explained the concept until he did in 1909. Empathy is not just putting yourself into a situation and feeling sorry for someone, it is actually experiencing their distress as though it's your own. It is imagining yourself as that person in that situation, and feeling grief or fear or abandonment exactly as they feel it. So you identify at a deep level with the situation, and you share the same perspective. Sympathy expresses care and concern, but it is you looking from the outside whereas empathy is you, more or less, being the other person and feeling it on the inside.*

'I don't understand how one can do that, Spiderman.'

'There, you just identified exactly why you can't. You used the word "one", very impersonal, Carol. But you shouldn't let that worry you. You have other skills and analysis like yours is rarely allied with empathy. Your ability to sublimate pain was developed by engaging your powers of analysis. You can't change that, but you can learn by understanding it. For you, this is a serious study, Carol. Here's how I see it, you have learnt how to not feel pain, now you have to unlearn that, so you can once again feel it. You have real work to do there. You can go on cutting

and burning yourself, that doesn't matter. But you have to understand the mechanisms that cause you not to feel that sort of pain. You have to separate the physical effects from the psychological causes. So let's start with tears. Why didn't you cry?'

'I do cry. Sometimes I can't stop crying.' *'I mean before the priest got hold of you.'*

'You know why. I trained myself not to feel pain, so I wouldn't cry when my father hit me.'

'And how did the priest change that?'

'He explained that children learn their attitudes to all kinds of authority from their earliest years, and that my experience had given me a negative and unhelpful attitude toward male authority. I had to learn to separate my personal experience completely, sort of quarantine it. Build a fence around it, and throw a cover over it, so it wouldn't keep interfering with my life. Then he introduced me to the Lord's Prayer.'

'But you already knew the Lord's Prayer.'

'Yes, but he made me think about it in other ways. To think of the Our Father as confirmation that the universe is driven by positive forces that exist to protects its young. He made it sound more like an affirmation of safety, not just a bunch of words. He explained it like this. It's not a very religious interpretation, but I got what he meant. Our Father who art in heaven, there is something more powerful than the individual. Hallowed be thy name, it doesn't matter how you name it, it represents something sacred as distinct from profane or worldly. Thy kingdom come, we hope to achieve something worthy. Thy will be done on earth, there are rules that we should live by here and now. As it is in heaven, wherever you live there are rules to be followed. Give us this day our daily bread, show us how to create a society that allows us all a fair chance. And forgive us our trespasses, don't hold our mistakes against us. As we forgive those who trespass against us, we should be charitable, understanding, and forgiving. And deliver us from evil, we can protect ourselves by following the rules.'

'Good, very nicely explained, Carol. But now explain what he was really trying to make you understand. I got all of the profane, but you didn't explain any of the sacred. When the priest took you through that, he had one objective in mind, didn't he?'

'He was trying to get me to understand the symbolism and to accept it.'

'So what is the symbolism, Carol? Explain it to me like he did to you.'

'That took nearly a year, I don't have that much time.'

'You forget, Carol. We are having this conversation in your head. I know what happened to you and how the conversation went. I'm just checking to see if you remember, just the salient points. The things you need to give voice to.'

'Please, please, don't make me go back there.'

CHAPTER FORTY

Carol is on the edge of panic. She's thinking of the nights she wept and no tears came, and how she wailed aloud at the walls of her bedroom, lying in the bed where her second husband had died suddenly a few months before. How she had sobbed convulsively, choked with no tears, and heaved and clutched the pillow. How angry she felt, how absolutely friendless and desperate, and still no tears came. She pleaded and her eyes burned with the heat of dry tears and begged to be relieved from her dark night of the soul.

There were nights when she never slept, days when she functioned normally, but was oblivious to anything, but the job in hand. From one day to the next, she had no memory of the day before. Every day, she relived the solitary panic of the night before. She went through the paces as though she were automated. Everything was done, but there were many things left undone that she ought to have done. Like mourning the death of a husband.

At the time of his death, a niece and her friend had been holidaying with them. They were both experienced nurses, so when he had sat up suddenly at 1.10 a.m. and let out a horrendous noise, half howl, half moan, she had leapt out of bed and called the girls downstairs to help her. She didn't have to wake up. She had been afraid to let go of the day and fall asleep ever since his first heart attack eight years before.

They got him out of bed and onto the floor to work on him. Her niece had said to her immediately, 'I wouldn't hold out much hope.'

Carol had switched into neutral, a gear she slipped into automatically whenever faced by a crisis. She called the doctor who arrived half an hour later, and pronounced him dead and wrote a death certificate.

The police attended, as was required of a sudden death, and she was questioned. The young constables were surprised at her coolness and calmness, and she overheard one of them questioning her niece about this in the kitchen.

'Is she always like this?'

The niece replied, 'Like what?'

'Well, I would have expected her to be upset or show some kind of emotion.'

Carol had then moved out of earshot, so she wouldn't hear how her niece replied.

The doctor had requested permission to do an autopsy for purely informational reasons, and she had agreed. It was grisly, though, seeing the huge oversewn *Y* on his dead chest.

The funeral was held at a nearby chapel. Friends attended from New Zealand, and two of them, lifelong friends from school, delivered eulogies. She made all the necessary arrangements in a catatonic state. There were flowers everywhere in her house and the neighbours' house. She greeted and farewelled friends after the funeral, at the house; and through all the expressions of sympathy, she shed not one tear.

This was remarked on privately by several people in the days that followed. She remained expressionless and moved as though stupefied.

It was mid-November 1992. She had a business to run, and she got on with it straight away. She felt as though she was someone else. She was not sorry for herself, and she didn't let herself feel sad. The day after the funeral, she sorted all her husband's clothes and folded them into neat piles, then rang the Smith Family and The Salvation Army. Whoever arrived first would get them. She left everything on the porch for collection. When she returned that afternoon, they were gone.

She sorted the sympathy cards and wrote a thank you to every sender. When the formalities had been dealt with, she rang their friend in Spain, the priest. He expressed his shock and asked how he could help. She asked him to come to be with her. He had teaching responsibilities and couldn't get away until the day before Christmas, and he could only get twelve days leave from the college, but he said at least she would have company for her birthday.

As soon as he arrived, he had noted the mechanical and detached nature of her behaviour; and try as he did, he could not make her shed a tear. In fact, he thought, in all the time he had known her, he'd never seen her get upset about anything. Not when she had called on him to rescue them from a police station in Spain. A 'misunderstanding' caused by a friend who was staying with them who had made a rude gesture at a pair of officers who were racing them on a motorbike alongside the car.

They had not been exceeding any limits. The guardia was just taunting a foreigner. Foreigners were not common on that part of the coast, and it was sport for the guardia. When they had stopped the car outside the apartment, Charles, their friend who was driving, gradually unfolded his well-built two metres plus, as he got out of the car and stared down the midget cop.

Charles, who was bilingual in English and Italian, told them they were sons of whores in Italian, very loudly, which seemed to work. At least well enough, for the pillion passenger had climbed onto his seat; and leaning over, holding the shoulders of the rider, had punched Charles, breaking his glasses. Charles had looked very angry, and Carol, in order to avoid a fight, suggested they go back to the pueblo to the police station and make a complaint.

The church was in the same square, so she had found the priest and taken him to the station. She'd done that because in those days, a Spanish village was run by the priest, the commander of the guardia, and the mayor, so the sides were equal. It was church versus guardia. A discussion was held and the matter closed.

She hadn't got upset either when her husband had crashed a car the priest had unofficially loaned them, on another occasion, for their use for three weeks. The car had been in his temporary care, while its owner was on holiday. After the accident, she had tracked him down to a restaurant where he was dining with other clergy, and coolly explained that he had become confused at an intersection and turned into oncoming traffic. The car was drivable, but had serious body damage. So the priest had arranged for the repairs, which they settled immediately and organised another car for them.

He'd witnessed another example of her cool approach, while he was staying with her that time. They'd gone to a local shopping centre and parked in a school zone area with restricted hours. Carol hadn't seen the signs. They'd returned half an hour late to find the car gone. He thought she'd be upset, but she had just gone to the nearest service station and asked where the pound was and what was their advice. They went on foot to the pound, which was close by, she paid the fine, and they drove home. He had thought it very odd. She had not even let slip a swear word.

The priest was considering all of this when he had told her there's no easy way to reach a hurting heart when the mind is stubborn. The three of them had been friends for twenty-two years at the time of the death, and they were easy with each other as though they were family.

Now, it seemed, it was time for him to move from friend in time of need to friend in deed. It was time to practise his profession.

CHAPTER FORTY-ONE

He had returned to Spain with the promise that he would keep in touch regularly. He left her with a few things to think about. He was very concerned by her apathy.

'Excuse me, Dr Arachnid calling. This seems like a good time to talk about tears. Do you remember how the priest explained tears to you? Do you remember how he referred to this vale of tears? That's the world, a vale of tears. Tears must be shed, I'm sure I remember him telling you that. And trespasses, sins, must be forgiven. He said that forgiveness is of prime importance. And in fact, forgiveness doesn't belong just to his church. It is a fundamental of all major religions and any successful society.

'Do you remember how he explained the father figure of the Lord's Prayer? He said it is symbolic of the father, forgiver, teacher, provider, protector figure in your life. A father who does not fulfill this symbolism is acting against the role nature has bestowed upon him. How much did that confuse you?

'Do you remember how he asked you to think about forgiving your father for his cruelty, or at least try to think past him? How he told you the importance of letting your hatred go? He said you can never really and truly love one person, while you are hiding hate in your heart for another?

'Do you remember the spiritual exercises he gave you? Yes, I know you do. You must have prayed a hundred Our Fathers daily. I know how hard you worked, and how after every midnight conversation with him, you would collapse exhausted with the effort of meditating, praying, and trying to get to grips with the memories you were dragging out of the past. I remember the tears you couldn't find and the shuddering of your body as you hurled abuse at the walls. I remember you clenching your fists and banging them against the bedhead in frustration. I remember the time you slammed your head against the door in an effort to hurt yourself, so you would feel the pain. And I recall exactly the night the dam broke and the floodgates opened, and you swamped yourself in your tears. How scorching hot they were, how salty, how strange it felt for you to be crying uncontrollably.

'Remember how he listened to you, and let you cry into the telephone at midnight. How he didn't hang up and leave you to cry alone, which is what you expected. Instead, he explained that your tears were cleansing tears, that you had to shed many more to make up for all the tears you had never allowed to escape.'

'And now, I can't stop. How bloody clever is that, Arachnid? I see someone cry, and I cry myself. I think a sad thought, and I shed another tear. And I don't mistake it for the sudden development of empathy either. My tears are simply out of control. Once upon a time, I didn't cry. Now I do. Yes, he opened the floodgate all right, but he didn't tell me how to close it.'

'I don't think you can blame him for that, Carol. He worked very hard with you, and he warned you what would happen if you let him lead you there. He told you that tears have to be shed. If you hold onto them, you could drown in your own grief. Don't blame yourself now, Carol, you had to do all this if you were to have any chance to be happy.

Speaking of which, you're doing quite well, really. You've come a long way these last few days.'

'I don't know, Spiderman. I'm remembering too many things, and it makes me feel stupid that I didn't understand all this years ago. I wish I could get it all over and done with today. You know there's stuff I tell myself not to remember because it's unpleasant. For instance, I don't remember the names of people I don't like. I have to struggle to find the word for the kind of cancer I had. I can't remember the names of the treatments I had. I don't just put things out of my mind, I actually forget things I don't want to remember. Now, dragging them all up to the surface makes me wonder what else is lying in wait for me. How much longer will this post-mortem last?'

'Let's see if we can sum it all up mathematically. You were seven when you told yourself not to cry. You didn't cry again until you were fifty-three. That means you didn't allow yourself to cry for forty-six years. You're seventy-five now. Do you realise that means you've spent more than half your life not allowing yourself to feel? That's a lot of pain denied and a lot of tears left unshed. But don't worry, you're progressing. The next step is trust. Trust yourself to live, and trust yourself to love. And remember that you won't love until you don't hate. You might need to revisit some of your life, Carol. Shall we look at the album again?'

'Please no, not today. I'm exhausted. Good grief, am I really having this conversation with myself? I must be mad.'

'No, Carol, you're not mad, far from it. And yes, in a way, you are having this conversation with yourself. Remember, you invented me to help you. You unconsciously summoned me from somewhere deep inside. Why do you think of me as a spider? I know how much you hate spiders, but I am not a real spider, I am a universal symbol of order and integration. Sounds pompous, doesn't it? The priest awoke me within you, and now that you have thought me into being, I must use my special powers to heal you.'

'Oh, God, this is too much for me to cope with now. I thought you into being? Special powers? The priest woke you up? I've heard all this before.'

'And you'll go on hearing it until you don't need to.'

'The only bit of this conversation I like is that you're not real. Please, leave me. I want to rest.' She puts away the photo album, which she hasn't even opened.

CHAPTER FORTY-TWO

Carol is exhausted and feeling frustrated to the verge of tears. How ironic, she thinks. First, I couldn't cry, now I can't stop crying.

She drifts on this thought, and happily, she's asleep in seconds just before the first tear slips down her cheek, leaving a shining path down to her pillow.

For a few minutes, she hovers in that layer of tiredness where her brain has not yet relaxed into theta waves. Occasionally, her eyes move lazily beneath her lids as though she is watching a very slow tennis match. The game's getting slower and slower, and then she suddenly falls over the edge and she is jolted awake, briefly.

She finally slips into delta waves, and she is being welcomed into her cousins' house on the farm. She loves being with them, but her visits are infrequent. Her father doesn't get on with their parents, so the only time they visit is when he's away somewhere. That's why her mother learned to drive, to be able to take her family to visit her brothers' families when she had the chance.

She's in her cousin Judy's bedroom, and she's going to show Carol something secret she keeps in the wardrobe. She opens the door and pulls out an old dressing gown, too small to be in current use. Put your hand in here, Judy whispers, indicating the pocket. She does, and what feels like dozens of little warm jelly beans jostle her fingers.

'What are they?' She whispers.

'Go on, you have a look, take a handful, see how many you can get.' Judy is pushing her elbow in encouragement.

So she takes a handful of wriggly things and discovers that the big pocket is full of little white mice! 'How long have you had them?'

'Just a few days. There were only four when I got them. Mum doesn't know yet, I don't know whether she'll let me keep them.'

'What do you feed them on?'

'Hen mash with bits of vegie. I just put it on the shelf in the wardrobe, and they eat it. I don't know what they're supposed to eat. They poo a lot, but it's easy to clean up. It's like little bits of black rice.' Carol is enchanted by the little white mice. Some of them are nearly bald, just little pink bodies with bright pink noses and tails, cute little feet, and naughty looking eyes. She's in a very happy place, and she's wondering whether she's in a dream or whether she really is with Judy. She remembers that it must be a dream. Can you dream that you're having a dream? Because Judy got cancer when she was thirteen. She had a sore knee in August and was dead by December. They were, more or less, the same age. Carol's last memory of her was seeing her wearing a green knitted beanie with one long hank of hair hanging out of the back. Judy had had lots of long hair. She had lost it all except one bunch in the therapy. It looked very weird. Judy had been buried just before Carol's birthday.

Carol knows in her dream that she is dreaming, and she doesn't want to be awake. She's thinking about Judy's hank of hair, and her dream thoughts return to her baby hair and her mother's hair. She dreams that she has a hair fetish and smiles in her dream.

'Hey, wake up, sleepyhead.' It's Mark, playfully pulling each of her fingers. She must have been in a deep sleep. The last thing she remembers is having a handful of pink and white mice. 'It's morning. You slept right through. I said goodnight to you, and you snored in response. Oink to you, I said. You didn't even stir, and I had the noisiest shower possible and you didn't even hear the water running or my singing. Here's breakfast then.' He hands her the tray. 'I'm off, got to be ready for a tenner this morning.' He'd always called his morning meetings tenners even if they started at 9.30.

Mark kisses her on the forehead and leaves. She attacks the toast and coffee with enthusiasm. I'll think about the morning while I shower. I might even sit on the verandah in the sun for a while.

CHAPTER FORTY-THREE

For some reason, Carol feels her bright mood dissipating as she showers and dresses. She decides not to sit in the sun, but goes back to her bed, smoothes the sheets, shakes the covers, and slides back in. She realises that her mood is slipping backwards into that dark place as she becomes aware of a momentary satisfaction about having made a decision. A decision? I just went back to bed! That's not a decision. What's happening to me? She feels flat and worthless. Does it matter if I don't get up? What's the difference? I can think just as well here in bed as I can outside.

She makes a feeble attempt to rally her spirits, but gives up. Maybe I'm supposed to stay in bed and rest. Maybe my body knows better than me. Or maybe I'm just bone lazy and can't be bothered doing anything. Maybe I'll stay here till I die. Who'd miss me at any rate? What seems certain to Carol is that she's missing something in all this soul-searching. Wait. Maybe I don't have a soul, maybe that's what's wrong. I'm looking for something that doesn't exist.

While she's considering this proposition, Carol becomes aware of a sensation of increasing heat radiating from a thin cord that's wrapping itself around her neck, and sending shock waves through hot fibres up into her nose and eyes. She wipes at her eyes, now hot with tears from the radiated heat.

'That got your attention, didn't it?' The cords are vibrating and right in front of her eyes, she can see translucent heat waves rising like sun shimmering off a radiant surface. *'You're getting warmer, Carol. You're getting close to another part of the puzzle. Let's talk about soul-searching. But first, are you searching for your soul? Or are you searching for something that's hidden in it?'*

'Right now, psycho-arachnid, I don't even know if I have a soul.'
'Oh, but you do. And that's a fact. It's been proven.'

'I'm over that religious stuff, psycho, it's only good as far as it goes. There are too many gods being promoted by too many religions and cults and so-called charities for me to choose one God above all others. In fact, I think that whatever force that exists for good in the world is being hijacked by a bunch of money-hungry fakes. Look at them, child molesters, murderers, kidnappers, I could go on—'

'Oh, please, don't, I get your point. But you don't get mine. The soul doesn't belong to religion. The soul belongs to the universe. So you can forget establishment religion and its offshoots. By the way, did you know that scientology is really just science fiction? L. Ron Hubbard, the founder, was simply a sci-fi writer in search of a tax-free money-generating idea. There was once a rumour, and I don't know whether it was true or not, that he had a bet with H. G. Wells that he could found his own religion by creating a plausible structure. He had looked round the world and realised that the fastest and safest way to make money was to establish yourself as a religion. People are so naive. They'll believe anything that makes them feel righter or more important or smarter than others. Take your pick.

'Rich religions attract rich people. Beliefs based on elitism attract even more people who want to think of themselves as elites. That's why Hubbard's Dianetics was so successful. It was designed to make you feel important for having been selected by your 'measured' potential.

'Remember that time in London when you allowed yourself to be recruited from the street, Shaftesbury Avenue it was, and you went upstairs to some semi-furnished rental office to have your potential measured? You were reading the leaflets there, did half the tests, and told your friends later that you were smarter than a tomato, that you had proved it by being tested. Someone said it must have been a dumb tomato.

'Of course, there were no signs outside saying that it was scientology, which already had poor press, but you knew who they were, and you wanted to find out how they recruited people. And just to be a smart ass, afterwards, you hung around as people were being lured upstairs and warned them that they were scientologists, a group of madmen operating offshore because Hubbard had been banned by the USA.

'I digress, I know, but it's important to appreciate that if a very ordinary sci-fi hack can turn himself into a demigod, and there is plenty of evidence to suggest that he genuinely had a god complex, then it might be a good idea to take a long hard look at some of the newer religions enjoying tax-free status.'

CHAPTER FORTY-FOUR

I thought we were talking about my soul? You said you had proof. Shit,’ thinks Carol, ‘if he’s right, I’ve read all this stuff without even understanding it.’

‘You have, Carol, you have read about the soul and the theory that it really is immortal. When you die, it will return to the universe. It will probably be recycled, and it may even carry with it a little of your own personal experience in this lifetime.’

‘In *this* lifetime, psycho spider? Tell me more. You know, well you must know, since you say you’ve been living in my head, what I believe. I think of my life as being the sum total of the past plus the anticipation of the future being experienced by me in the present. I have always believed that. Before I knew enough to challenge the “I am the Lord thy God, thou shalt have no other gods before me” idea, I’d figured out that I’m living in some kind of continuum. There, world without end, perhaps they got that bit right. But you’ve got my interest now. I’m beginning to like having you around.’

'Careful, Carol, you're not having me around. We are having us around. I am you, remember? And you are me. Sounds very esoteric, doesn't it?'

'Whatever, let's not argue. Explain what you meant by this lifetime. Do we believe in reincarnation as well? If you have a good presentation, I could probably buy that. But tell me about this soul that we share. Good grief, I'm starting to accept that this bloody spider is part of me.'

'I'm here, Carol. This bloody spider is part of you. We are as one.'

'Present your proof, doctor, of the existence of my immortal soul.'

'Very well, Carol. First, forget the idea that the soul is posited somewhere near the heart. That's what a lot of people believe. Think about this, the soul may be an integral part of the ego and the id and the super ego.'

'Hang on, hairy legs, how did we get to psychoanalysis? Explain yourself. I know about the ego, that's my sense of being, my self-esteem. It's the bit that checks between the conscious and the unconscious and allows me to make judgments about reality. And the *id*, if I remember correctly, is the bit that makes me want to let down someone's tyres when they take the last parking spot. I'd love to do it, but someone might see me. It's the superego that I've never been quite sure about. It seems to me to do the same stuff as the id.'

'No no no no no, Carol. But I can see how you conclude that. The superego is self-critical, it's your conscience, and it reflects what you've learned from those in authority like parents and teachers. It often represents the father, which in your case, we know, is a conflict for you. The priest tried to explain it to you. You may probably have concluded, Carol, that the driving force of your life is your attitude toward authority. To recap, then, the id reacts instinctively. The superego modifies that instinct to make it compliant with social standards. To put it another way, the id says go on, let the tyres down. The superego says that's no way to behave. Not because someone might see you, but because it is wrong.

We're a bit off the subject of the soul, but we're sort of in the right general direction.

'Let's start with the brain. It is a computer, a biological computer. It is human matter that contains billions of specialised nerve cells that transmit nerve impulses called neurons through long threads called axons. These axons make synaptic connections—'

'Synaptic connections? Really. Explain it please.'

'If you allow me to finish, synaptic connections are axonal firings through synaptic membrane. They are the information superhighways of the brain, which is exactly what the Internet was called when it was first introduced. Think of the brain as a computer-controlled train station, a communication centre that fires nerve impulses (neuron trains) through the many tunnels leading from it. The tunnels are the axons. The neuron trains are the nerve impulses that travel through the axons. The axon walls are made of synthetic permeable membrane, so that the neurons can use existing tracks. Those are the mental and emotional connections you've already established or create new tracks by making new axonal firings.

'Every time you do new mental puzzles, for instance, your neurons create new axonal firings through the synaptic membrane to arrive at a mental destination, which is your answer. And you have created a new neural path.'

'So I knew all this, did I? Are you really telling me that all this stuff you are saying now is somewhere in my head, that I've heard it or read it, and remembered it without being aware? How does that happen? Why and how don't I know that I knew all this? You say that we are as one except that you remember everything and I don't? What are you then, some kind of mind librarian?'

'That's not a bad analogy, Carol. Perhaps you've just mislaid the key to your own filing system.'

'Let's leave that for another day. Right now, I'd like you, or me, to explain to me where does my immortal soul fit in? What exactly is a soul? How do we know it's immortal? Can you see it? Can we touch it? So, Dr Arachnid, guardian of all things unremembered, Librarian of both forgettery and memory, get on with the explanation.'

'Two quantum scientists—'

Carol interrupts, 'Sounds like the beginning of a joke, you know. An Englishman, an Irishman, and an Italian walk into a pub. What exactly is a quantum scientist?'

'Carol, please try not to interrupt. This is difficult for me too, you know. You should have paid more attention when you were reading about it. I can only do my best with what you have exposed yourself to. Quantum relates to theories of relativity, and before you ask, the best definition I can give you for quantum is the physics definition from the dictionary. You probably don't remember, but at the time, you looked it up on the net.

'As I recall, we read that a quantum is a discrete quantity of energy proportional in magnitude to the frequency of the radiation it represents, or an analogous discrete amount of any other physical quantity such as momentum or electric charge. Discrete is the important adjective here. Think of it as many pieces of different information brought together to form something new. It might be a thing, a concept, an idea, or a memory.

'We're talking specifically about the brain. Inside each brain cell, we have structures called microtubules. The theory is that our experience of consciousness is the result of quantum gravity effects inside these microtubules. This is called orchestrated objective reduction. You can't see it, but it's there. A couple of world-renowned scientists proposed that in near-death experiences, the microtubules lose their quantum state, but not the information within them. Matter goes, memory stays. The container is destroyed, but the contents disperse and find new homes.

'Let me quote one of them, Dr Hameroff, Professor Emeritus at the Departments of Anaesthesiology and Psychology, and director of the Centre of Consciousness Studies at the University of Arizona. "Let's say the heart stops beating, and the blood stops flowing, the microtubules lose their quantum state. The quantum information within the microtubules is not destroyed, it can't be destroyed, it has no body, it just distributes and dissipates to the universe at large. If the patient is resuscitated, this

quantum information can go back into the microtubules, and the patient says I had a near-death experience."

'In the event of an unsuccessful resuscitation, or in the case of a normal death, it is possible that this quantum information can exist outside the body indefinitely, as a soul. Or call it what you like.'

'So, you're telling me that this proves my continuum theory, that some real scientists call it soul. I die but my soul lives on, albeit in another form. It remains itself, but contributes to something else, or it is changed in some way whilst retaining its integrity. We are all participating in some big universal consciousness soup. We are a mass of vibrating particles, vibration creates energy, energy can't be destroyed, but it can be redirected in order to dissipate it. Therefore, some aspect of all of us lives on and contributes to eternity, past, present and future. I am indestructible, or at least a part of me is, even if it's only a memory. I like it, psycho. It's a good theory, and it suits my way of thinking. I think I've got a grip on it. Perhaps that explains why I sometimes have memories of things I've never experienced. I'm tapping into some part of this continuum.

'At any rate, thanks for the memory, psycho, get it? Thanks for the memory? Would you like me to sing it? I wonder where I read about all that before. Why didn't I get it then? After all, if psycho's read it, I have too. Bloody hell, I hope I'm not losing my memory as well as getting it mixed up.'

'Shall we meet later then, Carol?'

CHAPTER FORTY-FIVE

Carol is almost dizzy with the excitement of knowing her theory has been confirmed, or sort of confirmed, by scientists! Real people.

Not some organisation or individual with an axe to grind. Actual scientists, not crazy God-botherers. 'Just wait till I tell Mark,' she thinks to herself. Then, 'whoops! I can't tell Mark I've been discussing my theories of existence and the meaning of life with a spider. I'll have to find another way of introducing it.'

Mark has already arrived home and appears at the bedroom door at that very moment. 'Hey, I thought I might have found you up and dressed today. You had such a good sleep last night. Oh, well, just a thought.'

Carol is somewhere between irritated that he thought she should be up and pleased that he's home. She's had a sudden brainwave. 'Hello, darling,' Carol flashes an uncharacteristic beam, and Mark smiles tentatively, aware that he is about to be sucked into a trap of some kind. It was *that* sort of 'hello darling'.

She hadn't pranged her car, that's good. She hadn't spent up big on something they didn't need, all good so far. He's intrigued. What the hell can it be?

'I've had an idea for our dinner at Colin and Judy's.'

'I thought we'd decided that we'd do something similar to last time?' replies Mark.

'Yes, we did, but I think I've got a nice little twist. I've been thinking about life.'

'Yeeeeessss?' Mark strung out the vowel and added an exaggerated rising inflection. 'Whose life? Yours or mine? Or the general?'

'Well, ours and the general, I suppose. Remember your stories about the fifth dimension?'

'What fifth dimension? I don't remember any story about a fifth dimension. Maybe you're thinking of a fifth dementia.'

'Ha ha!' Carol replies. 'Sarcasm is so low class. Mark, I'm serious about this. You called it the supernatural, but what you were talking about were fifth dimensional experiences. Why don't we use that as a sort of discussion theme for the evening? You've had some really interesting experiences, and I'm sure we all have had some kinds of weird encounters. I think that'd make for a really entertaining evening.'

Mark interrupts, 'Explain to me what your fifth dimension is first.

Please, madam.'

'Okay, I'll give it a go. One dimension can be expressed in a line like this.' Carol takes a pencil and a sheet of paper and draws a straight horizontal line. 'That', she points to the line, 'is a one dimensional line. It has no width, no depth, no height. It is a point that can move forward or backwards. It has only one measurable dimension. It looks like a line, it is a line, but it has no thickness. It is one dimension, 1D.

'Now if I add a vertical line to this horizontal one-dimensional line, we have a second dimension. With this, we can draw a circle, a triangle, or any shape we want. We have added a second physical dimension, and we can move in two directions, horizontal and vertical plus all points in between. We can now make a flat picture world that has no depth. This is 2D. Just like a child's drawing.

'Now, we add "projection" lines that give our otherwise flat shape a solid dimension, so it has a potentially physical, tangible presence. For instance, we draw the exploded view of a box then we join the exploded lines up, and we have a two-dimensional pattern for a three-dimensional box. We have added perspective in order to create a solid object. We use the drawing as a template, cut it out in cardboard, and join up the pieces to turn that box drawing into an actual box. We have created a third dimension, an object. This is 3D. The third dimension has given it body, presence, substance, tangibility. You can now pick it up and move it. You can't do that to a 1D line or a 2D drawn object.

'Now, think about this, we generally say that we are living in a three-dimensional world, but we're not. We're really living in a four-dimensional world. Our 3D world includes solid objects, but it doesn't include the perspective of time. We live in a world where time gives meaning to things. Think of a new car. Leave it exposed to the weather for ten years, and time changes it. Think of a newborn baby. Every day it is changing and growing. Why? Because of time. It still started out as a baby, but time changed it. Without the dimension of time, the baby would still be a baby. The new car would still be new. So time gives solid objects meaning in our world. 3D is fixed physical presence (the box you made), and 4D is that physical presence plus time.

'But we are *still* locked in time. We only exist in the here and now. We can remember the past and think about the future, but we can't *be* in either one. We can't go backwards or forwards in time at will. We can't speed it up or slow it down. At least, not yet, except in atom-splitting machines. Time is a fixed measure in our daily world.

'Now, 5D, the fifth dimension, will allow us to go backwards and forwards in time. Sci-fi writing is almost always set in a five dimensional, or more, world. And before you dismiss the idea of a fifth dimension completely, think about the theory of gravity. Think about defying gravity inside machines that fly. Seemed impossible six hundred years ago, but now, millions of people fly inside machines every day. In fact, at any one time, there are more than a million people flying. We can't yet fly into the past or the future, so we're fixed in the time we are experiencing now. For the present, that is.'

CHAPTER FORTY-SIX

'Woweee!' Mark is genuinely astonished. 'You did it. I wouldn't dream of dismissing your theory. You actually ex-plained that clearly in words with examples that I can nearly understand. You're a genius.'

Carol is flattered, thrilled, amazed, and thankful all at the same time. She's not losing her mind, not if she can get through five dimensions that easily. Perhaps her problem is just concentration.

'That's it, Carol. You know you're not going mad. Frustration gets the better of you, then you panic, then you lose the thread, and then you panic again because you can't remember where you started. The trick is to match the size of your bite to the piece of information you're planning to spit out. Take it slowly, and don't allow yourself to be sidetracked. That was amazing. Congratulations. See you later, soul sister.'

'I had no idea you knew all that technical stuff!' Mark throws his arms around her and kisses her ear and tells her she's a genius again. 'I've never ever given a thought to the idea of dimensions beyond seeing 3D movies and having a herd of elephants stampede onto my face.'

'So, Mark, my darling, what you were really talking about when you saw something before it happened that time, you actually were experiencing the fifth dimension. You have been there! You travelled forward in time and saw something happen before it actually did, and then you travelled backwards in time to see the event happen in its own time. That's very cool.'

CHAPTER FORTY-SEVEN

'Okay,' says Mark. 'What's the deal for our dinner date?' Mark is secretly over the moon with this sudden improvement in Carol's mental attitude. He's planning to push it for all its worth even if it means bringing the dinner party planned for next week forward.

'Well, let's talk with Colin and Judy first. You put the idea to them because you told that story about seeing something before it actually happened and everyone liked it. At any rate, why not talk to them and get their feelings about the idea. How about "Believe it or Not" as a theme? That offers plenty of scope.' Carol strokes Paco's ruff and runs his whiskers through her fingers and idly wonders if she were a witch what the duties of her 'familiar' would entail? Well, obviously, tail. She smiles to herself.

The conversation has tired her out. But she's happy to have held onto her train of thought long enough to explain it. And it was easy. She wasn't tense or nervous that she might 'lose it'. It was just like ploughing a field. Straight ahead, watching the furrowed clods of thought roll over and settle in neat lines.

She's thinking of Bonny the Clydesdale again, riding her to the river—the river and eeling. Best time to go eeling was at night. Break a rotten egg onto the water, duck egg preferably, they stink more than chook eggs, then shine a light onto the surface, and watch the eels as they shoot upwards from all directions to fight for the prize. Then gaff them out and flick them onto the riverbank.

She remembers Baron Petersen's barbed wire fence, strung with the bodies of eels drying in the sun. And the swing rope down at the creek. The creek was a sluggish pool created by a narrowing of the river on both sides, the surface almost covered with green weed, the river floor a murky mix of mud and big greasy river stones. The spaces between the weed were black and dangerous looking.

The river kids had a rope hanging from a willow. A big thick mooring rope knotted near the bottom, positioned so that the loose strands beneath the knot just skimmed the water when the kids rode it across and back. You had to have someone to give you a mighty push because there was no place to land on the other side of the river. It was all dirty reeds and marshy. The scary part was looking down as you swung out over the creek, and glimpsed your reflection in the black water between the creepy floating weeds.

The creek was full of eels, and the small kids were told terrible tales of children falling in and being attacked by hungry eels. You had to be ready to jump back to the bank you'd just swung from at just the right moment, or you'd slide into the horror below. Some of the older kids would throw the rope backwards with a huge effort, so they could grab it and jump onto as it swung past them across the creek.

Carol is at the river until Paco purrs her awake in the morning.

CHAPTER FORTY-EIGHT

Just as she stretches her arms above her head and braces her shoulders, Mark comes in with her breakfast tray.

'Well, you had a good sleep. I looked in a few minutes ago and Paco was draped right across your head and you were still asleep. You seem to be sleeping better these days. How are you feeling? Like facing the world yet?'

'Not quite, yet.' She produces a faint smile. 'What time will you be home today, darling?' Another darling, Mark notes. Things are looking further and further up. He places the tray over her knees and kisses her forehead.

'Probably around four-ish, I'd like to be away from the office early. Someone's having birthday drinks and they can be so tedious. Any reason why?'

'No particular one, I was just thinking of talking to Judy and Colin about dinner.'

'Done! My dear Carol. Agreed, organised, and invitations already sent out. I called them last night and came in to tell you, but you were already snoozing. They love the idea. In fact, Colin rang back and asked if we minded if they invited his brother with his new gay partner. I think we met Danny briefly at their Christmas do last year, but we haven't actually had a conversation with him. At any rate, we'll be sharing the evening with Danny and Manny whom Judy calls the Latin lover.'

'Oh, goody.' Carol is smiling. 'They know about the theme? What was their response?'

'Loved it, Carol. Thought it a super idea, and were going straight off to do some research, so we'd better be prepared for Medusa to rear any of her many heads. They'll have the Chef Chappie in to do the food and drinks, same as we did.'

Carol nods. 'Great idea. You don't think we might end up staying all night discussing or arguing?'

'Well, that would mean it was a success,' Mark replied. 'I'm off now, my dear.' Mark stops at the door and adds, 'Oh, by the way, they'd like to have the dinner this Friday. Okay with you?'

Carol agrees with another nod, and blows a kiss from her fingertips. She might spend the day brushing up on the afterlife.

CHAPTER FORTY-NINE

'Hmmm. Hmmm. Do you think we might be better off dealing with the here and now, or rather the past now? We can do the afterlife after we've dealt with the present, and the present after we've dealt with the past. How does that sound, Carol?'

'Okay, if you insist. What do I need to do?' She's feeling very amenable.

'Just go back to that small reference you made to the superego. It is often said to represent the father, inherited wisdom from the father. In your case, you inherited zilch. Nothing. And since you inherited zilch wisdom, you cannot allow this "nothing" to interfere with your life. If you can't use the experience positively, forget it. Forget him. He contributed nothing. Father figures are okay, symbolic fathers are okay, your father was not okay. Got it, Carol?'

'Actually, psycho sister, I think I do get it. I'm a lot more comfortable with the idea of finding a way of forgetting him rather than forgiving him.'

Carol is truly relieved. She is already busy creating a big, black box in her imagination. It is gigantic. She thinks a very small opening into the top of it, like a letterbox, but with a hinged cover.

She thinks of the little girl in the picture. The girl who looked exactly like her, but wasn't her. That picture had made her feel like she didn't exist, that her identity had been stolen, and had left her feeling that she was a nobody who wasn't wanted. She recalls the thrashings he gave her. And the time he slapped her head when she was sitting at the table in the corner of the kitchen, and he kept on hitting her as her head bounced from one wall to the other until her mother pleaded with him to stop. She thinks these memories onto an imaginary sheet of paper.

She recalls the work she and Barry had been made to do after school and at weekends. Excavating the clay and soil from under the same house where her head had bounced off the walls, grubbing and digging and filling buckets with it, and emptying them somewhere outside, day after day, while other kids played sport or went on family outings. It was back-breaking work. They had to bend double and dig. She had just started high school then. She adds the memories to the paper.

She recalls the random punches and verbal assaults, all of them wounding, physically and to her spirit. She remembers how he used to say things to hurt her and humiliate her. How he liked to bully her in front of the few friends she had. She remembers how he used to say, while hitting or bullying her, 'Careful, I've got a weak heart,' as though she were making him hit her.

He was punch-drunk, Margaret said. Had spent too much time in the ring, being pounded around the head. Once he started hitting, he couldn't stop until he remembered his weak heart and used that to put responsibility onto her. Margaret used to mock him and say, 'Do you have a wee horse to put in front of your wee kart?' She loved her for saying that. She was the only one of his siblings he still spoke to. They'd had some kind of falling out when their mother died.

Carol remembers her grandmother's death. Twenty-four hours of rosaries were said over her as she lay on her deathbed. Her body couldn't be removed until the family had sat the vigil. And everybody had led at least one rosary. The children were taken in to see her, and had to listen to the mutterings of 'she looks so beautiful', 'so peaceful', 'so calm', 'she's in heaven now'. It had sounded fake to her even then when she was ten. She looked as though she was asleep, that's all.

But the next day, she'd had another look at her just before they took her away, so that the coffin could lie in front of the altar in the church. She did look younger. Her face had smoothed out, gravity perhaps, and she definitely had lost some wrinkles. Perhaps death is just one long facial, the devil in Carol suggested.

'But I must finish this,' Carol reminds herself.

She takes all those memories and thinks them onto the same sheet of paper. It's now an enormous size. She folds the paper over and over carefully until it's too thick to fold further, and she ties it with imaginary string. She then takes an imaginary match and sets fire to it, and she watches it burn. Fat orange flames fading into blue at the sides until all that's left is a pile of grey ashes. In her mind, she picks up the ashes, careful not to let any escape on the wind of her movement, and feeds them through the letterbox hole, whispering *ashes to ashes, dust to dust, wrongs have been righted, now I will trust.* Carol smiles in her mind as she closes the hinged top and consigns the big, black box with the ashes to the forgettery.

Something flutters across her forehead, and she imagines that the spider has placed a soft kiss on her skin.

CHAPTER FIFTY

Tired out, she slips down in the bed, and tucks the sheet up snug under her chin. I'll just have a quiet snooze. She wakes to the sound of the dishwasher being unloaded. She slips into her dressing gown and pink polka dot slippers, and calls to the housekeeper, 'Hello, Mrs Rose. Lovely day, isn't it?'

'Goodness, you did give me a turn.' Mrs Rose stood up and shook her head a little. 'Bending does make one feel giddy, doesn't it?'

Carol supposes, correctly, that the statement was rhetorical. No response needed.

Mrs Rose continues, 'My, you do have beautiful china, don't you. Mine's all crockery, but yours is lovely, delicate, enough to make a cup of tea taste like nectar.' She adjusted the neck frill of her cotton print apron as she straightened herself.

Good lord, thought Carol. *Where did Mark find her?* She's perfect. House is always nice and clean, everything in its place, her kitchen skills are exemplary, and she even looks like a housekeeper.

Could have been dressed by Mrs Beeton herself. 'Believe it or not, Mrs Rose, most of our china was wedding presents. That's the benefit of having no children. Your beautiful things don't get broken.'

'Yes, madam, I suppose you're right. But with children, you don't mind the crockery getting broken. It's the way they break your heart that hurts most.'

Carol suddenly realises that she is talking with a real person. She's been in bed so long she's forgotten how it is to have an unexpected conversation. 'Mrs Rose, do we have time for a cup of tea? I'd love you to tell me about your family.'

'Yes, of course, madam. I was thinking about a cuppa myself, but I'm afraid I don't have much to tell you about my family.' She fills the jug and switches it on, reaches into the cupboard, and takes down a tin, which contains a delicious fudge slice and offers it to Carol.

'Shall I put some of these on a plate for us?'

'Lovely, Mrs Rose. Yes, please. Did you bake them?'

'Oh, yes, I make something different each week for Mr Mark. He has such a sweet tooth, and he's always very appreciative. It's nice to have someone to make things for.'

Carol feels slightly embarrassed that she's never shown any interest in her before. In fact, she thinks, *I've only met her the once when Mark introduced us.* She's only ever thought of her as the housekeeper, not a real person. *She's here in my house every day, and I've hardly ever set eyes on her. Except when she changes the bedroom linen twice a week. And then mostly,* Carol admits, *I try to avoid her.*

The tea is made, the pot's set to brew, it's turned three times, and Mrs Rose pours it into the violet patterned china. 'It's a lovely house,' she says, offering a matching plate with fudge slice to Carol. 'It was a lucky break for me that you've been poorly. My last house packed up and moved suddenly. Oh, I didn't mean it's lucky that you've been poorly. I meant this job came along for me at just the right time. Mr Rose died six months ago, and we didn't have much in the way of savings, so I have to work.'

'Sudden, was it?' Carol wants to sound interested, but realises that she's forgotten how. 'Had Mr Rose been sick or was it an accident?' It's a clumsy attempt, she knows. She must practise sounding interested in other people. She really needs to get up and around again. Go shopping, do something other than mope.

'You're doing something good right now, Carol,' a surprisingly soft and tender spidery voice whispers. *'She's a good woman and worth your while to listen to her.'*

CHAPTER FIFTY-ONE

'No, not an accident,' Mrs Rose replies. 'He was always an active man, but he chose a dangerous career. Eventually, it caught up with him, and it ate him up year by year until he finally gave in. Destroyed his mind, too many hits to the head.'

Carol is startled. Hits to the head? 'What did he do for a living?' she asks.

'He was a professional boxer, then for the last fifteen years, he's been in the ring doing training. Doesn't seem right, I used to say to him. "Why do you want to teach those young men to beat each other to a pulp? Just doesn't seem right." But he didn't listen. In the end, he didn't have anything much left to listen with. Great big cauliflower ears with nothing left between them. His mind went, turned into mulch. I'm lucky he had the stroke, or I might have been frightened to be alone with him in the house.'

Carol's mind flashes her an image of a big, black box with a hinged lid, and it endows her with sudden and astonishing strength.

She has closed and locked the door on the forgettery. She is a different Carol now.

She takes one of Mrs Rose's hands in her two hands, and says, 'That must have been terrible for you. Tell me what happened. I'm so glad you came to us. We're thrilled with your work. But tell me how many children did you have?'

Mrs Rose looks at her with a sad smile. 'We didn't have any of our own. At first, I hated the boxing so much that I couldn't bear the thought of bringing a child into a world where grown men beat each other around the head for money. So I had my tubes tied. I never told him, you know. I just went off and did it and never said a word to anyone. So far as my family knew, we couldn't have children. We weren't lucky. Lucky? I used to think, it would have been very unlucky for a boy child to have a boxing father.

'Then after about ten years, I started feeling sorry that we didn't have a family. It wasn't just that not having children made us different from other people. Most of my friends had families and used to talk about the children and swap baby stories, and I had nothing to say. So in the end, if you don't join them, you just drift apart. That's what happened with us at any rate. Our friends drifted away from us, and we drifted apart from each other.' Carol lets her hand go and offers her a tissue. There are tears welling in her eyes. 'Oh, I'm just being silly, you don't want to waste your time with my chatterings.'

'Actually, I do,' Carol says. 'And it won't be wasted time. It's a privilege to be invited into someone else's life, a rare privilege, and I hope I am worthy of it. Besides, our time is ours. There's no one here to tell us to hurry up. Tell me more. Why don't you bring your tea to the comfy chairs where we can relax.' Carol takes the plate of fudge goodies to the coffee table and settles into a chair with her tea, waiting for the housekeeper to join her.

CHAPTER FIFTY-TWO

'Where was I?' Mrs Rose places herself carefully into a chair twice her size and continues. 'Yes, before we were married, I wanted a family, but I had no idea then what boxing was all about. It's rough you know, madam. It's a hard life for the men, but harder for their wives and families. I'd seen enough in the first few months to know that I wouldn't have my own. But I was lonely at home on my own. I used to do a bit of secretarial work, but I soon thought I can just as easily do this and look after a child. So I told Mr Rose that I wanted to adopt. He was quite happy about that. Of course, he wanted a boy. He wanted a boy so much that I thought if I insisted on a girl, he would go off the idea completely. And I'd have broken my last straw.

'Then I had an idea. I'd go to the agencies and look for a boy who would be too slight or too weak to box, an unlikely candidate for adoption. Then the agency, I thought, would be helpful with the approvals and so on. Just to get him off their books, so to speak. As luck would have it, a couple of months after I started looking for a boy, Mr Rose was delighted that I wanted a boy. One of the agencies found the perfect candidate.'

Carol is entranced. She leans forward. Mrs Rose takes a deep breath, and wiping away an escaping tear, she has been silently weeping throughout the conversation. She says, 'They found me a bonny boy, 5 years old, good temperament, no mental problems. Lots of orphans at that age have already developed mental problems, but a hemophiliac! Absolutely perfect, so I arranged with the agency to take him for a few weekends to see if the three of us liked each other and it worked a treat. He was a clever wee thing. Entertaining, you know?

'The agency had warned us not to get him too intimately involved with us before the formal adoption, just so he wouldn't feel abandoned if anything happened that we didn't take him. One of the rules was that he shouldn't know what his prospective parents did for a living. They'd already checked us out all right, but we weren't to talk about work in front of him before the final decision was made. It was better, they said, that way. The less he knew about us, the less he would have to tell the other children, and the less he might have to be disappointed about if it didn't work out.

'Well, I knew that it was going to work out. I'd told the agency that I would not be telling Mr Rose that he was hemophiliac. He didn't need to know. We had enough income to pay for treatment, and the medical services paid most everything at any rate. Are you sure I'm not boring you, madam?'

'Boring? Far from it, my dear, Mrs Rose. Do you have a name? You could call me Carol, and I'd like to call you something friendlier than missus.'

'Oh, that's so kind of you. Are you sure it's not an imposition? Don't laugh now, my name's Rosemarie. How's that? Rosemarie Rose. Easy to remember, simple, like me, I guess.'

'Rosemarie, my dear housekeeper, you are far from simple. You are a delight, and I hope you'll be our housekeeper forever. I won't even use you as an excuse not to get out of bed. So tell me, Rosemarie, what is your boy's name, how old is he, and what does he do, and where does he come from? Everything, I want to know everything.'

'Well, he was a foreign boy. South American or Spanish, we were told. His parents abandoned him in Darwin when they went on the run for drug offences to escape Interpol. Just up and disappeared one day after they'd left him with a neighbour. Not a word to anyone.

'He was taken into state care straight away and had been there for only a month, happily, when we happened along. So he had not been traumatised as some children are, pushed from pillar to post with no one loving them enough to keep them. When we read his case history and saw his picture, we were both thrilled. They'd obligingly removed the reference to his medical condition. He didn't look that solid, but he wasn't thin like a string bean.' Rosemarie has relaxed and is looking into the middle distance, alternately smiling and weeping.

CHAPTER FIFTY-THREE

The trial weekends went well, and after we'd all three had a chat about the future, we asked him to decorate his own room. He was thrilled because his parents, well, the couple who abandoned him, had dragged him around with them from place to place. He'd never had a room to call his own, and he'd had no chance to make friendships with boys and girls of his own age.

'As soon as he started school, it was obvious that he was a good student, and Mr Rose was very proud of his school reports, which made a point of mentioning that he was always well behaved. Polite, you know, and good with names. He knew all our friends, and always asked after their families. He didn't play sport after school like most of the other boys. Instead, he asked if he could learn the piano, and then the violin. He was so good he was asked to join the school orchestra. I was thrilled that he showed such talent, and the school told me he could go as far as he wanted with the music. He played in the university orchestra as well, and they even performed a composition of his at the end of year concert. They were very sorry to lose him.

'Mr Rose was very disappointed when he understood that he would never be able to take part in most sports because of his condition. I had kept our doctor informed about what I was doing, and she was very supportive of the idea and agreed that it was better for Mr Rose not to know about the hemophilia before the adoption. He said he'd wished we'd known about that before we adopted him. I admit to feeling a bit guilty, but so far as I was concerned, it was Manuel or no one.

'At any rate, he graduated university with top marks. We never thought we would have brains in the family. It was such a shame Manuel and his father fell out. Well, it was a blazing row really, just before his twenty-first birthday. He'd never shown any interest in his father's boxing and had tried, always politely, to avoid conversation about it. But his father wanted to take him on a world fight tour to celebrate the twenty-first. He wasn't fighting, of course, but he'd put a good deal of time into planning a trip that included Manila, Las Vegas, and Tokyo, thinking that Manuel would be thrilled to see a world he hadn't ever been exposed to.

'I'd always used the excuse of his hemophilia to keep him away from the boxing and other rough sports, knowing that Mr Rose couldn't overlook the fact of high risk if he had an accident. We didn't talk about the hemophilia or boxing at home or with friends. And Mr Rose had plenty of opportunities to exhaust the subject with his friends at the club, so it didn't seem to be a problem.

'I didn't wrap him in cotton wool, but I did work very hard to protect him from that kind of discussion since I realised that he was a sensitive soul. I knew it wasn't Manuel's kind of thing, and I tried to dissuade Mr Rose from pursuing it, but he wasn't to be put off. Ultimately, he put the idea to Manuel very firmly and it ended badly. Mr Rose told him, rather crudely I thought, that as far as he was concerned, his ways were far too delicate for a son of his and that he needed something to make a man of him.

'That did it. Manuel was hurt, of course. He felt very let down. Their row was terrible, I was afraid Mr Rose might become violent. He was furious that his son didn't appreciate what he had worked at all his life. He wanted neither hide nor hair of him and told him so. It was very upsetting for me. He didn't even want him to visit for a meal.

'You should have seen the place while Manuel was with us. It was a picture. He had such a green thumb. When he left, the garden just grew and grew all over itself until you could hardly see what had been there. Nothing left but a jungle of weeds. At any rate, he left and that was that. For two years, we met in secret for coffee or lunch, but getting away to see him became more and more difficult when Mr Rose became ill. I couldn't leave the house for anything other than a few hours of work each day.

'Manuel and I talked with each other regularly, but his regular calls suddenly stopped. Then a week or so after his last one, I got a letter from him saying that he had been unexpectedly transferred to Singapore on a relief contract. Someone had gone off with a heart attack. It was all very rushed, and he hadn't had time to break it to me gently, so he thought he'd do it this way. He sent his love, of course, and said that he missed me, but it's not the same as a nice big hug, is it?'

CHAPTER FIFTY-FOUR

'Do you know how long the relief contract is for, Rosemarie?'

'No, I only know it was indefinite. Which might mean one month or ten years, I understand. I don't even know the name of the company. He was sharing an apartment in a building that belonged to a group of big businesses who used those apartments for short-term visitors like staff transfers. But he was looking for something more private that he could rent month to month. He said it isn't easy to find that kind of accommodation in a city like Singapore.'

'Well, at least he keeps in touch with you.'

'That's just it.' Rosemarie dabbed at the corner of her eye with her hankie. 'He doesn't know how to contact me now. And I don't know how to contact him now. He doesn't even know about his father's death.'

'Goodness, how did that come about, dear?'

'It seems we both moved house at the same time. I had a fixed line number for him, although it was mostly him who called me. We used to arrange a time when Mr Rose would be at the hospital for his regular treatments, so we were able to talk as long as we liked. I always waited for his calls because he fitted me in between his duties.

'He'd been over there for more than a year when Mr Rose passed away. I didn't know whether he'd be able to get away for the funeral, but I wanted him to know straight away. I had his home number, but I didn't have the work number for him. I didn't even know the name of the firm he worked for, so I had to wait for the evening when he might be home. But there was no answer. I called five times that night to find out that he'd just left that place, and they didn't have the contact for his new flat. Someone passing the door had heard the phone ringing and answered it. I was so shocked I just apologised and hung up. I should have called them back then and there and asked them to put a notice on their noticeboard asking him to call me urgently. I knew the place had a common noticeboard because that's how he'd found the Bridge Club he joined.

'Then the next day, the truck ran into the house, and I had to move out quick smart. It was lucky I was at the hospital doing the arrangements for the funeral. The accident destroyed the electricity and phone lines, the TV, everything, as well as the whole of the front of the house. You wouldn't credit it. Never rains, but it pours. Mr Rose passes away, a truck wipes out the house, and I find out that Manuel has moved all in the same few days.'

Carol reaches out, and takes her hand tenderly between her own. 'How dreadful for you. I'm so sorry. Did you have someone to help you?' 'Well, I had a lot on my mind, and first thing was I had to find somewhere to live. I didn't have time to think about everything. The social worker at the hospital made most of the arrangements for me. I found a small flat where I could just afford the rent. We hadn't had the house insured, you don't think about things like trucks running through your front room, and we weren't anywhere near bush fire or flood places, so we just didn't bother.

'I managed to save some furniture that I could clean up and use, so I wasn't too badly off. Could have done without all that grief at once though. Not being able to tell Manuel was the final straw. I called the only one of his friends that I knew here to find that he was off on holiday. I left a message, but never heard back. And without knowing his firm's name, I was lost. The old house number couldn't be transferred, so I got myself a mobile. But there was simply no way of getting a message to him to tell him my number. Oh, dear, am I repeating myself? I feel so helpless without him.

'I'm sure he would have come home for Mr Rose's funeral if he had only known.' She dabs her eyes and straightens her shoulders. 'But you don't want to know my troubles. You have to get over your own ill health. That's what's important for you.'

'Rosemarie, my dear housekeeper', Carol, suddenly aware that she is still holding her hand, squeezes it gently as she takes hers back, 'my health is nothing compared with what you've been through. If I can do anything, and I mean anything, to help you any time, be sure to ask me. You're my friend now, and I mean to help you as much as I can.'

'Oh, dear,' whispers Rosemarie, weeping quietly into her handkerchief. 'You are so kind. Thank you. But you must know that you have already taken a load off my mind by making me permanent. I didn't expect that. I am very grateful to know I am secure in that.'

Carol stands, helps Rosemarie to her feet, and hugs her. 'There', she says, 'that's a hug by proxy on behalf of Manuel. I have a few contacts in accountancy and banking who have offices in Singapore, I think I'll make a few discreet enquiries. Thanks for the tea and fudge slice, Rosemarie, I had no idea you've been spoiling Mark with your treats.' Carol puts her tea things on the bench and turns toward her. 'You've given me a mission. And, my dear, you may even be putting me on the road back to health. Thank you for that.'

'Now, aren't you glad you listened. This is just what we need, our mind on other things. Out of bed things.'

Carol finds herself nodding enthusiastically. God, I hope no one's watching me. I must look like one of those silly nodding dogs people have in the back windows of their cars.

CHAPTER FIFTY-FIVE

Carol is totally preoccupied now by Rosemarie's problems. She sets to work looking for E-mail addresses and telephone numbers of her and Mark's old commercial contacts. She's sure she'll turn up something to give her a clue as to Manuel's whereabouts.

Suddenly, it seems the afternoon has disappeared on her, and she remembers the 'Believe It or Not' stuff research she had promised herself to do today. She hasn't even got a start on it. Oh, well, there's always tomorrow.

'Hey, how's your day been? Still in your dressing gown, and I see an unmade bed. What has been happening around here?' Mark is cheerful and Carol is pleased to see him home and can't wait to tell him Rosemarie Rose's story.

'I've been doing some sleuthing. Over dinner, I'll tell you all about it. And I've been looking for some of those old contacts of ours in international financing. Accounting and banking people.'

'What on earth for?' Mark is surprised. *International financing? What is she getting herself into? Oh well, I suppose I should be happy she's found something to wake her out of the semi-catatonic state she's been in these last few months.* 'Tell me more,' he says encouragingly.

'Over dinner, over dinner, my dear, I will reveal all. Now, I think I might just primp myself up and check the wardrobe for something to wear. When is it we're going to Judy and Colin's? Tomorrow night? Sheeyit, I'd better get on and do that research.'

'I thought you were doing that today, my sweet dreamer. Or what were you doing instead?' Mark is surprised and pleased that she's looking forward to getting out of the house, finally.

'I was chatting with Rosemarie.' 'Who's Rosemarie?'

'Our housekeeper. Do you believe it? Her name is Rosemarie Rose!' 'Well', replies Mark, 'you can only hold her responsible for the first name I think.'

'I'll tell you about it later. Meantime, I'll do the wardrobe thing first.'

Mark is very happy to see her so animated, and can't wait to hear the reason for this sudden interest in being alive.

Carol scans the possibilities in her wardrobe and chooses a cat's eye green jersey pantsuit with a flattering cowl neckline, and selects the emerald earrings to go with it. No need for a necklace with that neckline. *Good Lord*, she thinks, *I'm actually getting back into the idea of living. I think I'm going to enjoy this.*

She holds the earrings against the suit and nods approval. As she returns the suit to the wardrobe and selects a day dress to slip into for dinner, she brushes a stray hair from in front of her left ear.

'Hulloooooo! Nice choice, Carol. You're doing so well, I don't think you need me. I may have to sulk to get your attention. We mustn't forget the research though. You may be needing me for that. Just to remind you of items you may have forgotten. There's so much packed away in here it's difficult, even for me, to find my way around. By the way, I've archived the forgettery. I don't think you'll be needing that again.'

'Well, if it isn't spindle-shanks himself. I thought you had deserted me.'

'I might if you don't show me some respect, Carol. I do not like that name. And before you answer me, remember we are talking with us. We need to maintain civil contact.'

'Yes, I'm sorry. Forgive me. I'm feeling reckless, that's why. I haven't been this happy in years. Your webship, sorry, worship.'

'Well, you deserve to be happy. You've put a lot of ugliness behind you these last weeks, and I do believe we've turned a corner. I'll just slip back into my corner again now, and when you need me again, I'll be with you.'

CHAPTER FIFTY-SIX

'That evening, Carol discloses what Rose has told her and tells Mark how much she wants to help her and perhaps they could put her on permanently. They could easily afford it.

Mark promises to do whatever he can, and is thrilled with the progress she is making.

Suddenly, Mark looks up and says to Carol, 'Why don't we offer Mrs Rose a permanent job?'

'I have,' says Carol. 'That's what we were just talking about. I'm happy to know I'm not the only one with a memory problem.'

'No, I mean a live-in, a permanent live-in position. Think about it. We'll be in New York in a couple of weeks, then I retire and after that. The world's our oyster. We can take off for weeks at a time. Months, if you want to. But if we do all that, who's going to look after Paco?'

'Oh, good God,' Carol gasps. 'I hadn't thought that far ahead. I was thinking of asking Rosemarie to stay over and be his companion while we go to New York. She likes him, and he loves to be rolled over and tickled by her. But what a splendid idea! We'd have a full-time housekeeper again. I love it. But she'd need her own private quarters, that would only be fair. How can we arrange that?'

'Simple,' says Mark, who secretly has been planning way, way ahead of Carol, and has rehearsed this conversation in his head a hundred times in the last few months. 'We renovate the flat above the garage for her, replace the drapes, and upgrade the bathroom to the twenty-first century. The space is a good size, just needs to be tarted up.'

'Mark! That's perfect, and I think she'll be over the moon. She won't be living in our pockets. She'll have security of tenure, and her own private space. She'll be thrilled. But how do we put it to her?'

'Like this,' says Mark, adopting a managerial tone. 'Mrs Rose, we are delighted with your work here, and since we're going to be spending a few months away each year, we would like you to accept a full-time position with your own apartment. There will be no rent to pay. We will draw up a private contract guaranteeing your security of employment and live-in accommodation, and it will carry a special clause formally adopting you as Paco's godmother. We will agree on an allowance per week for you. It will not be called wages, so you will continue to receive your widow's pension. You will inform us how many hours per week you wish our agreement to cover, and you may work those hours in as flexible a manner as required to suit our combined needs.'

'Oh, Mark, it's so perfect. When can we tell her? It will take such a load off her poor shoulders. She's had a horrible time lately.'

'Well, darling, we can sort out the flat in a week if we put our minds to it. She will have to give some notice of intent to vacate at her current place, so let's say, she will be here, if she agrees of course, as soon as she wants to.' Mark is very pleased with himself. What could have been easier?

They retire together, happier and more relaxed, for the first time in—it seems to Mark—years.

'One good turn deserves another, Carol. You have been a very good friend.'

For a brief moment, Carol thinks she is talking to herself. Then she remembers her multi-limbed alter ego.

CHAPTER FIFTY-SEVEN

It's the day of the dinner party, and they're ready to leave for Colin and Judy's, looking forward to the evening, and meeting Dan and his Man, Colin's secret nickname for his brother and his friend.

Carol, resplendent in cat's eye green pantsuit and emerald earrings, is hurrying Mark along, anxious not to arrive late. 'Are you ready yet, darling?' she calls. Mark appears from his dressing room, handsome in dark beige sports trousers, camel dress-velvet jacket, dark shirt and cream silk scarf.

'Wow!' exclaims Carol. 'Are you planning to make Dan think again about his man? You look divine!'

'Good, I was thinking of something that fitted "Believe It or Not", something appropriate to the subject matter. Seems like I succeeded. Divine sounds like just the right word.' Carol kisses his cheek and nibbles his ear. 'Down girl, you're too old for that,' responds Mark.

All four guests arrive at the same time at Colin and Judy's, so there's a short delay before introductions, while outerwear is hurriedly removed and hung in the hallway. The chef emerges from the kitchen, carrying a silver tray polished to brilliance bearing margaritas. Introductions are made, and the six make a toast for a happy evening and settle comfortably with their cocktail glasses.

Carol is checking out Dan and his Man. She remembers meeting Dan the previous Christmas and noticing how elegantly he dressed. Manicured hands and nails buffed to a soft shine, that's what gave him away, she thinks. His hands are too perfect for your regular guy. Good figure, tall, not so muscular that he looks butch, but definitely not in the market for my kind of girl. Or actually, any kind of girl.

She assesses the Man. High cheekbones, longish hair worn at just the right length, and with just the right amount of swing and shine to be lush. Well dressed, slim build, beige linen suit with waistcoat (she's sure he would pronounce it 'weskit'), tan brothel creepers (who would wear crepe rubber soles with such a nice suit?), crisp pale cream linen shirt, and paisley cravat. A paisley cravat! How enchanting. Carol hasn't seen a paisley cravat since the last issue of GQ she'd browsed in some fancy specialist's waiting room. Very presentable indeed, she approves.

Well, she thinks, *there's a handsome couple, it's enough to make a red-blooded girl weep for the waste.*

She feels a tap on her arm and looks around to see the Man leaning toward her, arm extended toward hers, she holds out her hand as if to shake his, but he slides his hand around and under her wrist and gently draws her fingers to his lips.

'Enchanted to meet you,' he says. 'I'm Manny, and I've heard you've not been feeling well of late.' He has the faintest somewhere else accent. 'I do hope you will soon be enjoying much better health. I am looking forward very much to this evening's conversation. Believe it or Not leaves the field wide open for all kinds of outrageous tales.'

CHAPTER FIFTY-EIGHT

Carol feels a little exotic thrill for no reason in particular, perhaps just the general strangeness of the evening's subject matter.

There's something in the air, she senses. Something quite exciting.

'Good,' she says. 'Feel free to share your outrageous tale with us.' Carol, wickedly, changes the spelling to tail in her mind as she speaks. Then manufactures a sneeze to cover her giggle.

'Sorry,' she apologises. 'Go to it, Manny. But first, tell us what you actually do. When you're not being outrageous, that is.'

Everyone's listening.

'Well, I'm an auditor by profession, but a philosopher by instinct. I'm a keen gardener, and I am delighted to be back here where I now have a nice piece of the universe that I can call my own. Or we can call our own.' He looks in Dan's direction.

Carol's about to ask where he is 'back here' from, but Manny continues, 'I'm really a renaissance man. I plant, prune, sow, and grow everything in my garden according to the phases of the moon. And I have had a 100 per cent success rate. I'm sure I'll be able to do the same again here. The soil looks good.'

'I love gardening myself,' says Carol. 'But I can't claim anything near 100 per cent success. Go on, share your secrets, this is interesting.'

'Well,' starts Manny, as he appears to launch into what is clearly a favourite subject. 'I use the moon. Did you know that the phases of the moon control the amount of moisture in the soil? At the full moon and the new moon, the soil contains more moisture. That's a scientific fact. And whether we're scientists, weathermen, or lay people, we can see the gravitational effect of the moon in how it pulls the oceans' tides.'

'Is that true even if you're nowhere near water?' Judy questions.

'Yes, it's true,' Manny replies. 'You don't need a river running through your garden, or even a lake a hundred miles away for the moon to moisten your soil. The same gravitation pull you see on big bodies of water where you can see changes in the tides of the oceans also pulls upon the subtle bodies of water. I use subtle in the sense of unseen. Underground rivers and lakes and aquifers all respond to this pull and cause moisture to rise in the earth. The moisture encourages germination and growth and seeds absorb most moisture at the time of the full moon. That's why it's the best time to plant.

'Each of the moon's phases or cycles, or call them quarters, lasts about seven days. The first two quarters occur during the waxing, that's when the moonlight is increasing between the new moon and the full moon. The third and fourth quarters are after the full moon when its light is waning.'

'I know tides are cyclical,' says Judy. 'But what causes high tides?'

'Easy, I can explain that. Our planet Earth is in a large gravitational field, which is influenced by both the sun and the moon. When the sun and moon are aligned with the earth, we have full moons and new moons. Gravitational pull is stronger, and therefore, tides are at their highest. If we go back to the four phases of the lunar month, at the new moon, lunar gravity pulls water up causing the seeds you've just planted to swell and burst. This, coupled with the increasing moonlight as the moon approaches full, creates balanced leaf and root growth as much growth above the soil as below. So there you are, your plants need moonlight as well as sunlight.'

Manny has obviously enchanted his audience. And he's very pleased with himself. 'Also, this first quarter is the best time to plant annual crops that grow above the ground and produce their seeds outside the fruit like lettuce, spinach, caulis, cabbage, broccoli, celery, and grains.

'In the second quarter, the gravitational pull is less, but the moonlight is stronger because the moon is getting bigger, and this creates strong leaf growth. Two days before the full moon is a good time to plant annual crops that grow above the ground, but produce their seeds inside the fruit. Like beans and melons and peas and peppers and pumpkins and tomatoes. And if your grass is a bit sluggish, and you want to encourage the lawn to grow, mow it in the first and second quarters.

'I think of it like this. During the first two quarters, the earth is breathing out, so the general emphasis is on above the ground growth during the second two quarters she is breathing in, so the general emphasis is on what happens beneath the surface.'

'Well, I'll be darned, Manny. I didn't know you were a gardener,' Dan exclaims.

'That's because you didn't know me when I had a garden. That's why I wanted the place we've just bought. You don't get into my secret past that easily.' He looks around. 'I hope I'm not boring you with all this bucolica?'

'No, go on!' three voices encourage in eager unison.

Carol breaks in, 'It's really interesting, and I specially want to talk with you about the effects of the moon on other things, but later.' Carol is flying high in her own head and probably doesn't need the margarita refill the chef is pouring for her. She has *never* felt this good!

Manny catches the chef's eye and says, 'Any time you need another litre of margarita mixed, let me know. I do an equally excellent one.'

Carol's about to say something else when Dan stops her with, as he gestures toward Manny, 'Meet my friend, he knows about gardens and mixes a marvelous margarita. He can help you with your garden, my dear, but only by appointment, and I'm his manager.'

'Go on, Manny, impress us with more, pardon the pun, lunacy. Lunar, see?' Dan's pun escapes Manny's attention.

Manny poses himself a rhetorical question. 'So what do we concentrate on during the third and fourth phases, while the earth is breathing in? The moon starts waning, light is decreasing, and her gravitational pull is drawing the moisture back down into the soil, concentrating energy into the roots into below the ground growth. So now's the time to plant root or below-ground crops like carrots and beets and onions and potatoes. Even peanuts. It's also the time to plant perennials and biennials and bulbs because this is the lunar period that most encourages active root growth. And it's the time to do your pruning.

'The fourth quarter is a period of rest. There's decreased gravitational pull and less moonlight, but you don't get to rest entirely. This is the best time to harvest and transplant and finish your pruning.

'So', comments Colin, 'you are proposing that gravity is responsible for my lack of gardening success?'

CHAPTER FIFTY-NINE

'Manny,' Carol intervenes. 'Do you know anything about the relationship between astrology and gardening?'

'Why ma'am, I believe I do, a little.' Manny smiles at Carol. 'Why do you ask?'

'Well, it's my pet subject. Normally, I would hesitate to say the word. Most people think astrology is what you read in magazines, but at least you accept that there's hard scientific proof that correlates the life of plants with phases of the moon. We, the whole world, accept that the moon affects tides and the growth of plants. Could it possibly affect other forms of living things like people? We know that it affects the breeding and migration patterns of fish and birdlife, why not affect people?'

Carol's winding herself up for a full swing at the subject. 'Why wouldn't we extend the same correlations to human life that we do to all things that grow? Why wouldn't we include humans also responding to the phases of the moon? We're all forms of life living under the same influences in the same world. How can you argue that one form of life is influenced and another not? Sorry, I know I'm going on a bit—'

'I don't know about astrology', interjects Judy, 'but if we're talking about the influence of the moon on life on earth, shouldn't we include the sun too? I remember my biology teacher saying that the sun is the ultimate source of energy for nearly all organisms. Photosynthesis can't take place without it, so that puts it right up there with the moon, doesn't it? And more, you can actually feel the effect of the sun. Stay out in it too long and you change colour!' She smiles impishly.

'Exactly,' agrees Carol. 'We see the effect of sun, we see the effect of moon, now what about the other heavenly bodies? And I wasn't thinking of you, Manny. Or you, or you, or you,' she nods at Colin, Mark, and Dan in turn. 'Is it not then reasonable to propose that, as planetary neighbours, Mercury, Venus, Earth, Mars, Jupiter, Saturn, Uranus, Neptune, and even poor Pluto whose status has been much discussed, might all share some effects? And, indeed, affect each other too as they are all sharing the same gravitational neighbourhood.'

'How did you rattle all those planets off so easily?' Dan asks. 'Carol used a mnemonic, Dan,' says Colin. 'My Very Efficient Memory Just Summed Up Nine. Mercury, Venus, Earth, Mars, Jupiter, Saturn, Uranus, Neptune. The initial letters create a sentence that helps us remember a sequence. We had the same science master, you and I, old starfish. Don't you remember my Very Efficient Memory was one of his favourites?'

'You're right. I remember now. I personally preferred Mercury's Volcanoes Erupt Mulberry Jam Sandwiches Until Noon,' rejoinders Dan, smiling as he now remembers old starfish, nicknamed because his facial skin was full of craters, and his moustache was stiff and stood out like the points of a star on either side of his nose.

'Well,' says Carol, scrutinizing closely both Colin and Mark. 'I use Most Very Elderly Men Just Snooze Under Newspapers. But getting back to my proposition, why is Earth affected by the sun and the moon and not our mnemonic neighbours when we're all part of the same solar system? The word "system" itself implies shared values of some kind.' Carol's picked up the baton and his running fast with it. 'Why do we use the word lunatic? Because early observation of changes in behaviour in people concluded that there existed a synchronicity between the full moon and erratic human behaviour. Notice I said a synchronicity, not a causal relationship. And by early observation, I'm not referring to within the history of western medicine. Early means since the dawn of time, since the first lunatic.

'Why do some hospitals avoid major surgery at the time of the full moon? Because their records reveal evidence of increased post-operative hemorrhage at full moon.'

'Gravity, it seems, affects all forms of liquid life. It's already destroyed my poor garden.' Colin is bemoaning his lack of agricultural success again.

'Speaking of which, where is the liquid life around here?' He reaches for the bottle of red from the sideboard.

Carol is not stopping now. 'Getting back to you, Manny, do you have an opinion about astrology?'

Manny shifts in his chair and thinks for a moment. 'Well, there are astrological calendars for gardening, and I know some people who use them. But it's actually not as simple as I said before. You need to be pretty keen to study it all. Carol', he looks around the other five, 'looks at astrology and people. Gardeners like me look at astrology and plants. We follow the rhythms of nature. And in my experience, the rhythms of nature coincide exactly with Carol's astrological signs, quite astoundingly so.

'For instance, the twelve signs of the zodiac are divided into groups by the four elements, fire, earth, air, and water. The three fire signs are Aries, Leo, Sagittarius, and they are characterised by the words "barren" and "dry". The journey of the moon in its particular phases through fire signs marks the times to cultivate the soil, to destroy weeds and pests, and to harvest root and fruit for storage. The three earth signs are Taurus, Virgo, and Capricorn. Taurus is a productive and moist sign and is second best for planting and transplanting. Best is the water sign, Cancer. Taurus is good for planting root crops and potatoes as well as leafy green vegetables, and especially good for vegetables that require hardiness. Virgo is thought of as barren and moist and good for some flowers and vines.

'You'd need to refer to a zodiac garden calendar for the specific year to be precise about which ones. Virgo's also good for weeding and pest eradication. Capricorn is characterised as productive and dry, so it's good for potatoes and other root crops and it encourages strong growth. This is the sign to graft and prune, to promote healing, and to apply organic fertilizer. That's my sign. I was born under Capricorn.'

'Good grief, he's a walking encyclopedia. Should be a garden gnome, sit where he's easy to consult.' Mark, who knows where the garden is, but not what to do with it, mutters.

Manny continues, unperturbed. 'Now, the air signs, Gemini, Libra, and Aquarius have quite different alliances. Gemini and Aquarius are barren and dry signs, suited to harvesting and cultivating and weed destruction. Gemini's good for melon seeds, Aquarius is good for onions. Libra is different again. Libra is semi-fruitful and moist and the best sign for planting beautiful and fragrant flowers, vines, and herbs. It's also good for root crops and vegetables with pulpy stems like rhubarb.

'So we've dealt with fire, earth, and air signs. Anyone up for water?'

'May as well go on, Manny, I've got a few minutes left on my Dictaphone.' Mark is hugely impressed by Manny's knowledge, but not wildly enthused by the subject.

'Yes, ignore that, Manny, he doesn't even know where the garden is.' Carol's keen to learn as much as she can. And the idea of a Manny gnome in her garden is quite amusing.

'Well, the water signs, Cancer and Scorpio and Pisces, unsurprisingly, are all good for irrigation. Cancer is the best sign for all kinds of planting and transplanting and grafting. Scorpio is also good for transplanting, and it's the best sign for planting sturdy plants, vines, tomatoes, corn, and squash. The last water sign is Pisces who shares the crown with Taurus as the two best signs for planting and transplanting. Moon in Pisces also stimulates root growth. If you want to retard growth and promote better fruit, graft, and prune when the moon is in its third and fourth quarter, and if you don't want your lawn to grow, mow it while the moon is waning.

'I've been collecting bits and pieces about gardening and plant biology for years, but now, the Internet has made it so much easier to access all kinds of information. So it's not all old wives' tales and superstition. There's a good bit of agricultural science involved too. If you're interested, the very best website, in my opinion, is gardeningbythemoon.com. Or buy yourself an astrological gardeners' calendar, which gives you day-by-day instructions.

'That's probably the best idea. The sun traverses the twelve signs once a year. The moon traverses each sign about twelve times every year. It can get very confusing if you're not following a daily guide.'

CHAPTER SIXTY

'Does anyone have a piece of paper I can write on?' Carol asks while fossicking in her handbag. 'No need, got one. That's really good stuff.' Carol addresses Manny. 'Fascinating. I'll certainly check out that website.'

'One thing though, you said you were born under Capricorn. It's not just the sign you were born under that identifies you astrologically. You are also strongly marked by your rising sign. That's the sign that is rising on the eastern horizon at the time of birth. It's called the ascendant. It often describes you physically as well as emotionally and mentally.

'The sign we call your birth sign is the sign the sun was in on the date and at the time, and in relation to the place where you were born. But many people are marked as much by their ascendant or rising sign, which you can have calculated by any astrologer, even a very ordinary one. This will show moderating influences, or perhaps it will emphasise the sun sign.

'The ascendant sign indicates your general approach to life. I'll give you a raw example of how it works, and may the universe forgive me for reducing an esoteric art to the level of a commodity. But here goes.

'Imagine that you are born in the sun sign of Taurus whose basic keywords are determination and interest in mundane affairs, and your rising sign is in Virgo whose basic keywords are service and detail, and your moon, which indicates your feeling approach, is in Capricorn whose basic keywords are position, honours, and ambition. Taking those three factors into consideration, you may be attracted to clerical work. That's a combination of mundane affairs of Taurus and the attention to detail of Virgo with the opportunity to be promoted through the ranks, position, and ambition of Capricorn.'

'So what happens with the other planets and stars?' Judy enquires. 'And what's my rising sign if you really can tell from appearance?'

'I'd be a fool to try that one, and besides, good astrologers don't make guesses. You are rather leonine in appearance though. Patrician features, good size head, a splendid mane of hair.'

Judy looks mildly startled. 'Well, I'll be you-know-what. It so happens that I had my natal chart drawn up when I was at uni, and my rising sign is Leo.'

'Good guess, that's all.' Carol continues. 'Manny made a great explanation supporting gardening by the moon, and no way can I imitate his eloquence. Astrology, as it applies to people, is too complicated, but I can tell you enough I think to show why it fascinates me. There are hundreds of volumes containing knowledge accumulated over centuries from observations made by astrologer/astronomers who were often one and the same person. Astrology and astronomy developed as sciences together, and yes, astrology was considered a science, and they both used the same information.'

'Do all horoscopes look the same?' Judy asks. 'Mine looked like a circle full of symbols with lines between them.'

'Well, western horoscopes look pretty similar. They're represented as a circle or wheel, divided into twelve houses and the twelve signs. Houses and signs overlap each other. They show the positions of the sun, moon, etcetera, distributed around the 360 degrees of the wheel, and are calculated for the time and place of the nativity. The twelve houses represent different areas of our lives, and there are various systems for marking the beginning and end of each. Each system uses a different way to divide the ecliptic.'

'What's the ecliptic?' Judy's really interested

'That's the apparent path of the sun around the Earth. The word apparent is very important in this case. It means how it appears to you from the time and place you are viewing it. At the same time, but in a different place, your relationship to the ecliptic would be different. And also, we know that the sun doesn't actually make circles around the Earth. It just appears to.

'But the idea, indeed theory, that the sun circled the Earth was the popular view until about 400 years ago when it was dumped in favour of the Copernican system, a new theory, at least for Europe, that the Earth actually moved around the sun. However, the old geocentric idea continued to be espoused and endorsed by the Roman Church until less than thirty years ago. Thirty years ago. Yes, can you believe that? 'The church clung to the gospel according to Ptolemy who, around 140 of the Christian Era, had documented a geocentric universe based on observation from Earth that everything that was seen in the sky was moving around the Earth. Apparently reasonable, but scientifically wrong.'

CHAPTER SIXTY-ONE

Dan, whose features have settled first into thoughtfulness, and now into something that suggests wickedness as he follows these exchanges, leans forward. He raises his glass. 'I propose a toast to the Holy Roman Church and her contribution to the advancement of science. The church,' he says, holding his glass high. 'Who will join me?'

Good-naturedly, everyone joins him as they toast the church. 'And now,' continues Dan. 'Let's toast those whom the church herself has toasted! I raise my glass to Giordano Bruno, a supporter of the Copernican system, burned at the stake in 1600 by the Holy Roman Church for heresy. And they made certain that he couldn't pollute the minds of the simple folk who turned up to watch the immolation by tying his tongue, so he couldn't address them. His writings were still on the *Vatican List of Forbidden Texts* in 2000, that's sixteen years ago. Do you believe that? It's true. Sydney has a radio station named after him. 2GB.

'And let us not forget Galileo Galilei, another supporter of Copernicus. That poor old sod was dragged off to the Holy Inquisition in 1633. He was already an old man, he was threatened with torture, and forced to recant. However, in 1992, you'll be glad to hear the holy church herself, albeit reluctantly, recanted its own judgment on Galileo and accepted, after twelve years of holy deliberation, that Galileo was right to support the Copernican theory!

'Do you mind, Carol? My apologies for interrupting you, but this happens to be one of my interests. Not astrology so much, but astronomy and the role played by the church in stifling scientific investigation. Even Archimedes, who shrugged off his mortal coil over two hundred years before the Christian era, had started speculating about the possibility of a heliocentric system. But European learning continued to be based on the Hellenic traditions of Aristotle and Ptolemy until Peurbach and his student Johannes Regiomontanus started the reform of European astronomy around 1400 and something. Nicolaus Copernicus was next on the scene in the 1500s. He continued the reform, and finally his theories were taken seriously by the scientific world, if not by Holy Mother Church.

'Copernicus built a heliocentric model of the universe because he was convinced that the Earth was a planet, and like all other planets, he believed that it rotated. Coincidentally, he was also a physician, lawyer, and church administrator. Copernicus died in 1543, the same year he published *On the Revolutions of the Celestial Orbs*, a book he curiously dedicated to Pope Paul 111, head of the religion which continued to persecute supporters of this heliocentric theory for centuries. Obviously, his holiness wasn't a great reader.'

Judy interrupts, 'Exactly why was the church so opposed to new theories?'

'Well, briefly, it simply didn't suit the picture that the Bible painted. The Bible describes a flat earth and a sky that forms a roof over it. It describes several instances of the sun and moon being controlled and commanded by Biblical characters. Look up Joshua 10:12–13 for one. That implies that the Earth is the centre of the universe. It was not in the church's interests to accept any other theory. If the Bible were wrong, then the teachings of the church were in error. If the teachings of the church are in error, the church no longer has control over its members. Everything could then be questioned, most notably the authority of the church. But over to you, Carol. Please go on. And tell me which system did you study?'

CHAPTER SIXTY-TWO

'The Equal House System, that's a western system that divides the horoscope wheel into twelve divisions of thirty degrees each, representing the twelve houses of the horoscope. Getting back to what I was saying before Dan, the iconoclast, took over, the beginning and end of each of the twelve constellations or signs of the zodiac is calculated and placed onto the horoscope wheel. And then the positions of the sun, moon, and planets are calculated and inserted. While the twelve houses are equal, the twelve signs are not all of equal length, so beginnings and ends of signs can overlap the houses.

'Your horoscope wheel, or your natal chart, is the map of the heavens at the exact time of your birth, provided of course you have that exact information. If you don't, there is a method to arrive at the correct moment of birth called rectification. Complicated and time-consuming, but it usually works. Or you can simply do what's called a solar equilibrium chart, which makes the assumption that you were born at sunrise and is general enough to give an overall impression, but not good enough to support detail.

'Apart from the sun, moon, and planets, there are various other sensitive points in the chart. Like the ascendant, which is the exact degree of the zodiac sign rising on the eastern horizon. As Judy told us, her ascendant is in Leo. And there are also various stars and constellations which have been observed to have special meanings. Once you have calculated the map, you then calculate the specific angles. That's the number of degrees between the many sensitive points and all the bodies whose symbols appear on your chart. Each type of angle has a meaning. 180 degrees between two planets or two sensitive points has a different meaning to 120 degrees or 145 degrees or ninety or sixty or forty-five degrees.

'The signs themselves are also divided into two groups, positive and negative. Then into three groups, cardinal, fixed, and mutable. Then further into four groups of the elements that Manny was talking about, fire, earth, air, and water. The signs each have a natural ruler from among the sun, moon, and planets. Each sign corresponds with the house of which it is the natural ruler. So the sun is the natural ruler of Capricorn. The natural domain of the sign Capricorn is the tenth house. So the sun is also the natural ruler of the tenth house.

'But it is rare that an actual natal chart shows natural rulers in their natural signs in their natural houses.'

'Back up a second, Carol. You've lost me again,' it's Dan. 'Why is the horoscope shown as a wheel?'

'Reasonable question,' says Carol. 'It's shown as a wheel because if you bisect it horizontally, that is, cut it in half, the top half represents the sky above at the time of birth and the bottom half, the sky below where you are.'

'Okay,' replies Dan. 'So the wheel is divided in twelve spokes to represent the twelve houses. What exactly does houses mean?'

Carol continues, 'Houses refer to periods or sections of your life. Briefly, and I apologise, very roughly, the first house indicates your instinctive approach to life, the second house your material possessions, the third house day-to-day occurrences, the fourth house family, right through to the twelfth house, which is the house of conscience. The equal house system places equal importance on each aspect of your life.'

'So explain again the signs and the houses?' Dan has been trying to visualize as Carol speaks, and has now arrived at a wheel full of lines and symbols and has lost his starting point.

'With pleasure,' replies Carol, quite pleased that Dan is participating. 'The houses roughly relate to activities of your life and attitudes to those activities, and are of fixed size on the wheel in my system, thirty degrees each, or one twelfth of the 360 degree circle. In this system, they're always numbered one to twelve anti-clockwise from the ascendant. The signs correspond to solar months, which move clockwise around the wheel. If you're born at sunrise, your sun sign will be rising on the eastern horizon. That is the left of the horizontal line, which bisects the wheel. If you're born at midnight, it will be opposite on the right called the descendant. Midday, it'll be close to the midheaven, the point immediately above at the time of birth.

'Sometimes, the general pattern created by the distribution of the celestial bodies in a chart can offer some quick clues about the person. The astrologers' skill at blending the many tendencies shown in a chart is the single most important ingredient in astrology. Anyone who can read an ephemeris and knows the formulae for calculating exact positions can erect a chart. The tricky bit is interpreting it. It takes a rare ability to deliver a sensible, sensitive, and accurate reading.

'The Equal house system was generally, in the sixties when I studied, considered to be the most practical system in that it offered good information about character, personality, and potential. Whereas some systems have a deeply spiritual application, this system shows the practical path of least resistance, likely problems and likely areas of success.'

'So', interrupts Dan, 'all that theory's terrific, but can you offer us a short, please, argument in favour of astrology? Like proof that it works?'

CHAPTER SIXTY-THREE

'I'll try.' Carol accepts the glass of wine Mark is offering her. 'Thanks, darling, but let me give you my definition of astrology first.'

'Right then, the definition first. That's my girl.' Mark smiles at her.

'This is the bald definition. Not what it purports to do, but what it is. And you won't find this in any book you look up. It's my personal definition. Astrology is the formalisation of a system, which assigns spiritual, metaphysical qualities to numbers, which represent actual physical measurements between celestial bodies and the earth, and celestial bodies with each other. What does the system purport to do?' Carol doesn't expect an answer, so she continues. 'It supports the notion that what happens in the viewable sky over the course of the year has some significant, measurable, theoretical relationship with what happens in the lives of the people who are viewing it. Observations that validate synchronicity in the relationship between man and the stars have been recorded over thousands of years. After all, there wasn't a lot to look at, so people looked up.'

Colin, who has been listening closely, ventures, 'I see that your problem is getting proof that it works. It's both theoretical and empirical, but without the possibility of scientific proof.'

'Perfectly defined!' Carol returns. 'You can't scientifically prove the existence of something without controlled tests. For tests, you need groups of people who share identical data plus a control group. But the very premise and nature of astrological analysis is based on unique personhood. Just sixty seconds of difference in the birth time changes the natal chart.'

Colin interjects, 'Unique personhood? What about this? Two babies are born to mothers in adjacent beds at the same time. Won't they have identical natal charts?'

'Yes, but the chart only describes potential. What those babies do with the same energies and same inclinations indicated by their charts throughout the course of their lives could be very different. And opportunity depends greatly on economic circumstance. Your chart is not your destiny. It is a map of potential, of possibilities, and probabilities shaped by your educational and economical reality. For instance, one child may be born into poverty below the palace stairs, whilst the princeling is brought into a world of opportunity above stairs. Both born at the exact same time in the same building.

'There is actually an example of precisely this with one of the sixteenth or seventeenth century European monarchs. The above stair baby became king with a stable of fine horses and a kingdom to rule. The below stairs baby became the trusted stableman with a secure job and a stable of fine steeds to care for. Damn, I wish I could remember who it was. It was part of a study I did about fifty years ago on astro twins. Now, there have been so many studies published I haven't been able to track that one down.

'So there we have it. I have to be content with believing in a system that can never be proven. I might be better off starting a church. But I put it to you again. Is it reasonable to assume that the sun and moon affect everything that lives except the lives of people? And why should they be the only celestial bodies that affect everything? If we're affected by one celestial body that we can see, would it not be reasonable to assume that we are affected by all celestial bodies we can see? Maybe even some that we can't yet see? After all, we are affected by things we can't see.' Carol's becoming playful. 'Wind, for instance, you can't actually see wind, you can only see the effect it has on things exposed to it. Perhaps it doesn't exist at all.'

'And', interjects Judy mischievously, 'menstruation is based on the concept of the lunar cycle. Perhaps the moon only affects lunatics and women!'

No one's brave or silly enough to take that one on.

CHAPTER SIXTY-FOUR

The chef, who has been handing around the hors d'oeuvres, has now produced a huge circular tray with a sumptuous selection of finger foods. Wine is being poured and idle cocktail chatter is in full swing as Colin addresses the room.

'While we're in the esoteric realm, well, at least talking about things we can't see and things that many people would deny the existence of, I've been doing some work on chakras recently.'

The conversation quietens as brother Dan comments, 'I thought you didn't approve of stuff like that.'

'I didn't, you're right. But now I know something about it, and I can tell you that chakras are real and they do work. And I was surprised to learn that chakra theory has some relationships with Carol's pet subject. Just think, though, how often do we dismiss something because we know nothing about it?' Colin smiles self-effacingly. 'That's what I did, and I'm truly ashamed of it. It took an old patient coming back to me to shake me out of my smugness. At any rate, he did, and I was totally shaken.

'Anyone here interested in how they work? I ask because I'm getting to believe more and more in the holistic approach. Not just to physical health, but to the whole of life. The more I read, the more I suspect that a lot of stuff I have dismissed as twaddle and nonsense may have real importance to my life.

'I didn't believe in out of body experiences, for instance, but Mark had one. His story convinced me. There's a lot of things going on in the world, behind the scenes, so to speak. Hidden influences. And a lot of overlap between theories.'

'But tell us about the chakras,' Mark steers him back to the nitty gritty. 'I touched a little Thai boy on the head once, and I was told very quickly not to do that. The head is considered sacred to Thais, the most sacred part of the body. It's where the kwan resides, the spiritual force of life. For Maoris, too, the head is the most sacred part of the body. Does this have anything to do with chakras?'

'Not exactly.' Colin settles himself into a sitting position, legs crossed, on the floor. 'The chakras are the seven major centres of energy in your body. And each centre has a physical position in the body, each refers to special functions of our being, each is represented by a different colour. Altogether representing the colours of the rainbow from red through to violet, and each has a different vibration.'

'Have you noticed how spooky this party's getting?' Judy comments, and everyone shifts a little on their chairs.

CHAPTER SIXTY-FIVE

'Imagine that you're sitting on the floor exactly like me. Try it if you want to, but it's not really necessary. Now, imagine a line from where your tailbone touches the floor straight up inside your body to your head. Your chakras are all positioned along that line. Starting with the base of your spine, there's the root chakra, which represents our foundation and the feeling of being grounded. It is associated with emotional issues affecting our survival, money, and food. Its colour is red.

'Now, move up to the lower abdomen about five centimetres below the navel and five centimetres inwards. That's the sacral chakra and is associated with our ability to accept others, connect with them, and how we face new experiences. It pertains to our sense of abundance and well-being, pleasure, and sexuality. Its colour is orange. Further up in the upper abdomen and stomach area is the solar plexus chakra, which represents our ability to be confident and in control, so it has to do with our self-worth and self-esteem. Its colour is yellow.

'In the centre of the chest, just above the heart, is the heart chakra, which unsurprisingly represents our ability to love and is particularly associated with joy and inner peace. Its colour is green.'

Colin is indicating each location as he speaks. 'The fifth chakra is the throat chakra, again, unsurprisingly associated with our ability to communicate, express ourselves, and how we handle truth. Its colour is blue. The space on the forehead between the eyes is the third eye or brow chakra. This has to do with our ability to see things in proportion and focus on the big picture. So it's associated with wisdom, imagination, intuition, and how we make decisions. Its colour is indigo.

'The crown chakra is the very top of the head and represents our ability to be fully connected spiritually. It's associated with inner and outer beauty and the experience of pure bliss. Its colour is violet.' Colin gets up off the floor where he's been tracing with his fingers from chakra to chakra from tail bone to crown.

'Now that I know where they are', Dan asks Colin, 'what do I do with them? Besides, I thought you were a physio or osteopath or something?'

'I still am, but I started doing a bit of yoga and meditation lately, and got interested in the spiritual side of it. Probably a sign of an increasing sense of my own mortality. Then one of the class tutors offered to introduce me to chakra theory and practise, and it just seemed to make absolute sense. It relates very well to a lot of problems I've come across with patients, so I decided I'd find out all about it. Apart from that, I'm delighted with how it's helped me understand more about my own treatments.

'But getting back to specifics, the chakras act as centres through which our energy flows. If one gets blocked, it interferes with the natural flow of energy and causes pain or illness. You know from the symptoms, which chakra is doing the blocking or interfering, and once you identify it, there are specific treatments to remove the blockage and release the energy. You know that annoying little multi-coloured spinning disc you get from time to time on your computer screen? It happens when you've asked it to multi-task, and it seems to have to spin its wheels while it works out what you want first. That's exactly how I think of my work with chakras.

'The disc is spinning until I locate and clear the blockage. And in order to clear the blockage, I have to choose exactly the right colour from the disc and treat the chakra associated with that. Coincidentally, chakra is a Sanskrit word for wheel. Neat, isn't it? How did my computer know that? Every organ, gland, and body system is connected to a chakra, and every chakra colour has its own frequency. When our body frequency is at its optimal, we are balanced, we feel well, alert, and healthy, and our vibration is in sync with the law of vibration. That is we are in tune with each cell in our body, and each cell is vibrating at the frequency it was designed to.

'We are part of an entire vibrating nature. The law of vibration applies to all things, sounds, colours, the cells in our body, the food we eat, everything. "Nothing rests, everything moves, everything vibrates," I quote Albert Einstein in 1905. Gautama Buddha said in the fourth century before the Christian era, "We are the same as plants as other people, as the rain that falls. We consist of that which is around us. We are the same as everything."

'Every living element of our body, of our entire world, radiates a vibration or frequency that can be measured in hertz. The level of frequency is measured by the vibration rate and wavelength. The longer the wavelength, the lower the vibration frequency. Even our thoughts emit frequencies. We might extrapolate, might we? That balanced thoughts, or should we say positive thoughts, contribute to overall balance and unbalanced thoughts, negative ones, detract from that balance.

'Sound and resonance have been found to affect us physiologically and psychologically. Witness the current experiments with music with the elderly. Listening to old tunes stimulates memories of earlier times, memories that would have been lost without the stimulation. And experiments are being conducted with difficult cases of autism with astonishing success.'

'Hang on a second,' Judy interrupts. 'Talking about waves, where do brain waves fit in and what exactly are they?'

CHAPTER SIXTY-SIX

'I can explain that one, Judy,' Mark leaps into the conversation enthusiastically. 'I did a bit of research on those when I was reading about out of body experiences. The easiest way to understand them is to go from highest to lowest. Theta waves have a frequency range of forty to 100 hertz. Think high cognitive function, learning, memory, and information processing. Too high, anxiety and stress. Too low, depression and learning disability. You stimulate your theta waves through meditation.

'Beta waves have a frequency range of twelve to forty hertz. This is the awake condition, conscious thought, logical thinking, problem solving. Too high, adrenalin, inability to relax, stress. Too low, ADHD, daydreaming, poor cognition. You stimulate beta waves with energy drinks and coffee.

'Now, we get a bit more interesting. Alpha waves have a frequency range of eight to twelve hertz, and they bridge the gap between our conscious thinking and our subconscious mind. Too high, daydreaming and inability to focus. Too low, high stress and insomnia. Alcohol and relaxants are used to stimulate alpha range. Some drugs, like marijuana, have a very effective reaction.

'Theta waves have a range of four to eight, considered slow, and they induce daydreaming, sleep, and are connected with deep feelings of raw emotion. Too high, inattentiveness, impulsiveness, hyperactivity. And too low, anxiety and stress. You influence theta waves with depressants.

'Delta brainwaves are the slowest recorded in human beings. From zero to four hertz, and are common in infants and young children. These are the restorative and healing waves that induce deep sleep. Too high indicates brain injury or severe ADHD or learning problems. And too low, poor sleep and inability to rejuvenate the brain. You influence delta waves with depressants and sleep.' Mark stands and performs three exaggerated bows toward his audience who mime stamping and cheering.

'I say, professor,' congratulates Manny, extending his hand to clasp the master's. 'Jolly good. What say you, class?'

Mark responds, 'I do hope you're not taking the proverbial.'

'No, what's that?' asks Manny. 'I was just taking the piss.'

Everyone relaxes and laughs. 'I wish I had a record button on my phone,' Manny adds. 'I really was impressed. You'd make a good teacher.'

'I was,' Mark replies. 'I taught Classics. But I interrupted you, Colin. Please forgive me.'

Colin starts again, 'Now, here's an interesting thing. Did you know that when someone is really nasty to us, causes us to feel real emotional pain, your body can actually store that emotional hurt? Many a time I've only been able to relieve a patient's pain after talking with them. Sometimes, it's just a casual reference they make that puts me onto the trail, and after a comparatively short examination, I've been able to identify where the hurt has been stored. The pain is often a deep knot in a muscle. It doesn't feel to my fingers like an injury, it really feels like something that's been buried and hidden a long time.

'That's what I meant about taking a more holistic approach. Everything, I now believe, is connected. And many different disciplines are capable of identifying the same problems through different pathways. Therefore, the more I know about different disciplines and skills, the more help I will be to my patients. I just wish I'd learned a whole lot more a whole lot sooner.'

Mark leans toward him. 'I might just ask you to run your fingers down my spine one day, Colin. I think I've got a few knots that need undoing.'

CHAPTER SIXTY-SEVEN

'Colin, that's interesting…very interesting and I certainly support your holistic approach.' Manny, hands in pockets, looks around, almost as if to check that everyone's listening.

He is the master in front of the class.

'Let's hang onto what Colin's told us about Chakras and how his seven major centres of energy are associated with the seven colours of the rainbow.

'You know that Gautama Buddha taught that we consist of that which is around us. And Einstein told us that the Law of Vibration applies to all things. Quantum Physics tells us that everything has its own rate of vibration and that vibration is energy.

'We are all part of an entire vibrating nature, Einstein said. 'Well, here's another interesting thing—there is a very specific and provable relationship between colour and music!'

'How does that work?' asks Judy.

Colin, too, is leaning forward with interest.

'The seven colours of the rainbow, which we know are related to Colin's Chakra energy centres—are also related to the major musical chords!'

'I think I can see where you're going with this' Judy says 'music creates sound, sound creates vibration, energy created by vibration is measured as frequency, frequency is measured in hertz. And in sound—this means the number of pressure waves per second that move past a fixed point.'

'Which is the same' Manny interrupts 'as the number of vibrations per second that the particles make as they transmit the sound!

'So there we have it!

'Now that we can see that all these things are related, it's no surprise that there must be a measurable relationship with music, which is sound whose frequency and rate of vibration is measured as hertz-and colour.

'Here's the thing—each colour of the rainbow is related to a major musical chord. So first, we need to understand the colour spectrum—how colours are isolated and identified—in this case as their equivalents in musical notes.

'Suddenly we're back to Sir Isaac Newton—he isolated the colours of the rainbow by passing a beam of sunlight through a prism. When the light came out the other side, it had separated into rays of seven different colours, the very same colours that match your Chakras—Red, Orange, Yellow, Green, Blue, Indigo, and Violet.

'Then he discovered that when the light rays were passed through the prism again, they turned back into white light. If he passed just one ray through the prism, it retained its own colour. So he concluded that white light is composed of the seven different coloured rays.

'He was dealing only with colours that are visible to the human eye. And the eye, just like the ear, only registers what we can see and hear. There are oodles of subtle colours that we can't discern just like there is a wide range of upper and lower sound frequencies that we can't hear.

'For instance—most people can't hear dog whistles, because they're beyond the range of normal human hearing. What sounds like a low hissing sound to us is recognised as a whistle by the dog.

'Now, counting the steps we can understand so far—we have Colin's seven major chakras identifying the seven major energy centres in the body.

'And we have Professor Isaac Newton's seven colours of the rainbow that correspond with the seven Chakra colours.

'And now I'm going to show that the frequencies of the seven notes in the musical scale match the seven colours!

'All of which will confirm, to even the most skeptical, that there are specific relationships between the human body, colour and sound.'

Manny takes a piece of paper from the sideboard, gets a pen from his jacket pocket and as he's talking he draws a horizontal rectangle 7cm by 2cm.

He then draws a horizontal line through the centre of the rectangle.

'Now, I'm also going to divide this this rectangle perpendicularly into seven equal sections. I love that magic number seven!

'In the boxes of the top line we write the seven colours of the rainbow with each box representing a colour in spectrum order. From left to right—RED or MAGENTA, ORANGE, YELLOW, GREEN, BLUE or CYAN, INDIGO and VIOLET.

'The lower boxes are going to name the notes of a a musical scale creating parallels that connect colour and sound—this is the partnership that is the structure of all musical chords!

'Let's take the C major scale for example and we call these boxes from left to right C D E F G A B, with C being middle C.

'Now—we select the first, third and fifth colours which correspond to the musical notes C E and G. What we find is that RED YELLOW AND BLUE which are the primary colours are aligned here with C E and G the three notes of the C major chord! Primary colours—major chord! Musical colours—colourful music.

'Music demonstrates the idea more entertainingly by creating sounds that we can all listen to and enjoy.

'Chords are a combination of three or more notes in a scale.

'And the major chords are the basis of all other chord structures.

'Judy' he indicates a shelf loaded with CDs. 'see if you can find some music that would look like a rainbow, please.'

Judy obeys, and checking titles along the top shelf she says 'How about this one? 'Over the Rainbow'—what could be more appropriate?'

Manny thanks her and while Judy attends to the music, he continues 'As I said before, there are many more frequencies in the sound spectrum, as there are also many more colours to the colour spectrum. But frequencies outside of our hearing range are beyond our ability to appreciate, just as our eyes can't register the many subtle shades of colours.

'These days there are Apps that demonstrate this amazing relationship. Imagine a surface the size of a card table that's divided into squares showing different shades of different colours—as you touch each square you produce sound—the musical notes represented by that particular colour.'

'Does that mean that lighter and darker shades of the same colour would work the same way by producing higher or lower pitches of the same note?' Judy asks.

'Yes, notes repeat themselves the higher up and lower down in frequency. Even if you're not a musician you probably know that notes of the same tone, but different pitch are called octaves.

'There is a USA Government standard for musical pitch. A-440 is the official standard and if you're a pianist or piano tuner this means that the strings for A above middle C should vibrate at 440 cycles per second. Higher A will vibrate at 880 cycles per second—twice A above middle C—and A below will vibrate at 220 cycles per second—half A above middle C.

'Light waves are also doing this. Other electro-magnetic waves like xrays, radio waves and microwaves all behave similarly.'

Carol, who prefers the metaphysical to the physical plane, and tends to be a bit impatient when dealing with government bodies and Rulemakers, is incensed by the idea that a government can set a standard for a musical note. Of course she knows that someone has to set standards but she feels like having a gripe about it right now.

'Don't you just love that the Government has an official standard for musical pitch? Isn't there some musical body, or Academy whose job that should be? God knows the way governments interfere these days we could end up with a president who institutes a new Inquisition that declares that E equals middle C.'

Manny politely invites Carol to 'relax and enjoy it' and continues 'Thank you Carol for reminding me that E=MC squared. Which should remind us also of Albert Einstein, the real Maestro here.

'This was all theorized by Isaac Newton who was a mathematician, physicist, astronomer, theologian and author. Then, two hundred and thirty-six years after Newton was born—along came Einstein, the man who proved it. E=MC squared is the most famous equation in the world.'

'He won the Nobel Prize for that, didn't he?' interjected Carol.

'Actually, no. Most people think that this theory won him the Nobel but it was actually the Law of the Photoelectric Effect—he was awarded the Prize for his services to Theoretical Physics.

'Come to think about it—the law of Vibration, Quantum Physics and the Theory of Relativity are the philosophical and scientific bases for bloody near everything.'

CHAPTER SIXTY-EIGHT

'Manny, before you get overexcited.' It's Judy interrupting again. 'Do you know exactly how a piano is tuned?'

'Happen I do, ma'am.' Manny can be quite charming with that exotic little accent of his. 'You've seen a tuning fork, it's an acoustic resonator made of dense steel and has two prongs. Each fork is tuned to a different frequency or note. You hold the fork on its side and strike it, one prong only, about one third down from the top against the heel of your hand or a rubber object. If you're tuning by ear, strike the tuning fork, and the note you are tuning then listen for the beats as the sound from the piano interferes with the sound from the tuning fork. The two will beat less and less frequently, and as they tune to each other and reach the same frequency, you no longer hear any beating.

'Or you can hold the fork close to the piano string that carries the same musical tone, and the string will raise its vibration automatically and attune itself to the rate at which the fork is vibrating. This is the principle of resonance, which states that when two frequencies are brought together, the lower will always rise to meet the higher.

'Luckily, our brains were smart enough to select a nice manageable section of the electromagnetic field to use. So we have seven colour frequencies and seven sound frequencies to be used by our eyes and ears for sight, hearing, art, music, painting, song, and writing. Everything, in fact.

'All of this means, in fact, that if we could hear colour, we would hear music. A painting would sing to us. A piano piece would paint a picture. Imagine how your world would look. Imagine the metaphysical implications.'

'Hey, you're talking about synaesthesia,' Colin interjects. 'Some people can actually do that. I've come across it a few times in my practise. Hearing colour and seeing music are real conditions. I can vouch for that. As I said before, I've been in practise long enough not to dismiss stuff just because I'm not familiar with it. People call things pseudoscience if they sound a bit esoteric, but there may a bit more to these borderline systems than we give them credit for.

'Who in the western world would have thought of colour therapy or aroma therapy a hundred years ago as being part of everyday life? We'd have assumed they were cranks. But now, you can find your local aromatherapist in the directory. There's even an app for it! The idea's not new at all. The ancient Egyptians used colour for curing ailments, and there are papyri dating back to 1550 BCE that list colour cures.

'Colours had metaphysical meanings then. It wasn't until the Greeks got in on the act that colour became science only, physics not metaphysics. And the Chinese practised colour healing two thousand years ago!'

'Getting back to where this conversation started, what on earth is synaesthesia?' Carol questions.

Colin explains, 'It's a weird thing where the brain is crosswired and somehow the senses are co-mingled. You've heard about people who automatically associate a number with a colour? They actually see the colour when they see or hear the number. Like the number five is always red, or three is always blue. Well, surprisingly, it's not actually all that rare. It's one of the forms of synaesthesia. Some people do it with music as Manny said. They hear a note, and they see a colour.

Some people do it with taste. They hear a word, and they get a taste. Not the taste the word suggests. They might hear tree and get the taste of bacon.

'As I said, it's not that rare. Around one in two thousand people have the condition. And it's genetic, so it goes from parent to child. There are different kinds of established tests to detect different kinds of synaesthesia. Try having another drink and saying that quickly five times.'

'Does anyone know what causes it?' Carol asks. 'I mean, why or how does the brain become crosswired?'

'It's thought that because all mammals are born with far more brain cells than are needed, the brain goes through a period of pruning where only the connections and brain cells you use and need survive. If you have the synaesthesia gene, the pruning happens differently, and your wires are crossed.'

'I could name you a few politicians who were pruned in the wrong phase of the moon,' says Manny. Everyone agrees. 'Truth is beauty and beauty truth, that is all ye know on earth and all ye need to know.' Manny appears to be addressing his drink. Brow furrowed, he focuses tightly on his margarita, apparently willing it to defy gravity and leap through his parted lips. Disappointed, he shakes it until it vibrates to the key of Ooommmmmmmm. 'Time to go home,' he says.

'But not quite yet.' He eyes the sideboard, which is gradually being populated by interesting looking platters.

Colin finds himself already looking forward to another such evening. It's not often you find a group of people who can make you feel so relaxed and are so interesting. Dan and his Man are enjoying themselves, as are Carol and Mark, and the evening still has a while to go. Carol is so relaxed she's scared that if she has another drink, she'll drift off into oblivion.

She feels a faint fluttering in her ear. *'We are having a good time, aren't we?'*

She smiles and nods and leans back onto the springy cushion, using the arm of the chair to rest her glass. She's afraid that if she doesn't hang onto it, someone will fill it, and she'll have to drink it.

CHAPTER SIXTY-NINE

Mark pours himself a glass of red from the sideboard where the chef has left it, while he was preparing the post-prandial delights. 'Do you recall that little out-of-body experience I had?'

'Creepy. Yes,' Judy responds. 'Don't tell me you've had another one.'

'Another one what?' Dan asks and looks at Mark. 'We're into bodies big time tonight. What's all that about?'

'Manny will explain it to you later,' replies Mark. 'But let me continue. My lovely wife, Carol, mentioned something about the soul earlier today when we were discussing what we might contribute to the conversation tonight, so I thought I'd do a bit of research into it. Turns out, he fixes Carol with an accusing stare, she'd got there before me. I looked on her laptop and found she'd been reading up on a theory of quantum consciousness.'

'Yes, darling, I was,' Carol revives herself sufficiently to reply. 'But it's too difficult for a little mind like mine to grasp, so I left it for you.' She responds to his stare with an elaborately mimed show of humility.

'Well, briefly, folks, a couple of very important people in the quantum physics field have put forward a good argument for the existence of the soul and a lot of other very important people agree that it's got legs. That scientific enough for you folk to follow? They don't suggest that the soul has body. But they do suggest that something of us lives on after death, and that something becomes part of universal consciousness. My soul is immortal, and it will contribute to the universe. They have some interesting evidence to support this. But first, are we all agreed that there is such a thing as an out-of-body experience? I've had one myself.'

'Finally,' sighs Dan. 'This sounds like the kind of weird I like. Out of this world weird. Not science weird.'

'Sorry, Dan, it's science weird as well. To put it briefly, I was experimenting with astral travel, and I saw something happen outside the house a few minutes before it actually did, if you get my drift. My astral self travelled outside my bedroom door. I had the impression I was floating in mid-air and I witnessed a specific scene. A few minutes later, what I had seen as my astral self actually happened right in front of my actual self. In exact detail, which means I saw the whole scene before it happened. Perhaps I bent time or something.

'Well, I had a browse around Carol's secret website looking for OBEs, out of body experiences, and came up with some interesting stuff. A survey of 380 Oxford students showed that 34 per cent of them had had an OBE. That's how we professionals refer to it.' He grinned at Carol. 'Which means that I'm a sort of special one in three person.

'The same website details an experiment conducted by a Dr Charles Tart, Professor Emeritus of Psychology at the University of California, amongst other highly regarded professional achievements. He published this experiment in the Journal of the American Society for Psychical Research. A young woman was placed in a room with nothing but a bed, a shelf, a clock, and a window through which she was observed from another room. She had electrical devices hooked up to her head to detect brain wave activities.

'She was able to leave her physical body, which remained lying on the bed, and read a five-digit number, which was written on a piece of paper placed flat on a shelf too high for her to be able to see even if she were standing. She reported the correct positioning of the paper as well as the number written on it. The odds of guessing a five-digit number at the first attempt are one in 59,000.

'The experience of the OBE coincided with abnormal changes in brain-body activities, but because she was only being observed and didn't move from the bed, the physiological data are limited by her only being able to report how or what she was feeling after the event. Checking the evidence and thinking about the general timing of the experiment, it seemed to Dr Tart that her OBE occurred in conjunction with a non-dreaming, non-awake brain wave stage, which showed predominant slowed alpha brain activity and no activation of her autonomic nervous system.

'It sounds like some sort of trance-like state.'

Mark fossicks in his breast pocket and produces a piece of paper, from which he is now reading. 'Quoting Dr Tart, he wrote, "In summary, this brief study found a fairly clear-cut correlation between several of Miss Z's (she was the lab rat) reported OOB experiences and a physiological pattern characterised by a flattened EEG with prominent alphoid activity, no REM or skin resistance activity, and normal heart rate." Please don't ask me to enlarge on that, all I can tell you is that alphoid has something to do with DNA and chromosomes. I did metaphysics, not physics.

'Lots of people who have OBEs (not Order of the British Empire) are apparently not aware of it until something triggers the memory. For instance, there are literally hundreds of reports of children who actually die in drowning accidents and then return to life. Some can give very detailed descriptions of how they felt and what they were seeing, of watching their surroundings change colour, and then experiencing a feeling of floating without body. They return to life by either divine intervention or rescue, but they had already been pronounced dead.

'In many cases, no one has told them that they drowned or died until some trigger in later life brings the whole experience back to them. And they are able to have the prior death or near-death condition, no breathing, no heartbeat, confirmed by family members. After all, I don't suppose you'd tell a 3-year-old they'd been presumed dead for ten minutes.

'There are medically documented examples where all readings have flatlined. The patient has been pronounced clinically dead, only to return to life later with stories of white light, light tunnels, voices calling them back, telling them it is not yet time to go or offering the choice of death or life. Ernest Hemingway reported a weird but brief death or near-death experience that affected him for the rest of his life. He was wounded by shrapnel during World War I near Fossalta in Italy and went to convalesce in Milan. He made a cryptic reference in a letter to his family saying, "Dying is a very simple thing. I've looked at death and really, I know."

'Years later, he explained to a friend that a big Austrian trench mortar bomb had exploded in the darkness, and he knew at once that he had died. He felt his soul, or something, coming out of his body "like you'd pull a silk handkerchief out of a pocket by one corner". It flew around and then came back and went in again, and he wasn't dead anymore. He remained deeply affected by the experience.

'Some children actually remember being born. No one has told them of the circumstances surrounding their births, yet they report details years later that only their mothers or those present at the birth could have known.'

CHAPTER SEVENTY

'What about people who remember past lives?' Judy offers. 'I was surprised to find how much really interesting information there is about reincarnation. I was looking for unchallengeable examples and came upon this one on iisis.net. researched by Ian Stevenson, MD, from a work called *Old Souls* by a Tom Shroder. These are all well-known people.

'It's about a Lebanese girl, Hanan, who was born in the 1930s, who was married at twenty to Farouk, and had two daughters, Leila and Galareh. After the birth of her second daughter, she developed a heart problem and was advised not to have further children. In 1962, she had a son. In 1963, after the death of her brother, Nabih, in a plane crash, her health began to deteriorate, and she started talking to Farouk about dying.

'Two years before her death, Hanan told Farouk that she was going to be reincarnated and have lots to say about her previous life. At thirty-six, she went to Richmond, Virginia for heart surgery. She tried to telephone her daughter, Leila, to tell her what was happening, but couldn't get through. She died of complications the day after her surgery. Ten days after Hanan's death, Suzanne was born to a woman who reported to Ian Stevenson that "I dreamed I was going to have a baby girl. I met a woman, and I kissed and hugged her. She said I am going to come to you". The woman was about forty.

'Later, after she had seen Hanan's picture, she thought it looked like the woman in her dream. At sixteen months, still little more than a baby, Suzanne pulled the phone off the hook as if she were going to talk to someone, and said over and over, "Hello, Leila." No one knew who Leila was. When she got older, Suzanne explained that Leila was one of her children and that she was not Suzanne, but Hanan. The family asked, "Hanan what?" Suzanne replied "My head is still small. Wait until it is bigger and I might tell you."

'By the time she was two, she had mentioned thirteen names of people her parents had no knowledge of. Her husband, Farouk, her parents, her children and brothers, all from her previous lifetime as Hanan. Eventually, the two families met, and although Hanan's family was skeptical at first, they became believers when Suzanne was able to recognise pictures of their relatives and name them accurately.

'Suzanne also had a piece of information that nobody outside the family knew. That before the operation, Hanan had given her jewels to her brother, Hercule, with instructions to divide them between her daughters. Before she could read or write, Suzanne had scribbled a phone number on a piece of paper. When the families met, they found that the number was the same as Farouk's, but the last two digits were transposed. As a child, Suzanne could also recite the oration delivered at Hanan's brother, Habih's, funeral.

'At 5 years old, Suzanne would call Farouk three times a day. And when she visited, she would sit on his lap with her head against his chest. Farouk, who is a career policeman, has accepted that Suzanne is the reincarnation of Hanan, and over the years, Suzanne has identified scores of people Hanan had known and had provided a variety of information that only she could have known. There is also a striking physical resemblance between Suzanne and Hanan.

'Makes you think about how we view life, or do I mean death, doesn't it? There are thousands of cases just like this being collected and investigated all over the world at any one time. I found this one compelling. And being so clearly laid out, with so many checkable facts, it's an important one to serious past life and reincarnation researchers, since it demonstrates uncontestable parallels. They look for all kinds of indicators.

'The physical resemblance, the involvement of a spirit being, Hanan's announcement of her coming death and reincarnation. Relationships renewed through reincarnation, Suzanne with her past life husband. This is called a split incarnation, which assumes that with only ten days between the death of Hanan and the birth of Suzanne, the soul of Hanan was already animating Suzanne's fetus, while Hanan was still alive. Indeed for almost the entire pregnancy.'

'Holy hell,' comments Dan. 'Do you guys realise that everything we've been talking about is in the realm of spooky and/or weird and yet it's all actually happened!'

CHAPTER SEVENTY-ONE

Judy's so pleased with the impact her story has made that she makes them another offer. 'How about a Muslim boy who was killed by a tractor and reincarnated as a Hindu? I bring you this with impeccable grounds for proof. This one also includes Xenoglossy, a word I never knew existed. Allow me to explain what that is. A child spoke a language that he had never learned, but would have spoken it in a previous life. It really got my attention because Muslims don't believe in reincarnation or Hinduism for that matter.

'Mushir Ali is a Sunni Muslim who lived in Kakori, a town in the Lucknow district of Uttar Pradesh, India where Urdu is spoken. Mushir was the primary breadwinner of the family because his father, who was very religious, devoted himself to prayer and the family lived off alms and donations. Mushir supplemented the family income by selling fruit and vegetables at the area markets.

'He was driving the horse cart he had rented to take a load of mangoes to the Lucknow market in the early morning of thirtieth of June in 1980 when his cart collided with a tractor, just a little more than two kilometres from his hometown. He was mortally injured, suffered fractures to his ribs on the right side of his body, and died almost immediately. Mushir was twenty-five.

'The following February, in Bazbagar, another village in the same district, Bishwana gave birth to Naresh Kumar, a baby whose body showed the defect of a depressed area near the middle of the chest and slightly to the right. She and her husband, Guruprasad, were lower middle class Hindus.

'At the age of 1, Naresh said the word "Kakori", Mushir's home village, and the Urdu word "kharkhara", which means horse cart. The family did not speak Urdu. At two years, Naresh started to assume the Muslim posture of kneeling and saying namaz, the ritual prayers of Muslims. He would do this alone, but if he noticed people looking at him, he would stop.

'He would play at pretending to drive a horse cart, tying a rope to a cot, and making sounds as though to gee-up the horses. In addition, he was heard speaking some words in Urdu. This is evidence of Xenoglossy, a language learned and retained from a prior lifetime. When he was four, he started to elaborate about a past life in which he had lived in a town called Kakori where he had been killed in a collision between another vehicle and the horse and cart he was driving to market with a load of mangoes.

'Haider Ali, the father of the dead Mushir, used to visit Bazbagar on Thursdays to pray for villagers and collect alms and donations. When Naresh learned to walk, he used to follow Haider Ali around the village and claim that he was his father. He called Haider Ali "Abba", meaning father, and told him he wanted to go home with him.

'Naresh insisted that his family take him to Kakori, so much so that Bishwana decided to ask Haider Ali for assistance on the grounds that he was both from Kakori and a Muslim. She needed help for the boy. She had no ulterior motive.

'Haider Ali did not seem to want to get involved himself, but advised Bishwana to take the boy to the grave of a Muslim saint in

Mazar, thinking that this would stop the boy talking about a previous life. The family did so, but the child continued to talk about his previous life. Even if, at any stage, Haider Ali had suspected that the child could be a reappearance of his dead son, Mushir, he would not have risked saying it for fear of criticism from the Muslim community who did not believe in reincarnation.

'Guruprasad finally decided to take Naresh to Kakori together with some friends for support. Without knowing where he was going, Naresh led them to the house where Mushir had lived. And inside the house, he identified several objects that had belonged to Mushir including his cap and the contents of his suitcase.

'He also recognised and named members of Mushir's immediate family. He told them about a bank account that the family had at the time of Mushir's death and about money, which was owed to Mushir at that time but was repaid after the death. Ultimately, both families accepted Naresh as the reincarnation of Mushir Ali, and presumed that the birth defect on Naresh's body reflected the trauma and rib fractures inflicted on Mushir when he died in the accident.

'Now, you have to admit this kind of stuff is super weird. Again, the investigators and past life researchers, including Ian Stevenson MD, noted important principles of reincarnation in this story. The change in religion, past life talents, and behaviour, geographic memory, Naresh was able to locate his past life home, Xenoglossy, birth defects reflected in the physical body of the reincarnated son, and relationships renewed between past and present lives.

'How spooky is that?' Judy asks the other five.

'I think I'll come back as a margarita,' mumbles Manny.

CHAPTER SEVENTY-TWO

'Wow. Just wow,' says Dan. 'Now, I definitely need a chaser of something.'

'You have a chaser after something, Dan.' Mark reminds him. 'Not before. You know, like after spirits. A shot of whisky and a chaser of beer.'

'I think we've had a fair dose of spirits tonight, brother, so go ahead. We've all earned several chasers.'

'Be my guest,' Colin indicates waiting bottles of wine and port on the sideboard, which is voluptuously laden with strawberries dipped in dark chocolate, petits fours, a selection of cheeses, toasts, and wafers of every description, fruit kebabs, brandy snaps, and meringues.

'Brandy snaps!' yelps Manny. 'My favourite, I adore them. Mum always made them for special occasions. I used to watch her rolling the mixture around the wooden spoon handle and hope that she would crack one. She used to make a big display of spoiling or nearly dropping one, so I could have it. Brandy snaps! Love them. Darn tricky getting the cream into them though. And I feel cheated if I just get a bit of cream poked in each end and nothing in the middle.'

'Well,' says Carol. 'Manny, you and Dan must come for dinner one evening soon. We could do the same thing if it wouldn't be too boring. The whole dinner party thing, I mean, not necessarily the spooky stuff. We have a housekeeper whose specialty is brandy snaps.'

'Count us in,' Dan confirms. 'I'm fond of a brandy snap myself. You don't see them these days, too much trouble I suppose. Or just too old-fashioned for the frenetic food freaks who seem to have taken over our television screens. I never thought I would get such a buzz out of seeing a soufflé collapse. And they take it so seriously, those contestants.'

'Mmmm,' Mark muses. 'I wonder what it says about us as a community that we derive so much pleasure from watching people making fools of themselves, or humiliating other people by putting them into carefully stage-managed unmanageable situations. Time was when entertainment was about enjoyment and laughing or learning. Nowadays, it's about seeing someone come a cropper in front of an audience or fall off the stage stoned.'

CHAPTER SEVENTY-THREE

'Let's lighten up a bit, folks.' Colin reaches for the CD remote control and challenges. 'I'm going to turn on some music and see if we can remember where we were the first time we heard it. We can do sixties. No, that would rule out Manny, seventies, eighties, or nineties. Anything after that in the pop field would rule me out.'

'I can do rock 'n roll,' Manny protests. 'My mum used to play the music from her teenage and twenties years endlessly.'

'Okay, let's rock and roll,' says Colin. 'I'm just going to hide these brandy snaps for a while. The first right answer gets a brandy snap as a prize.'

'That's okay,' says Judy. 'I prefer petits fours.'

'Done!' says Colin. 'I'll hide them as well.'

'Okay, first question, folks. Name three Little Richard hits.' 'Easy peasy, pass the petits pleasy,' Judy answers. '*Long Tall Sally*, *Tutti Frutti*, and *Rip it Up*. I heard nearly every Little Richard hit at my presentation ball. They had a rock and roll hour. Thank you.' She reaches toward the plate being proffered. 'I'll have these three. Now, it's my turn to ask. Who's for brandy snaps? Brandy snaps next prize. Can you handle four? Name four Elvis hits.

'Okay, Dan, you're first.'

Dan rattles them off, '*Heartbreak Hotel, Don't Be Cruel, Hound Dawg* and…' Dan's stuck for a fourth. Manny hums softly close to his ear, *love me tender, love me sweet.* 'That's it, and *Love Me Tender*. That's four brandy snaps, I believe.'

'Forget four, Dan,' says Manny. 'I get two, one for helping and one for being right.'

'Now, I get to ask the questions.' Dan looks around and asks. 'Who can give me three hits from Bill Haley and the Comets?' He presents the question like a professional quizmaster, complete with three fingers in the air followed by a mimed drumroll.

'Razzle Dazzle,' offers Carol. 'And I'll take the petits fours, thank you, *Rock Around the Clock* and *See you Later Alligator*.'

'Hey, Manny, speaking of See you Later Alligator and clocks, don't I have a conference call at midnight?' Dan takes out his phone and taps it, brings up the diary. 'Yes, it's tonight. Tarnation. I wish I didn't have to go, but this is important. It's a hook up with Sweden, US, and South Africa. We're all contributing to a compendium-type publication, and we have to check that we're not doubling up or treading on each other's toes, so to speak. And it's covering some of tonight's subjects in a way. I think I'll have a few out-of-left-field ideas for my fellow fizzios. Manny, do you mind if we leave these good people now? It's a quarter to already. If I don't get there by midnight, I'll be turned into a pumpkin. I'm so sorry,' he looks around the group.

'Thanks, Judy and Colin, great party, folks. Our compliments to the host and hostess for a most engrossing evening, and what a great idea to get a chef in. Thoroughly enjoyed myself, and I love it when I go home feeling I've learned something new. Thanks to all of you.'

Manny is getting into his coat when Carol sidles up to him and asks, 'Are you available for house calls? I might need some help with the garden. How can I get hold of you? Do you have a card or something? Do you mind my asking you to help me with the garden?'

'Good Lord, no. I'll be pleased to be of agrarian assistance to a charming lady. But I don't have a card at the moment, sorry. Ask me next week after I've picked them up from the printer, but I'll give you my direct line at work. That'll be better than the home number. I'm not there much at any rate. If you call during the day, work's the place you'll find me. Darn, I'd forgotten about those cards.'

Manny tears a page out of the notebook beside the phone and writes down his number, as Carol adds, 'Don't forget to put your name too. I want to know who to ask for in case you're in a meeting or something and someone else takes the call.'

Suddenly, Carol is alert again and remembers she was going to ask Manny where he'd just moved from. But she can do that when she calls him. They'll have more time to talk then.

'It's all there.' Manny hands her a neatly folded page, which she slips straight into her handbag, so she won't lose it.

They say their farewells and promise another dinner together and rush off.

CHAPTER SEVENTY-FOUR

'That was such a great way to spend an evening,' says Colin. 'And we haven't even finished dessert yet. Good lord, you could almost call it a midnight feast.'

'Did you know that there's an actual medical condition connected to midnight snacking? It's called night eating syndrome and affects about one and a half per cent of the general population. Mostly adults and', he pauses as he fixes both Carol and Judy with an accusing stare, 'more women than men.'

'Bloody hell,' Judy comments. 'There's a fancy name for everything these days. It used to be called night starvation. It hadn't yet reached the status of a syndrome. Granny science used to recommend a hot milk drink at bedtime. The theory was that during the night, you don't produce as much melatonin and leptin, but your nightly drink of hot milk cocoa increases the level of the tryptophans that produce the serotonin, which helps you sleep. Or something like that.'

Colin assures her, 'Not a lot has changed, you'll be happy to know, my dear. Seratonin still helps you sleep. Night snackers still prefer carbohydrates because they stimulate production of insulin, and that helps increase the level of tryptophan in the brain. That's why a lot of night snackers find it hard to lose weight. Half their calories are consumed at night. Granny was half right.'

The four finish their post-prandial pleasures and decide to call it a night—a jolly good one.

Everyone feels much more scholarly. They agree that Dan and his man are top value, and look forward to a repeat performance. Carol has her second wind, and is telling Mark how much she has enjoyed the dinner, the company, the stories, everything. Just the kind of evening she loves. A bit like being back at a uni get together, but at a much more elevated level. Mark feels that his efforts have been fulfilled and feels hugely gladdened at Carol's recovery. He still has no idea why she had taken to her bed for so long. He counsels himself against pursuing it.

In the car, calmed by the motion of the vehicle, Carol is relaxing into reverie. She has bowls of beads in front of her and lengths of chain. Suddenly, she creates an arrangement that pleases her, and she starts laying out the beads in her head in colours and sizes, making a beautiful pattern. Each row of beads is laid in a semi-circle and has a length of chain to connect it with the next. It feels perfect to her.

'And', just a susurration in her ear, *'it's beautiful, Carol, just like a web with the dew still upon it, slightly weighted down, but connected in a lovely suffusion of shades. We were amazing this evening. We really got it together. We should indulge ourselves more often. We like conviviality, don't we?*

Carol nods and says, 'Yes.'

'Yes, what?' asks Mark. Carol snaps into the present quickly and says, 'Yes, I was going to say, yes, we must do it again. It was thoroughly fun. Nice people. Dishy Dan and his marvellous Man, what a waste.'

'Not to each other,' says Mark. 'They seem to be very fine indeed. Splendid company. I wonder what Manny's story is.'

They finish the journey in silence, and immensely satisfied with themselves and each other, they shower and snuggle into bed together. Any connubial thoughts Mark might have been entertaining were quickly lulled into a deep and ultimately restorative sleep.

As Carol dreams the tranquil night away, she is back with the beads, making the final selection of colours and chain lengths. She is happy. 'That's perfect,' she whispers to herself.

'Yes, it is,' she answers. And she picks up the new necklace and places it against her skin. Just the right length, she whispers. *'Yes, it is,'* she answers. We will wear it in our dreams. *'Always. You have restrung our life, and it looks beautifully balanced. Its colours are harmonious and soft with just enough connecting links. It's very pretty, Carol. And all the beads and links have been used. All the connections made.'*

Why do I feel so happy? Her dream self looks into the mirror and sees a shadow fading into the distance. It looks like someone she knows. It is. It is her.

Suddenly, it's Sunday morning; and Mark, already up and dressed for golf, hands her a breakfast tray, places a gentle sweet kiss on her cheek, and goes off to the game of golf, maker of so many fine-weather widows.

Rosemarie will not be in today, she remembers, so she finishes her croissants with the deliciously edgy cumquat marmalade and sets about planning the day in her head.

First, an invigorating shower. 'Well something to wake me up,' she corrects herself as she remembers it's only a few hours since she had a shower. 'Then I'll see what we need to make the new flat habitable. No, not just habitable, homely and welcoming. I think we should spend a little bit extra in the bathroom. I wonder if there's room for a corner spa. That would be nice, I'm sure Rosemarie would like that.'

So she busies herself for the full day, making lists. Things to do.

Things to buy. Things to look into. Look into is the catchall list.

'Do you remember', the leggy voice caresses her ear as it slides into her mind, *'how you used to think of your life? How many problems have you put behind you? How many things have you consigned to the forgettery? Do you think the day is worth getting out of bed for now? Of course, you do. And do you know why?'*

'No. Why?' Carol knows full well why. She has arrived at a place of peace in her life. But she's interested in what the psychiatrist says.

'Exactly!' says psycho spider. *'Exactly. We are at peace with each other and with the world. You don't want to kill me, and I don't want to die. We have a life to live. We are free. Free because of what you have done.'*

'What have I done?' Carol feels a slight panic. Has she done something without knowing? What does psychosister mean?

'There, see how close we are to being together forever? One minute I'm psychiatrist. There's nothing wrong with us, Carol. We don't need a psychiatrist. Then I'm psycho spider, better than spindle-shanks. That was very hurtful. But psycho spider is not as good as psychosister. We're nearly there. We are nearly I. It's getting to be very exciting, Carol. I'm getting a bit shaky about it. I love the necklace, by the way. Lovely design, beautiful balance of shape and size and colour. We are very talented. And it suits us. Here comes our husband.'

CHAPTER SEVENTY-FIVE

Mark arrives home a half hour earlier than Carol was expecting, and he presents her with a voluminous voluptuous (why aren't there more *V* words in my vocabulary? Oops, there's one) bunch of jonquils. She can almost see the fragrance hanging in the air. They are flagrantly fragrant, absolutely overwhelming. She is stunned as much by the sheer vulgarity (another *V* word) of the size of the bouquet as by the aphrodisiac effect of the perfume.

'Shall we have dinner out tonight?' Mark is trying to keep his tone casual, aware that they went out last night until late, and that Carol has been in bed all day every day for the last several months. He might be overdoing it. There is a long pause, while Carol considers the proposition.

'Yes, let's.' She says enthusiastically. 'I know it's shockingly self-indulgent, and I should be feeling exhausted. But I'm not! What's happening to me?'

Mark takes her into his arms and presses his face against hers. He feels close to tears, he is so relieved. 'I think, my darling, that whatever devil kept you in that bed has vacated this house forever. It is wonderful to have you back in the world with me. Back in my life.' He wants to tell her how terribly, terribly worried he has been, how he had questioned himself endlessly about how he might have contributed to her malaise. But wisdom prevails, and he stays silent.

Dinner was a delight. They went Italian and finished the evening with the most magnificent mascarpone with dark chocolate cream dessert followed by two macchiatos. 'I hope I'll sleep after this, Mark, it's very strong, but also very delicious.' Carol licks her lips daintily, and despite the hour, she still looks very animated.

Over dinner, they discussed Rosemarie's new apartment and the furnishings. Mark agreed that the spa was a good idea, and it was left that Carol would organise the furnishings and furniture, and Mark would handle building adjustments, plumbing, and electricity. They agree to make the offer to Rosemarie the following day.

They shower and retire, delighted with the decision to employ Rosemarie. Paco will be so well cared for. He may not even miss them.

They are both infinitely more content. Their marriage had returned to the sweet harmony it had gradually drifted away from. Mark is exultant and far too hyped to sleep immediately. Carol slips into bed, tired from so much unaccustomed activity, and is almost asleep before she has adjusted her pillow.

CHAPTER SEVENTY-SIX

Carol sighs deeply and murmurs in her sleep. Mark, just finished reading, switches off the bedside lamp and settles down for the night.

Carol is murmuring. He catches a couple of words only. *Necklace* and *web*. That's a funny combination, he thinks. 'I wonder what sort of dream she's having. I hope she's not putting a necklace on that spider she was frightened of.' Mark, then, muses more seriously. 'I wonder what that spider business was all about. She was absolutely hysterical about that shadow. Never seen her like that before. She's always been so cool and confident, everything under control. Even when the rest of the world's panicking, Carol's calm, making lists, and ordering people about. Women are strange creatures. I'd love to know why she decided to take to her bed, though.

'Oh, well, tomorrow we'll be getting on with the apartment, and we'll both be too busy to think about anything other than finishing that off and flying off to New York. Which reminds me,'

Mark's finally drifting off, finding it hard to keep hold of the thought. 'Reminds me of what?' And then he's asleep.

Next morning, they start their makeover plans and Carol goes off to see corner spas. She chooses an apricot blush spa and over the top silver swan accessories. Gold would have been vulgar. Then pale grey with an apricot fleck tiles for the floor, walls, and spa surround. A charming combination, she thinks. She knows Rosemarie's fond of apricot because she commented on her bed and bathroom linen in the cupboard.

By the time she arrives home that afternoon, Rosemarie is just about to leave, and Carol asks if she could spare a few minutes to 'help with something special' after work tomorrow. She happily agrees.

Carol tells Mark as soon as he's in that the scene is set. Tomorrow will be the beginning of Rosemarie's new life. Little does she know how much truth there is in that thought.

As Rosemarie finishes work in the kitchen the next day, Mark and Carol ask her to make them all a cuppa and, adds Carol, bring some of those little fudge numbers you spoil Mark with. The three of them sit at the dining room table. Rosemarie's nervous. Could they have changed their minds? Of course not. She relaxes and pours the tea.

'Now, Mrs Rose,' starts Mark.

'Rosemarie, please, if you don't mind. Just plain Rosemarie.' 'Right you are,' Mark continues. 'I'll come straight to the point then. We'd like you to become part of our household. No, our home.' He pauses, surprised that he isn't delivering the much more pompous speech that he had prepared.

'Yes,' says Rosemarie. 'You've given me a permanent position. And I'm very happy with that.' She feels a little uncomfortable. She has already agreed to be permanent. What does this mean?

'Oh, I put that badly, my dear Mrs Rose. You will forgive me if I continue to address you like that just for a while. It may take me a while to adjust, you know. I'll try again. My dear Mrs Rose, we are delighted that you have accepted the permanent role with us. But we are so very happy with your work that we would like to make you another offer.'

Rosemarie is stunned. 'An-n-nother offer?' she stammers.

'Yes. If you accept, you will have a separate apartment with us. That is, you'll live in, but have your own place. We're going to refit the area over the carports and garage. It will be a roomy lounge, a dine-in kitchen, fully equipped of course, and you can choose the appliances. A bedroom with en suite, complete with your own spa. And I think we can squeeze in, or out, a small balcony big enough for a small table and a couple of chairs.'

'Oh, no, sir. Oh, I'm, I'm, I don't know what to say.' Rosemarie is bright red and tears are beginning to glisten in her eyes.

'Well, say nothing until I finish what I have to say. We will decide together, all three of us, how many hours per week you will work. You will have a better idea than us of how much time the house needs. You will have a private income. It will be fair and reasonable recompense, but it will be set at a figure that will not interfere with your widow's pension. You might think of it as a retainer. I'll have our accountant draw up a proper contract, private between us, but binding nonetheless, so you will have absolute security.'

Rosemarie appears dazed and totally unaware that tears are rolling down her reddened cheeks.

'The contract will cover everything you want it to, and we will be pleased for you to take it, before signing it, to anyone whose advice you might value on the subject. Paco will have his place in the contract, of course. He will be naming you as his adopted aunt. If, after thought, this idea appears attractive to you, you will move into the apartment as soon as it is finished. So over to you, how does it sound so far?'

'I'm... I'm... I don't know what to say. Do you really mean you would want me living here? Of course, it would be a dream. But could you really mean it?' She is still totally unaware of the tears rolling down her face.

'Rosemarie,' Carol reaches across the table and takes her hand in hers. 'It would help us so much if you would accept the offer. Mark is retiring at the end of the year, and we're hoping to spend a few months each year travelling. It would be the perfect answer for us. We're off to New York for Mark's conference in two weeks, so we could treat it as a test. What do you say? We sort out the terms now, and you can sign it when we come back from New York. Or not, as you wish.'

'I don't think there's any chance of me looking a gift horse like this one in the mouth, Carol. This is so unexpected. I'm over the moon. Just to be made permanent took such a load off my heart and mind. Oh, sorry to be blubbing like this.' She wipes her face with a hankie. 'I can't believe it.'

'Well, you'll be hearing a bit of noise coming from the area over there during the next few days. It's all organised. They start work tomorrow. And just to give it an added touch of reality, Rosemarie, here's a picture of the en suite and spa. We ordered it today because even if you decide you don't want to live in properly, we can always let it as a granny flat. But it does look a bit fabulous, doesn't it?'

Rosemarie has the brochure in her hand, which is trembling. 'I never saw myself with anything so grand as this.' She wipes another waterfall from her cheeks. 'Oh, dear, I don't know whether I'll be able to sleep tonight.'

'Just remember to give your notice in at that place. You can move here the minute it's finished. One week, they said, and we'll keep them to it. Start packing, Rosemarie. We're going to start planning your welcome party.' Carol escorts her to the door and turns to Mark. 'That went well. What do you think?'

'Just as well you didn't leave it all to me,' Mark replies. 'I'd have done a runner with all those tears.'

CHAPTER SEVENTY-SEVEN

The days passed, and finally, the workmen complete the apartment. Fittings are all in. Rosemarie is trying, desperately trying, to keep her mind on the housework and not on her new place, which she has promised she won't peek at until it's ready for her to occupy. Furniture in interesting looking wrappings seems to be being delivered daily.

She has given her notice at the old flat, and she has already packed the few possessions she has left, ready to leave at a moment's notice. She's spending a lot of time plotting with Paco. She plans to have a special bed there for him, so when the folks are away, he'll have a familiar place to be. She doesn't know that Paco has no plans to sleep alone except outside during the day.

Carol, too, is busy planning. She's checking temperatures in New York, planning what they will do in the ten days extra they are tacking onto Mark's conference time. They'll hire a car with a driver, and well, that's as far as she's got. The details can wait. More important is the wardrobe. Should she take a full suitcase or a half-empty one? The full one would be this year's fashions, which will not be right up there with it for New York. So half-empty wins.

She'll pack just enough to see her through a couple of days, and she'll buy the latest of everything while there. That makes much more sense. And that will put her ahead of the season back home. Excellent!

Mark continues to be amazed at the change in her. Not the same woman as a few months ago, and even younger, brighter, more outgoing than the Carol of a few years ago. Whatever it is, Mark knows he could make a fortune bottling it.

'Oh, look what I found in my bag!' Carol says to Mark. 'It's Manny's contact number. I'd almost forgotten about him with all this excitement.

'I'll call him right now. He won't have left yet. The clock in the hall shows quarter to four.'

She dials the number and is told by Jenny, the receptionist, that Manny is not available and won't be back until next Monday. The receptionist sounds quite chatty, so Carol ventures a question. 'He's not on holiday, is he?'

'Oh, no, it's not a holiday,' Jenny chirps. 'He's tying up the last of a case he was working on when he left Singapore three months ago. He was transferred to Sydney before it was complete, and as the auditor, well, he has to sign off on it.'

Carol is stunned. Singapore? Auditor? Three months ago? No, no, no, it couldn't be. Could it? No, it can't be. The name on the page from the notepad she has says Manny R. Flores. Rose's son is Manuel Rose.

She thanks Jenny, and just as she's about to put the phone down, she adds, 'Jenny, I wonder if you'd help us. We're planning a surprise for Manny's birthday. He's a close friend of a family we know very well, and we've all been wondering what on earth we can get for him. We want it to be really special. You know him, do you have any ideas?'

'Well, he's keen on gardening, and he's just moved into a new place. Perhaps a fancy something or other for the garden, a birdbath or something. Have a look at that place near to where he's moved. They're having a big sale, and they always have super stuff. They import directly, their prices are a bit steep, but it's much classier than your average place.'

Carol thanks Jenny, and says she'll call and let her know what they decide, since she's been so helpful. She is well pleased with her afternoon's work.

Manny, auditor, Singapore, gardener—she searches her memory. Could she be imagining it? Manny, their Manny, Dan's Manny is an auditor. Rosemarie's Manuel, isn't that the same name as Manny, works for an accountancy place. They have Singapore in common. But Dan's Manny's here and Rosemarie's Manuel is there. But there's more—they're both garden lovers.

That's just too much, Carol thinks. It would be awful is she were wrong, but wonderful if she's right. What to do? Then it dawns on her. First, they need to know the name of the company Manny works for. Colin can ask Dan for that. Then they need to find out where Manuel works.

That means Mark making a few calls and some discreet enquiries amongst his financial contacts. And then wait to see what that turns up. Even Mark's been bitten by the investigation bug. He starts making calls immediately, taking the slip of paper with Manny R. Flores' contact number with him.

Half an hour passes with Mark busy on the phone when, 'Success!' he shrieks from the home office. 'Come here, Carol! We're onto something.'

'What is it? What have you found out?'

'Well,' says Mark. 'I called Carlos because he's worked for damn near every company in the country. Singapore, I mean. And he knows everyone. And he's Spanish.'

'What's that got to do with it?' Carol asks, then from the back of her brain somewhere, she drags out Rosemarie's reference to Spain or South America when she was talking about Manny's adoption.

'Almost everything,' Mark replies. 'He knows Manny R. Flores personally, and says he's a top bloke. And they have a mutual friend in Singapore, a corporate lawyer who just happens to have helped a Manuel Rose change his name to Manny R. Flores. The *R* is for Rose, his family name, Flores is simply because the rose is a flower. He didn't know much more than that he'd had a terminal row with his father before he left Sydney for Singapore and changed his name soon after he got there. He hadn't told his mother, and Carlos swore me to secrecy. The father was a pugilist. Your basic thug.'

'Wow.' Carol's gobsmacked. Manny is Rosemarie's son and he's here! And she doesn't know. So why hasn't he called her? 'Mark,' she says. 'You remember what she told me? Manuel hadn't called her for a week or two, and when she tried to call him to tell him his father had died, he'd moved flats and jobs and the office had no way of contacting him. Then the truck ran over her house, and she had no telephone as well as no house. Even if he'd tried to call her when he was settled somewhere, he wouldn't have got an answer. Who knows what he thought?

'And if he'd tried to visit her when he moved here, he'd have found nothing but a hole in the ground. The people around that area now are all in transit from one place to another. You're lucky to hear any English spoken. No one would be interested in where she went or what happened to her. But why wouldn't he ask the police for help?' Carol trails off.

'Probably', answers Mark, 'because it would have been a bit of a convoluted tale to tell. I am this person, but I changed my name to this person, and I'm looking for my mother, and I don't know where she is? My guess is that having the mind of an auditor, he'd want things nice and tidy and in their place before he started looking for her. After all, he's been backwards and forwards from Singapore so much, and he was getting nervous about having no piece of turf to call his own. That's why he was so keen to buy a place.'

'Do you know how long he's known Dan?' Carol asks. 'They bought the place together, so they surely must have known each other longer than a few months.'

'Colin said they met on a twenty-day cruise through France and Germany a couple of years ago. So it's not a new bromance.'

'Well, my darling, where does that leave us?' Carol looks puzzled. 'Well, my lovely, I would say that leaves us with one hell of a big party to arrange, and I would anticipate a truly impressive display of waterworks from our housekeeper.'

CHAPTER SEVENTY-EIGHT

Mark and Carol decide on a plan. Manny's due back the week after Rosemarie moves into the apartment, so at least that will be a fait accompli.

First thing then is to consult Colin about how best to tell Dan. Dan will decide how to tell his Man. 'I'd like us to be there when they are reunited,' Carol insists. 'You don't think that would be too intrusive, darling?' Mark is sympathetic to the idea. He'd like to be there too.

This will be a huge event in the lives of Manny and Rosemarie. They both know how deeply Rosemarie has grieved for her Manuel. It would add ten years to her life to know that he is alive and well and within her reach. Carol is still in planning mode.

'How about this,' she offers. 'We get Dan and Manny in on it. We prime Rosemarie for a big surprise. Actually, it's her birthday, so we could slip it in under the wire without detection, so to speak. How good is that? The perfect reason for a celebration, a new year, a new place to live, and here's the surprise, a new life. So we do a birthday shindig here in our place, perhaps a late afternoon cocktail thing. And because she's entitled to have the day off on her birthday, she won't feel bad about us getting the chef fellow in. Makes sense so far. We'll invite Colin and Judy and Dan and Manny and invent something to make sure she's inside when Manny arrives. It would be too much of a shock for her to see him standing at the door.

'We invite Rosemarie for 4 p.m., and tell her that Dan will knock on her door to escort her when the time comes. After all, a girl can't arrive at a cocktail party without an escort. Dan stays here. Manny goes and does the honours. We give them an hour to get over it, Manny brings in Rosemarie, and then the party starts.'

They're both thrilled. We'll call Judy and Colin tomorrow and get them over to write the script. I think we should leave it up to Colin as to whether he gets Dan involved at this stage or not.

But Carol decides suddenly that she can't wait till tomorrow. She needs to get the plan going right away. She won't sleep until they have it settled. So she calls them, and despite the fact that they're on their way to bed, they insist on celebrating right away. Minutes later, they're at the door with the news that Dan's on his way too. And Dan is jumping out of his skin by the time he arrives.

He hugs and kisses everyone, and then he hugs and kisses each one again. He is overcome with emotion, tears are gathering in his eyes, and his voice is shakey as he says this will heal the deepest wound in Manny's life. 'And it will make our life together perfect. I can't tell you', he's almost whispering, his voice is trembling, 'how happy you are making me now and how excited, delirious, Manny will be. He says he feels half dead with the grief of losing contact with his mother. He thought changing his name would help him get over it. He kept the *R* in his new name in memory of her. He realised that without her, he could have been dead or desperately unhappy in some other life.'

'Oh, God, am I really hearing this? Please tell me I'm not dreaming. Pinch me.' Judy leans over and gently pinches his cheek, her fingers wiping the tears that have finally escaped. 'Dan, darling, it's real. All of it.'

'Now we just have to make sure we stage-manage the reuniting, so that no one has a heart attack.'

Dan goes on telling his story as if he hasn't heard her. 'When he saw that there was no house, only a hole left he was shattered. He asked around, but nobody knew anything. They knew about the accident, that's all. They didn't know who was living there. He called his mother's sister in Perth, only to find that she had died a month beforehand. There were no other relatives to try. He was planning to see if he could find her through one of the housing places, but he hasn't been here long enough to start. He knew he would have to be prepared to follow up on every lead, and he'd need to be in the country to do that. Well, now he's in the country, and you, guardian angels, have done it all for him.' Dan shakes his shoulders as if to remove a heavy weight and says, 'Tonight, I will sleep. Thank you both. I can never repay you.'

'And neither can we,' add Judy and Colin.

That evening, before they make their way back to their homes, the five of them make a toast to serendipity.

'It's a fair bet that we'll all sleep sweetly tonight,' Carol says as she slips in beside Mark. Mark grunts and rolls onto his back, already in twilight land.

CHAPTER SEVENTY-NINE

Carol wraps her arm across Mark's chest, snuggles toward him, and kisses him on the neck. He stirs and grunts again.

Paco is dreaming, paws twitching, and flexing in his sleep. His tail is alert, swishing like a feather duster flicking imaginary flies off Mark's pillow where he lies flopped over its corner.

The morning brings bright sunshine and a tray of croissant and coffee for Carol. 'Did I dream it, or have we really solved the problems of the universe?' She asks as she shrugs off her sleep and sits up to receive the tray.

'You didn't dream it. You made it happen. You waved your wand and the fairy tale happened.'

'You didn't dream it,' Mark replies. 'You must have waved your wand because everything I want is happening. And everything Rosemarie wants is about to happen. And Manny is going to be a very happy person too. I think I like playing guardian angel. It seems we are moving into a new era.'

'Yes, darling, it does look that way. Did I really spend months in bed? It really didn't seem that long. I felt so confused and worried, and I can't remember now what I was so worried about. I feel good about everything. Things that were a burden before, like things I wish I'd never done or things I knew I should have done and didn't, they seem to have melted away. *Je ne regrette rien.*

'I feel so different. I had a really strange dream last night. I was looking in a mirror, and I could see myself waiting at a bus stop for a bus that never came. I knew it wouldn't come, and yet I went on waiting. Then I realised I had the keys to my car in my pocket.'

'Yes, my dear Carol, we are driving our own car now, and we can go wherever we like. We can look in the rear vision mirror to see how far we've come.'

'That's funny,' replies Mark. 'I had a strange one too. I dreamed we had lost our way somewhere. I was looking for a map. It was a map of Spain. We were there looking for your place on the beach. I'd left the book open at the Torrenostra page. I was sure I knew where I'd left it, but I found a necklace. Weird.' He bends down to retrieve the napkin that has slipped off the breakfast tray. 'Good grief, how did that get there? That's the map I was looking for in my dream. Where did that come from?'

'Where does what come from?' Carol looks over the edge of the bed where she'd watched the napkin sliding over. 'Oh, that? That's the book of maps of Spain I ordered from Amazon just after we decided on going there. You remember? Well, it arrived yesterday. I left it on the bed. It must have slipped off. I left it open at the page that takes us from Barcelona to Torreblanca. It must have closed when it fell off the bed. I left a post-it note on the page. Let's take a look at it now.'

Mark opens the spiral bound pages at the yellow sticker and holds it out to Carol. 'Look,' he says. 'Look inside that plastic spiral, there's something stuck in there.' He looks more closely. 'It's a dead spider. Big one too. How on earth did that get there if it only arrived yesterday?' Carol upends the book and shakes the spider onto her hand. ‘It’s very dead,’ she says. ‘Maybe it hitched a lift with the maps in your dream.’

‘Let’s go, Carol. We’re on a new journey now.’

‘Or maybe he’d used all of his threads and had spun all the webs he needed. There’s a right time for everything and everything should happen in its time.’

THE END

Photo Image by
Russell Cockayne/Christian Moulay.

The author is 75 and this is my first book, a work of fiction, of fact and of truth. I have spent most of my life writing, in various ways within advertising and marketing, in New Zealand, London, Barcelona, New York and Sydney.

Outside of earning a living, I have written to distract myself from reality. My stories and poems are about animals and objects, gentle loves as far away from the everyday world as possible. I have always been interested in symbolism and when very young I wrote a poem about a nightingale who fell in love with a rose and in the pure consummation of his love he was fatally pierced in the heart by the thorn of the rose. I was later disappointed to find that a Persian poet had had the idea before me.

My husband and I live in rural New South Wales, with a cat (Ruler of the Universe) and a garden full of birds.

The story I have written is coloured by my having observed the first signs of Alzheimer's in someone close to me and then the later quite rapid deterioration. I was intrigued by the way the afflicted mind has sudden flashes of lucidity but the moment of true memory is overcome by the accompanying realisation that time there will be brief.

Such an experience causes one to look constantly for signs in oneself.

ACKNOWLEDGMENTS

I am grateful to the following substantial and professional websites, from which I have adapted material:

near-death.com
youramazingbrain.org
hiddenlighthouse.wordpress.com
gootar.com
nderf.org
chakraenergy.com
humansarefree.com
iands.org
mindbodygreen.com
iisis.net
altered-states.net

Each of these sites provides well-researched data and/or fascinating observations and intriguing propositions, and is worth further investigation by interested readers.

My thanks to the webmasters and designers of these sites for making extensive information so accessible.

Lightning Source UK Ltd.
Milton Keynes UK
UKHW010926090720
366271UK00003B/737

9 781953 048066